I AM NOJPATH

PROLOGUE

1

He never liked it there; Irvine, California.

There was something about it that irked him. Maybe it was the ominous whistling that crept through the cracks in his window frame every night or the loud rolling of glass bottles down the inclined road that he called his street. He couldn't pinpoint it, but it was there.

Then, there was his wife. They'd been married 10 years, but he still couldn't explain her. They had their tussles and their disagreements and always seeming to have the "Life would be so much easier if I was single" moments. But nevertheless, she was the fire that he didn't mind standing over because it kept him warm. She was the cloud that he didn't mind standing directly under because the rain that came down from it cooled him down and left him feeling refreshed. She would always be a mystery to him, in more ways than one, but he didn't think he could ever love anything more.

Maybe that's just who he was: Jackson Arron Yardley. He had never thought of himself as a comfortable person, either with himself or his surroundings. There was always something in the back of his mind that kept him from loosening up and enjoying himself. He wasn't boring, by any means, but he could be tense. Hannah was probably the only thing keeping him sane, even though she always called him out for being tense. She'd try to get him to go for fun drinks with their friends, or go on fun days out to help him have fun with nothing on his mind, but he could never be like that. He was never the easy-going type. Maybe the traumatic childhood that he'd had, he learned to always be wary of people, and never relax enough to allow a situation to get the best of him.

His mind kept wandering as he snapped himself back into the real world, back behind the counter of Coffee Bravo, a small coffee shop in Culver Plaza. He stood leaning on the black marble, eyes darting from patron to patron as he sipped from his glass of water. Then, he turned his attention to the world beyond the sparkling clean windows - that he'd cleaned himself – to the passers-by that had decided to go to Starbucks instead. Consuming the last few refreshing droplets of water, he turned around and headed to the staff room to get a quick refill. The customers were extra boring today, so he wasn't in any rush to get back.

There was an elderly man – Keith, or something plain like that – who regularly spent the entire time reading the local newspaper and taking short, pointless sips from his plain black coffee. His head was buried in the pages and his hands were turning black and powdery from licking his finger to turn the pages. There was a young, 20-something couple that sat opposite each other holding hands with their outstretched arms. They sat glaring longingly into each other's eyes, sipping a shared lemonade through two different straws. Classic millennials.

It was a slow day in Coffeetown.

Jackson placed his small plastic glass under the nozzle of the water cooler and pressed the button, waiting for it to fill to an acceptably hydrating level. He felt his phone vibrate in his back pocket, startling him and sending a weird sensation through his butt cheeks. He took his attention off the water and retrieved his phone. Flashing up on the screen were multiple pointless notifications; emails from betting websites, a reminder that his car insurance was due for renewal and a few sports articles that were recommended for him to read. He swiped all of them off the screen and what remained was a text from his wife – which was weird because she rarely texted him while he was at work, she was too busy for that.

Jay, something's happening. Please come home.

He quickly texted her back asking for clarification. He was beginning to get nervous and his palms were getting clammy. He had a knack for quickly overthinking every situation and feeling the worst would happen at any given time. The reply from Hannah came almost immediately. He took a calming drink of his water and looked at the new message.

I think people are trying to break in. They're outside. I'm scared.

Now he was really nervous. He could feel his heart beginning to beat faster, almost pounding out of his chest. He rushed to the bathroom and dialled her number, taking a few deep breaths to settle himself as he waited for her to pick up. She did so after two rings.

'Jay?' Hannah said quietly and quivering.

'Hannah, what's wrong? What's happening?' he replied.

'I-I-I don't know. I can see a few people outside. They're all in-in-in black, and they're talking amongst themselves. I opened the window a little bit so I can hear them talking.'

'Just, stay there, okay?'

'But I can see them. They're walking toward the door. They're hiding their faces. What do I do? What do I do?'

'Don't move, okay? I'm coming now. I'll tell my boss that I have an – I don't know – a personal emergency at home.'

He hung up before she could respond, shoved his phone back into his pocket and burst out of the bathroom door. Coincidentally, his manager came around the corner at the same time and had to slam his feet on the ground and lock his eyes to stop, and avoid being bowled over.

'Damn, Jackson, the stink that bad, huh?' he joked.

'I gotta go,' Jackson replied, hurriedly taking his apron off and throwing it onto one of the brown leather chairs that filled the staff room.

'Wait, what? It was just a joke, man. I'm sure it doesn't smell that bad.'

Jackson stopped in the corridor outside the bathroom and turned back to face his manager.

'Look, Pete,' he said, a sense of urgency creeping into his voice, 'this isn't about you, this isn't about work. I have to go. I'm not going to tell you why because, no offence, it's not your place to know. But it's an emergency, and I have to get home. So, please, just let me do this.'

Pete could see the worry in his eyes and could hear the trembling in Jackson's syllables. He raised his palms, conceding the argument, and nodding politely to let him go.

'I'll cover until you get back,' Pete said.

Jackson thanked him and turned around, bolting around the edge of the counter and almost breaking the glass panels of the door on his way out. He groaned to himself and started to run away from his regular life making coffee and serving lukewarm breakfast food. He liked the regular life; it kept him sane and grounded. Suddenly, everything came falling apart around him. He had one of those feelings that he couldn't shake; a worrying feeling when something was about to go horribly wrong. He couldn't stay away, though. He wanted to avoid it for as long as possible.

But no.

Instead, he headed towards the black hole that was opening up before him.

2

Jackson's thighs started gradually aching as he powerwalked down each street and over every crack on the paving stones. He narrowly avoided being run over multiple times, but he couldn't afford to wait for the **WALK** symbol to flash up.

Weaving through the human traffic, he felt his phone vibrate in his pocket again. Without breaking his stride, but slowing down a little, he took it out. His favourite picture of Hannah popped up; a ridiculous caricature of her looking down at her phone wearing her favourite business outfit. She looked beautifully stupid and he always smiled when he saw it. He wiped his hand on his pant leg, still clammy, and swiped across the screen. He heard nothing for a few seconds and heard Hannah breathing heavily down the line, not even bothering to say hello.

'Han?' Jackson asked, panting.

She whispered something inaudible and began breathing louder but slower, trying to calm herself down.

'Hannah, what's wrong?' he asked again.

'They're inside. Where are you?' she asked, quietly.

'I'll be there soon, there are so many people on the streets, it's hard to go really fast. My legs are hurting but I'm coming for you, I promise.'

'I can hear them moving around in the house. I can—'

'What? Hannah? What?' he said with a raised voice, getting increasingly concerned.

'They're walking up the stairs, I can hear them talking. Art? I think one of them is called Art? Please hurry, Jay, they're outside the door.'

'I'm nearly there. Hang up and quickly call the police. Then just, hide or something until I get there.'

She tried to calm her breathing again, doing everything she could to be quiet and avoid detection. He could hear the shaking in every breath she was taking as if she were getting ready to jump out of a plane with no parachute. He slowed down into a jog and then receded to a brisk walk. The strain on his thighs and his calves was becoming too much, tightening every time he placed a foot on the ground. He also felt like he was going to pass out. He felt like he was still young at 34, but he had little to no stamina. Missing the chance to go to the gym for the thousandth consecutive day was beginning to take its toll on him.

He let out a loud *argh* and then picked up his speed again, doing his best to get home before it was too late. It was a 25-minute walk, but there was no way he could afford to take that long.

'They're going in all the rooms, what do I do?'

'Call the police and hide, Hannah. I told you what to do,' he replied adamantly, 'In the wardrobe, behind the door, under the bed, I'm not really bothered. Just, please don't put yourself in danger.'

'I can see your baseball bat next to the door, I can reach it.'

'Hannah, no!' he shouted, knowing that she was conjuring up a plan.

A few people stared at him as they passed; shouting down his phone and sweating.

He could hear her strain and stand up through the phone, breathing quieter and quieter as she crept towards the door.

'Hannah, don't do this! I know what you're trying to do, and it's not going to end well. I mean it. I'll be home soon, just stay hidden. Stop being so stubborn. Call the police! Please!'

'I want to be strong, like you. I want to stand up for myself, Jay. I don't want to be a coward anymore.'

'You're not a coward. You're strong, we both know you are. Promise me you won't do anything stupid. You don't have anything to prove, not to yourself or to me.'

She took a deep breath, frozen in place for a few seconds, not saying a word. Jackson picked up his speed. He knew his wife. She was never going to promise him anything. If she felt like she could do something, there weren't many people who could convince her otherwise. He was not one of the people who could.

He could feel his eyes beginning to sting, clouding his vision as he ran towards his wife and his impending nightmare.

'I love you, Jackson Yardley,' she whispered softly before hanging up the phone.

He screamed in anguish – getting a few more confused stares – and dropped his phone back into the pocket that it came from. Then, the adrenaline kicked in. He'd never felt a rush like it. All of his weakness and fragility just simply disappeared. His pain receptors softened and he felt energised.

So he ran. He ran harder than he ever had before.

3

By the end of his sprint, he was lunging rather than running – like he was an Olympic long-jumper getting ready to take off into the sand. His legs felt shaky and weak; a trembling tower of bone that would topple with the slightest bit of pressure. The adrenaline prevented that from happening. It propelled him and he couldn't stop even if he wanted to.

    People were looking at him with eyes filled with confusion and judgement as he passed them. He paid them no mind. He'd never see them again so he didn't care what they thought about him. There were more pressing matters that he had to attend to.

    Reaching the corner of his street, Jackson slowed to a stop to regain the feeling in his calves and to stand up straight properly. It was a small cul-de-sac, only holding six houses – albeit they were quite sizeable. There were two along each side of the street and two more at the bottom. He put his hands on his hips and breathed deeply towards the sky, inhaling and exhaling with the force of a small hurricane. Looking towards his house, the second one down on the left side of a street that had been vibrantly decorated with different potted plants and white, marble-esque concrete driveways. There was no-one there. He looked confusedly up towards his bedroom window, questioning the entire thing and thinking Hannah was playing a weird practical joke on him.

It wasn't funny, though.

The front door was shut, still glimmering and showcasing its lime green paint job, fresh from a new coat. The bedroom window was slightly open; wide enough for someone to peer out of and remain inconspicuous. He walked up to the door, feeling a sense of urgency but being crippled by his tightened calves and the heart that was almost forcefully pumping out of his chest. He took a few deep breaths and opened the door, immediately shouting Hannah's name as soon as his foot crossed the invisible border of the doorway.

Silence.

He couldn't hear anything from upstairs. No creaking of floorboards or rustling of coats to indicate Hannah was coming out of her hiding spot. The only noise that rudely filled the air was the incessant ticking of the clock that hung above the fireplace in the living room. The world was talking in metaphors.

Tick. Tock. Come on, Jackson, get a move on. Go find her. Tick. Tock.

It got louder the more he focused on it, eventually becoming unbearable, and he had to resist ripping his shoe off and launching it at the wall. He edged closer to the foot of the staircase and shouted her name again. The silence whistled through the air, taunting him and sending slight shivers down the back of his neck. He glanced quickly around the downstairs area, through the living room, and across the open-plan kitchen. She clearly wasn't down there, she would have revealed herself if she was.

He took a few steps up the stairs, listening out for any sound that could tell him what happened. When he got halfway up, he heard the slightest groan from the back of the upstairs corridor near the bedroom door. Then he heard a small squeak from something shifting along the washed-oak wooden floor. He hurled himself up the rest of the stairs towards the source of the noise.

Getting to the summit, worsening the strain and the burning on his legs, he saw it.

He saw *her*.

Hannah was sitting slumped against the bedroom door clutching at her stomach with her left hand. Blood was seeping through the gaps in her fingers, staining her nails and leaving a thick puddle on the floor between her outstretched legs. Jackson stood frozen in place, horrified by the scene that was in front of him. He didn't know whether to concentrate on the blood coming from her stomach or the fact that she didn't have any pants on.

Her head was bowed slightly and her eyelids were fluttering. She shuffled again, still not able to look up at her husband, not even knowing that he was there. She just sat, one hand holding the wound, and the other hand wrapped as tight as possible around the baseball bat.

4

Jackson's heart sank.

Hannah's near-motionless body looked weak and pale. Her eyes were only half open and she was staring blankly at the floor beneath her. She looked like she was deep in thought, analysing the various shapes of blood droplets as they fell miserably from the tip of her finger, and joined with the puddle between her legs.

'Hannah?' Jackson whispered, overcome with emotion, his eyes welling up at the sight of her.

She slowly tried to lift her head up to look at him, but it took most of her strength to do so. He rushed over to her side and knelt down, avoiding the blood. He moved the baseball bat away and cupped her hand between both of his.

'Hannah, what did you do? I told you to hide,' he muttered quietly.

'Did... Did... Did I do good?' she replied.

'I told you to hide. Why couldn't you just listen to me this once?'

'I... I wanted to... be strong and show you... I could take care of myself,' she couldn't hold on to her emotions in her weakened state, as the tears began freely running down her cheeks.

'We've already had this—'

'Did I not make you proud?'

He could feel his heart breaking with every beat; pieces cracking off every time he heard the genuine sadness in her voice. He placed his index finger under her chin and softly directed her head upwards so that they could make eye contact.

'Listen to me,' he calmly said through his own tears, 'you've made me proud for the last fourteen years. Ever since we met, there's never been a day where I've not looked at you and not felt like the luckiest man in the world; the proudest man in the world. And I refuse to let this be the last day I ever wake up next to you. I refuse to let this be the last moment that I see life in your eyes – your beautiful eyes.'

'I'm not gonna make it, Jay.'

'You are. You have to. Please.'

As they stared intently at each other, telepathically reminiscing over every memory that they had together, he could feel the grip from her hand weaken and the colour slowly drain out of her face.

'I managed to hit one of them with my bat, though. I... I gave it a good swing. Hit him... right on the— on the side of the head,' she said proudly, flashing a tiny smile.

'You can tell me all about it when you're better, okay? Tell me when you're better.'

'But I'm... I'm not gonna get better, Jay. I've... come to terms with that. You... you need to.'

'I can't accept that. I'll never accept that. You're the love of my life and I'm not ready for either of our lives to end right now.'

He reached behind him and pulled out his phone from his back pocket, still making sure to maintain a grip on Hannah's hand to gauge how much life she actually had left in her.

'I'm gonna call for an ambulance, they're gonna come and get you and you'll be back on your feet in no time, okay?'

She slowly and painfully shook her head, fully accepting of her incoming fate.

'They... they hurt me,' she whispered, losing her voice.

'They hurt you? I know they did, babe, I can see it,' Jackson replied, dialling 9-1-1.

'They... took... my trousers off me... and...' she couldn't finish, she seemed too traumatised to say the words.

'Hello? Hello?' Jackson said into the phone, a sense of urgency clinging to him like a leech.

Hannah smiled at him, her eyes fluttering as the once-vibrant sky blue that emanated from them turned a sad, steel grey. He maintained eye contact as he spoke to the operator on the other end of the line.

'9-1-1, what's your emergency?' a young man said.

'My house has been broken into and my wife's been stabbed. Please, you have to hurry, she's fading really fast,' Jackson told him, mouthing to Hannah to stay with him.

Her grip was loosening. Her eyes were fading.

'Okay, sir, we'll get an ambulance and a police cruiser over to you as quick as we can,' the man replied calmly but sympathetic. 'Can you tell me your address?'

Jackson gave him the details, paying more attention to his wife than the phone call.

Grip still loosening. Eyes still fading.

'Hannah, please stay with me. There's an ambulance on its way, alright? They're gonna patch you up,' he told her, still on the phone.

The operator was telling him something but he zoned it out. He was counting down the seconds in his head that he had left with her; looking into her eyes, seeing her chest move gently in and out.

'You're gonna try and stay with me, aren't you?'

She didn't reply to him. She flashed a small, cheeky smile and looked deep into his eyes once more. Trying to gather her breath was a struggle as she tried her best to form another sentence.

'I... love... you... Jackson... Yardley.'

Then, she gave up.

Her hand went limp and her eyes floated closed. He tried to say her name but could only get halfway before stopping. He couldn't bring himself to say it anymore for some reason.

He stared at her, but she could no longer stare back. His wife had died in front of him in a way he could never have imagined.

He collapsed to the floor and sat next to her, facing the stairs and waiting to hear the grinding sound of the sirens coming to save someone who couldn't be saved. He rested his back on the wall behind him, still holding her hand.

No-one could ever make him let go of that hand.

I
Three Months Later

5

The funeral had come around quicker than Jackson wanted. A few short weeks after watching her die, he was watching the small wooden box that she would forever be living in – a glazed dark brown with small gold dots around the opening – being lowered agonizingly slowly into the ground.

The crowd of people, most of whom he'd never met before, all looked the same. A machine had churned out mourning faces and black suits. Did they even know her? Maybe they knew *of* her, but did they *know* her?

He had stood up in front of all of them before they lowered her down. They were staring at him with expectant, but sorrowful eyes. He couldn't even look at any of them; standing there with their heads directed towards him, some with their hands in her pockets and some hanging them in front of them as a sign of respect. Before any words could come out, or his dry mouth could muster any distinct sound, he coughed a few times and took a few breaths. He scanned the room for anyone that he knew, any face that looked familiar, but other than her family and two of the friends he'd known for years, everyone was a stranger.

'So,' he began, clearing his throat again, 'I'm not really sure where to begin here. I'm not familiar with a lot of the faces here, but I'm sure you all knew Hannah in your own rights. Me? I knew her in a way I never thought I could. I knew her tiniest tendencies. She'd scratch the index finger on her left hand when she got nervous. She always liked her coffee with exactly one and a half sugars in them, as if she'd count every grain as it fell into the cup. Stuff like that, y'know?'

He looked around again, like someone invisible to everyone else was standing in front of his podium holding up a card that read 'PAUSE FOR REACTION'.

'No. I can't. This—This is too soon,' he said abruptly, triggering himself as a few tears dripped from the corner of his sunken eyes. He squeezed them shut to stop himself, and tried to laugh it off, but it didn't work. His emotions weren't listening to him and he was too weak to do anything about it. He couldn't help but stare at the coffin. He imagined himself having x-ray vision, trying to visualise Hannah's body lying motionless inside of it; eyes closed, hands folded into her chest, dressed to the nines in that dark green dress that she loved. He developed funnel vision at that moment, like the opening credits of a Bond movie. The crowd of people around the 6-foot hole faded into blackness and a lens highlighted his wife's coffin.

Then his thoughts drifted to the three men that she had described with some of her final breaths, and the one that she'd managed to strike with the bat. Then, almost as quickly as the thoughts entered his mind, they left again.

He was right. It *was* too soon.

And he was going to make sure he found out why.

Jackson had relived that day, those few hours, in his head multiple times over. He found himself revisiting those feelings more often than he would have cared to admit. The colours, the emotions, the sights. Everything was so vivid and it was ruining him, one unbearable minute at a time.

He hadn't slept in his own bed since that day. He couldn't bear to go back, not even for one night. He'd spent most of his time staying in various hotels, following the cheapest deal wherever it took him. But he needed to subject himself to the pain if he wanted to heal and move on. He needed to go back and get his things and find somewhere stable to live. But that wasn't even the priority. He needed to find those three men and understand how his life had unravelled so quickly.

He'd found a more permanent, yet still temporary home in a low-key hotel on Sand Canyon Avenue. It was a sleek building, cream-coloured on the outside and looked like a generic block of flats from Florida in the 1980s. The rooms weren't much different. They looked modern in general appearance, but the white walls, brown sofa and darker brown furniture made it look like an old person's home. He had to settle in, though, while he searched for a permanent apartment in which to get his life back on the track that it still should have been on.

He left his room and walked swiftly to his car, not looking around or paying any attention to his surroundings. The drive to his former residence didn't take very long. It was the middle of the day so there was no congestion and the sun was mild but not overpowering. The roads were warm and smooth and he could see everything in the distance clearly without furrowing his brow.

He stepped out of the car and some of his nauseating feelings returned. He remembered standing in front of the door and just waiting, studying the surroundings for concerning activity.

Who knew a door could be so traumatising?

The police tape was gone and the house looked good as new, ready for new owners that don't know that someone was murdered in the upstairs hallway. To him, it was radiating with an odd, concerning aura. It was like he was about to step into a haunted house and he was on an episode of one of those Ghost Hunter programs. But maybe it was haunted. It had a reason to be. Or maybe he was trying to come up with any reason he could to not actually enter the house and just turn around and go back to the hotel. He'd been avoiding it for 3 months and felt like it needed to be more. He could just not step foot in the house again and just buy all new stuff when he gets a new apartment. The new tenants can just have all of his clothes and his possessions.

But that was preposterous and he was being weak. She wouldn't want him to be weak.

But almost on cue, he heard someone shout his name from behind him as he began to take the first few steps up the driveway.

'Jackson?' Ms. Renshaw, his neighbour shouted from across the street.

He turned around and saw her smiling at him from her own doorway. She was aging but not elderly, probably mid-50s but he could never tell. She probably used lots of products on her face to reduce wrinkles so she could look as young as she felt.

'Oh, hey, Ms. Renshaw. It's been a long time, huh?' he replied, happy for the distraction.

'It *has* been a while, yeah. Where've you been living lately?' she flashed an inviting smile and he felt obliged to walk over the street to have a proper conversation.

'Y'know, just living the "travelling man" life; going from hotel to hotel until I settle down. It's been rough, but it was bound to be, wasn't it?'

'I'm really sorry for your loss, I don't think I've told you properly yet. She was a lovely woman, and it's really, really sad what happened. Have the police told you anything about it?'

'Thanks,' he said, 'but no, they haven't. I don't know who it was, and the police said there wasn't enough evidence to start a manhunt, so to speak. I'm still kinda processing it myself. I know it's been months and all that, but it's still not easy.'

'I know how you feel, sweetie,' the look on her face made you want to share your life story. The odd twinkle in her eyes and the crooked sincerity of her smile made her seem trustworthy. 'When my husband died, it took me so long to actually enjoy something. Everything seemed so bland, it all reminded me of him and I couldn't smile, and I couldn't laugh.'

She took a more comfortable stance, leaning on the side of the door frame and crossing her arms. Even though they'd never been close in reality, he always found if she started a conversation, he'd end up revealing lots of information about his life and he'd even feel comfortable telling her things he'd never told anyone before. She had that effect on everyone she met.

'The only thing that kept me going,' she continued, 'was little Arthur. He took it really hard when his dad died, he wasn't that old and he had no-one to really bond with. I've never been much of a sports person, so his dad always done all that kind of stuff. It's funny, actually, because that's what helped me feel like myself again. When it was just me and Arthur, I could see him slipping into some kind of unhappiness so I took him to an Angels game. He's always been a big baseball fan – got that from his dad.

'We sat in good seats, those pretty expensive ones behind home plate, and I let him explain everything to me when it happened. It got him really excited and it made me smile so much. He loved teaching me about it because it let him express himself in a way he could never do with me before then. After that, I just accepted that it was me and Art, and I got better.'

Jackson smiled, somehow happy to have heard the nice story and peculiar words of encouragement from her. But the smile didn't last long. He made a connection that he didn't think he'd be able to make that close to home.

They're walking up the stairs, I can hear them talking. Art? I think one of them is called Art? Please hurry, Jay, they're outside the door.

Suddenly, he felt relieved. He knew where to start on his journey to find out why Hannah died and it had literally been staring him in the face. Maybe it'd be easier than he thought, even though it took 3 months for him to get there.

'My son's actually in town if you want to meet him,' Ms. Renshaw said, 'I'm sure it would both do you the world of good to have a friend right now. He's about your age, I think, maybe a little younger, but you might find you have something in common.'

'I don't know, I—'

'I'll go fetch him,' she interrupted, obviously not allowing 'no' to be a valid answer.

She disappeared into her house for a few minutes and Jackson was left standing there, starting to feel awkward and that his neighbour was setting him up on a blind date. He also felt nervous. If he'd made the right connection, he was about to meet one of the people who killed his wife. He'd be able to look right into his eyes and have a faux-friendly conversation with him to see what kind of person he was.

Before he could get lost in his brainstorm, Ms. Renshaw re-emerged from the darkness of her house with an excited smile plastered over her smooth face. Immediately behind her, and towering over her 5'3' frame, was her son. He was relatively skinny but had wide shoulders, looking like he was just about ready for a midlife crisis. His oversized SLAYER t-shirt hung loosely over his pale, white torso and the rips in his jeans showcased his unattractively hairy legs. He had a thick head of ginger hair that had been horribly stuck to his head with a thick handful of mousse or gel, with the end of his fringe hanging delicately over the side of his face. He smiled at Jackson, in a generic-greeting sort of way, and ran his fingers through his fringe, returning the hanging tufts to the top of his head. In doing so, he revealed a small scar on the side of his head, surrounded by a faint purple bruise.

They exchanged pleasantries as the mother ventured back into the darkness to give the two men some time alone. They stared awkwardly at each other, ready to have an equally as awkward conversation about life that they both knew was forced.

'I'm sorry about your wife, man,' Arthur said eventually.

'Yeah, thanks,' Jackson replied, knowing it was fake and just to maintain his image of innocence.

'Really, man, that's a tough break. I've not been too lucky in the relationship department myself but I imagine losing someone like that after being with them ten years stings like a bitch.'

'Well, we were married for ten, but together for fourteen,' Jackson was stern and almost monotonous, not wanting to prolong the conversation any longer.

Almost on cue again, Ms. Renshaw shouted for her son from inside. He heard her cough and then say his name again, getting closer until eventually, she emerged again from the friendly abyss.

'Jacob's on the phone for you. D'you want to take it?' she asked him.

The name triggered something inside. It was a few minute details on his face but Jackson's self-proclaimed eagle vision caught it. The corner of his mouth twitched ever so slightly and his pupils dilated. It seemed like his heart rate increased and he got nervous like his mom had revealed information that he didn't want anyone to hear.

He awkwardly snatched the phone out of her hand and walked into the house, waiting until he was out of earshot to say anything. Jackson heard faint whispering in the distance but nothing he could comprehend. Ms. Renshaw remained at the door like she was waiting for him to say something else or tell another story. He fidgeted in place, deep in thought and plotting in his mind.

'How long is your son gonna be around, do you know?' he asked her after a short, awkward silence.

'I don't know, he only lives in Sacramento so he tends to just come and go without telling me. A few days, I imagine. Why?' she asked.

'Well the conversation we just had was pretty brief, he didn't really say much so I was gonna see if he'd want to go for a couple beers, just so we can have a better conversation. Like you said, I need a friend,' he forced a laugh and she returned her own.

'I'm sure he'd love that. I'll let him know and you can organise something.'

'Great. I'm sure there's a lot for us to talk about,' Jackson said, still plotting.

She smiled at him and he smiled back, both genuine this time.

But for two different reasons.

6

The motel was comfortable but it wasn't *his*.

The smell was unfamiliar, like an aged mixture of cherry blossom and wood varnish, and the decorations were bland and generic. The paintings hung at certain intervals around the four walls and featured various abstract interpretations of the California coast. Jackson was sitting at a medium-sized desk, painted a fake mahogany colour and chipping on the underside. He had a small lamp in the corner, helping him focus on the numerous different pages of notes he had accumulated throughout the night.

There were small bits of paper with scribblings on scattered around it, some were balled up and lying next to the wicker basket he used for a bin that lay solitary in the corner next to a long, potted plant. To his left, there were notes he had transcribed from a phone call he'd had with a real estate agent earlier in the night. Like he would have guessed, having to disclose that someone died in your house – he told them she died, he couldn't say that she was brutally murdered – definitely deters any prospective buyers. It doesn't seem to help the market value either. But he was convinced it would sell eventually, even if he took a massive loss on it.

He just wanted rid of it. There was no way he could even step back inside, never mind live there again. But that was another topic for another day. There were other things he needed to focus on.

He looked at the blank sheet of paper in front of him, brainstorming in his head and fiddling with the stolen motel pen in his hand. There were many things he wanted to write but he needed to make it coherent for himself, he needed to understand.

He brought the pen gently down to the crisp sheet of partridge, letting his hand flow majestically across the line before lifting it off again. He'd only written two words, but they were important words; a good place to begin the rest of the plan.

ARTHUR RENSHAW

There were many avenues he could now go down, but he needed to be smart about it. This would need to be something meticulous and well-executed. He wanted to be slow and precise, but once he saw that name, everything came bursting out and he couldn't control it. The deep-rooted anger that he had tried to suppress came flowing from heart, to limb, to pen.

He just had to roll with it and see what came up.

ARTHUR RENSHAW – POSSIBLE SUSPECT, ONLY SUSPECT ATM
HE GOT A CALL FROM JACOB? IS HE INVOLVED? NEED MORE
GO FOR DRINKS WITH HIM, SOMETHING LIKE THAT GET HIM TALKING, HE NEEDS TO TALK

A KNIFE MIGHT WORK – DO YOU HAVE A GOOD KNIFE?
FUCK SAKE
TRY NOT TO KILL HIM, THAT'S NOT YOU
IS IT? IT COULD BE
LEAVE THE MOM ALONE, SHE'S NICE
LOOK FOR PRIVATE PLACES – ABANDONED IF POSSIBLE

He'd been scribbling for what seemed like an hour, but after he came up for air and tapped the screen of his phone to wake it up and check the time, it had only been ten minutes. He looked over what he'd written and a confused look took over his face as if he were looking at someone else's work. He couldn't even remember writing most of it, it was just ramblings. But the more he studied it, the more he made sense of it, the more he felt like it was information that he could put to good use, providing he was committed enough to do his research and not mess it up.

He could definitely be committed. There was *no* doubt in his mind about that.

After accepting the quality of the notes, he returned his pen to the paper one more time. He wrote one sentence at the bottom in thick, block capital letters, underlining it multiple times to make sure he got it through his head.

DO IT FOR HANNAH

7

Jackson was prepared.

Maybe not mentally, but everything else was there.

A few days after his initial scribblings, he had managed to make plans with Arthur to go for a few beers. He'd written down a few questions on a piece of paper, like he was hosting the Presidential Candidates debate, and tried to memorise them as best he could. He didn't want to be too direct, he wanted Arthur to feel like it was his decision to spill all the information and it wasn't forced out of him. He had to cover his tracks if anything happened.

What was that phrase, again?
Plausible deniability.

Jackson stood gazing into the 5-foot mirror hanging on a narrow wall near the front door, staring at his outfit choice and taking comfort in the fact that he still had a bit of confidence in himself. He had paired a slim-fitting pair of black jeans with a plain white short-sleeve t-shirt. It was a chilly night so he'd chosen a fashionable grey denim jacket, with small rips and tears across it that were purely for the aesthetic.

Giving himself a slight nod into the mirror, he turned around and ventured into the kitchen and 'cased the joint', eyeing up the different appliances and utensils. In a small metal-wire pot near the toaster, he spotted a stainless-steel knife with a sleek 8-inch blade that was glimmering through the knife guard that it came in. Jackson reached over and grabbed it, slotting it carefully into the inside pocket of his jacket, allowing the thick black handle to protrude out of it and irritate his underarm. He took a few collecting breaths, doing last minute checks around the place to make sure he wasn't forgetting anything then left his room.

Hurrying through the lobby and out the rear doors towards the parking lot, and instantly felt the blow of the lukewarm wind that splashed gracefully across his face. It had recently stopped raining and the air felt clear and refreshing. He took a brisk walk through the almost bare lot and towards his luminescent-white Jaguar XE. It was a Christmas gift that he thought couldn't be topped. His dad had outdone himself that year and he didn't even expect another gift from him until the day he died.

He set off into the sunset, chasing the horizon in a car that aggressively purred every time he pressed his foot down on the acceleration. It didn't take him long to get to the Renshaw residence; at least he didn't think it did. He was too preoccupied to notice.

He parked on the side of the road, a little bit further down from the house, as much into the corner of the street as he could get without blocking a driveway, and turned the engine off. Getting out of the car, he noticed an eerie quiet about the environment, like Silent Hill without the fog. Maybe it was the picturesque sunset casting deep orange shadows onto the sidewalk or the purple tinge that dressed the sky in the distance. It was fit for a painting, but it didn't feel as tranquil.

Walking slowly up the street, suddenly feeling a lot more aware of the knife in his inside pocket, Jackson started noticing everything around him, down to the finest detail. He noticed the couple that was strolling by at the top of the cul-de-sac, fingers interlocked and deep in conversation. The man was dragging his feet, scratching the soles of his cheap sneakers on the rough, sand-paper-like concrete.

He noticed the small Jack Russell standing guard at the window of the house that he was passing. It was standing statuesque, glaring at him with deep green eyes that screamed 'evil'. It had an aggressive snarl forming on its face, like it thought that every passer-by was going to try and break into its house and steal everything. It was small, but it packed a big punch.

Then, as he progressed upwards, he noticed his house. It radiated with an off-putting aura. It made him feel uncomfortable, but he couldn't look away. He could see *her*. He could see the paramedics rushing up to her, realising that they were too late.

How could he possibly live there again? Every time he visited, he felt nauseous and had sickening flashbacks and visions of her death and all of the blood.

Can you still tell there was a bloodstain in the wood? Have they replaced the flooring upstairs? No. Jackson, stop it. Shake it off.

He did as he was told and rid himself of the oncoming panic attack and the solemn, angry look that was plastering itself over his face and walked up the light grey concrete path that led to the door of the

Renshaw's house. He tapped lightly on the small glass pane near the top and stepped back, waiting for either one of them to answer. After another louder knock, he noticed a tall shadow approaching the doorway. Arthur.

The Renshaw son opened the door with a smile that he'd give to a co-worker that he didn't know very well. It was fake, Jackson could tell it was. Arthur didn't really want to go but his mother probably would have forced him to; saying it would be good for him to make a friend while he was in town, that it would be good for him. Hannah would have probably said the same thing to Jackson.

No. Stop it. Shake it off.

Arthur looked every bit the part of the "I do not want to go" role Jackson had thrust him into. His casual attire made Jackson feel overdressed and out of place. He had on a loose-fit pair of dark blue jeans and a light grey *Metallica* t-shirt that didn't go together. His hair was combed back and stuck in place with mousse but parts were beginning to flop down to the side of his face. Jackson greeted him with a monotonous tone in his voice, knowing he didn't need to make that much of an effort with the conversation.

'So, where we going?' Arthur asked as he shut the front door behind him.

'I know a good place not too far from here. It's fairly quiet which is good, I'm getting old and I can't deal with the loud music any more,' Jackson replied.

'Aren't you, like, 30 or something?'

'Well, I mean, yeah, but I still have weak ears. You know... actually, never mind.'

Both men walked awkwardly to Jackson's car. Arthur complimented it as he stopped next to the passenger door; the first, and possibly only, bit of genuineness that would come out of the night. Jackson thanked him and walked around to the driver side.

He sat down and fastened his seatbelt, making sure the knife in his pocket wasn't visible. He placed his hands on his lower thighs and casually wiped the sweat and clamminess that was, unfortunately, forming on the surface of his skin, trying not to draw attention to himself and the fact that he'd never been more nervous in his life.

Arthur put his seatbelt and stared confused at the dashboard and the steering wheel, wondering about the inactivity and noticing Jackson's fidgeting.

'Hey man, you okay?' he asked.

He got no reply. Jackson quickly scanned the surrounding area, making sure the Jack Russell in the nearby house wasn't watching and checking all of the mirrors to see if there was anyone around. Knowing they were alone, he swung his left arm around and punched Arthur square in the face as hard as he could. As soon as his knuckle made contact, he heard a satisfying mixture of two different noises. He heard Arthurs pained groans, and the satisfying crunch of his nose. He looked as the blood dripped majestically down in a tidy line from his nostril to his upper lip.

He cocked his arm back again and returned it for a second go.

Arthur screamed out in pain again, clutching at his nose to prevent the blood from soaking into his pants. Jackson looked at him, watching the blood drip over the webs in his fingers as his hands were cupped around his nose.

    'Change of plans. You're going to stay right there and you're not going to move a fucking muscle until we get where we're going. I've got a knife in my pocket and I will gut you if you do something wrong. You got that?' Jackson said, shaking his hand to alleviate some of the pain.

Arthur gently nodded, focusing all of his attention on his broken nose and the searing pain that was taking over his entire face. Jackson hummed, satisfied, and finally turned the engine on. He took one last look at Arthur as if his suffering was a source of happiness for him, reminding him of what he'd just done, and checked his mirrors again. Not wanting to waste another moment, now that the metaphorical wheels were in motion, he drove away from his old neighbourhood and towards to the next part of his plan.

8

A few weeks before, when he had been running errands on the outskirts of town, Jackson had stumbled upon the location he was currently at. It was a small, one-story building that used to be a garage, but had long been abandoned. It was situated on the side of a long road with very few houses around and he'd never noticed a high volume of foot traffic through the area. There were a few thick trees decorating the perimeter, casting a protective shadow over it and preventing him from being easily spotted.

Inside was everything he'd need for the job at hand. On the back wall was a long desk attached to the wall, upon which were several apparently-unwanted tools from the previous owner. There was two thick concrete pillars either side of the centre of the room. Arthur sat leaning on the side wall, legs bent with his knees sticking up, and his hands bound in front of him. He was contorting his face trying to ease the pain of his broken nose that he could no longer tend to. The bleeding had stopped, which he was glad about, but there were still a few small blood stains on his t-shirt and on the crotch area of his jeans that he'd been unable to contain.

Jackson stood leaning on one of the pillars, staring down at his victim, watching him act as if he were the only one in the room. He was sitting so casually like it was a normal occurrence for him to be kidnapped. They hadn't made eye contact or spoke at any point during the 20 minutes that he'd been sitting down. Arthur had only looked up from the ground once or twice, and that was to inspect the room and the tool desk on the wall.

'Y'know,' Jackson finally said, almost forgetting what his own voice sounded like, 'my wife had this thing that she used to do when we got into fights. It's just like what you've been doing since we got here.'

Arthur looked up from the ground with a condescending look on his face, showing his clear lack of interest in anything that was about to be said.

'Any time we got in an argument,' he continued, 'she'd do anything but look directly at me. I'd try to sort it out, make things better, but she was so stubborn and sometimes wouldn't let me. She'd give me a word here and there, but flat out refused to look directly at me. Maybe it was because she might forgive me and get over it if she saw me, I don't know.'

'Look, man, I really don't care,' Arthur replied.

'Well, you're gonna have to care because these stories are the only thing keeping you alive right now.'

Arthur smiled and let out a small chuckle, amusingly shaking his head at the vague threat.

'That's not you, man. You look too boring and office-y to kill me. We'll just sit here for a while and then you'll get too sweaty, too nervous, then you'll either let me go or leave yourself and I'll stay here until

I can manage to let myself go. I saw how much you were sweating when we first got in the car; this is clearly the first time you've done anything exciting with your life.'

'Unlike you, huh?'

'What do you mean?'

Jackson stood up straight and crossed his arms, looking judgmentally down at Arthur.

'Can you really act innocent when you're bound here?'

Arthur laughed, sounding genuinely perplexed at the man stood in front of him, and shook his head. But that feeling didn't last long.

'Funny, is it?' Jackson began, getting closer to him and taking the knife out of his pocket, making sure not to pull the guard out with it. 'Is it funny that you went to rob a house that was just opposite your mother's?'

He punched Arthur again in the face, feeling the impact of cheekbone on his knuckles, while an exciting shiver shot its way up his spine.

'Is it funny that you got two of your friends to come with you because you're *that* much of a pussy?'

Another punch, this time in the nose. Arthur screamed out in pain, his eyes beginning to well up.

'Is it funny that you saw a woman when you got upstairs and decided to have a bit of fun with her?'

He punched him in the stomach this time. The fat cushioned the impact but he still felt the brittleness of his rib cage. The tingling sensation intensified and the adrenaline began to kick in.

'And the funniest part is; the part that I think you'll laugh at the most, is that you proceeded to attack this woman for *no good reason*,' he held the knife up to Arthur's face, 'she attacked you with a bat and that's why you have that bruise'—Jackson tapped the blade of the knife on the side of his head—'on your head.'

Jackson could see the terror coming into Arthur's eyes via his tear ducts. The temporary twinkling in his hazel eyes began to dissipate and fall distressingly slow down his bruising cheek in the form of a tear. The expression on his face didn't change and he couldn't take his eyes off the knife. There was intent in Jackson's eyes. Pure, unabated intent.

'Now,' Jackson continued, 'it is *beyond* my grasp why you decided to brutally stab and murder this woman, but I can almost guarantee that you will not be leaving this building alive. But it's up to you how many pieces you end up in.'

The sweat beads came in bunches. They swam in synch across Arthur's forehead, then slowly trickled downwards to find shelter in his thick eyebrows. His face was turning slightly paler, and as much as he tried to mask it to keep up his façade, he was beginning to get terrified.

Jackson saw it. He was going to use it.

'This is the thing,' he started, crouching down to stare into Arthur's eyes, 'I've never done this before – as you probably guessed as soon as you saw me. I'm not the 'office-type' like you thought, but I do make coffee for a living which is pretty much just as menial. What *is* important about that, is that I have no idea where this weird tingling sensation that I'm currently feeling in my head is going to take me. This is a type of adrenaline I'm not sure I've ever experienced before and I want to ride it until it subsides. Do you understand?'

Arthur nodded slowly, scared and confused at the same time. He was just as unsure as Jackson about where his day was headed.

'Okay, good,' Jackson finished.

He lifted the knife up to Arthur's face and lowered his voice, speaking softly as if he were talking to a young child.

'All I want from you is a sincere apology, and the names of the other two guys who helped you kill my wife. That's it. Maybe a proper explanation as to why you did it.'

He received only a blank stare in return. Jackson raised his eyebrows and tilted his head, like he was staring into his soul, looking for life – and more importantly, a response.

'Aw, come on, I know you want to say something. I'm not scary, see? You said so yourself,' Jackson said again.

'L-l-look man, you don't have to do this. You don't have to ruin your life just because of me. Just, um, just let me go, yeah? I promise I won't tell anyone,' Arthur replied.

He knew his bargaining wouldn't work, but it was all he could think to say. Nothing else was coming to his mind. He had conflicting thoughts, feelings, that were zipping around his head like blades on a ceiling fan. They were going too fast for him to make anything out of, so he just had to blabber and hope for the best. All the while, the sweat beads were getting thicker, and there were becoming more of them. He could taste the blandness of them as they dripped from his top lip to his bottom, sneaking inside his mouth every time he tried to speak. In a way, he was just thankful that he hadn't pissed his pants.

A disappointed look went over Jackson's face as he sat in front of Arthur and crossed his legs. The answer he'd just received was embarrassing, even by his standards.

'And what in the hell was *that*? Is that really all you could come up with?' Jackson asked, perplexed.

He lifted the knife up to Arthur's face again, this time so that the tip of the blade made a soft indent in his cheek. He went cock-eyed trying to look down at it, a deep terror in his eyes.

'I need something better than that. I'll ask you again; who are the other two guys that helped you kill my wife? I want you to think properly about this before you answer.'

Arthur couldn't get the words out. His eyes were strained and he couldn't take his attention off the knife touching his face. He could feel the cold steel against his sweaty cheek, sending a shiver up and down his spine – and not a pleasant one.

Jackson looked at Arthur expectedly before turning his attention back to the knife. He smiled, both proud and excited about what he was about to do. He took his free hand and placed it on Arthur's neck in a light chokehold, pushing back so he had a firm grip, before applying pressure to the knife. The tip inserted itself into Arthur's cheek and he cried out in pain, mostly because he didn't think he'd actually get hurt.

He made a shallow incision just under his left eye and dragged the blade downwards, stopping just above his lip. The blood trickled out slowly and majestically around the blade, with some droplets finding their way onto Jackson's hand. The sweat on Arthur's face found a new home inside the wound, and the stinging was intense; the pain even more so. His breathing quickened to try and power through it but it didn't help. He was overwhelmed, suddenly realising how weak he was and how low his pain tolerance was.

'Okay, okay, fine,' Arthur cried out, 'I give up. Please, just—just get that damn knife away from my face.'

He scrunched up his face, closed his eyes and tried to slow his breathing. It didn't work very well, the stinging kept coming. The cut might not hurt as bad if he wasn't sweating so much. It felt as if somebody had poured salt all over him and it was creeping into scars he didn't know he had.

'Now we're getting somewhere,' Jackson replied.

Arthur tried his best to speak throughout his quick breathing, stopping every few seconds to collect himself through the searing pain.

'Their names are—are—are Jacob Davies… and Grey Sullivan,' he said.

'Much better. Much, much better,' Jackson replied as he stood back up.

'But—but it wasn't all me. I'm not the leader or anything. It was—' Arthur's eyes darted back and forth a few times; thinking on the spot '—it was Jacob, yeah. It was his idea. He paid us to come with him, saying he had something huge planned.'

Jackson tilted his head, taking in the information that he'd just been given, trying to decide whether it was complete bullshit or not. He held the knife up with his thumb and index finger, like he was a Crime Scene Investigator looking at evidence, and watched as the blood followed the laws of gravity and swam down the blade edge and onto the tip, before falling gracefully to the ground and forming a small puddle in front of him.

'I'n't that beautiful?' he asked.

Arthur wasn't paying any attention. He was sat slumped against the wall, his face becoming paler with each agonising minute. He'd decided to just let the blood run down his face, into his mouth, and off his chin.

'Majestic,' Jackson said, talking to himself at that point.

He crouched down again, grabbing the knife by the handle once more. Arthur looked to him, but his eyes were dazed and blurry like he was in his own little world. Jackson clicked his fingers in front of his face but didn't get much of a reaction. There was no startling, there was no noise. Arthur's eyes regained some colour as his attention turned to Jackson, but they still looked far away. Jackson smiled; an oddly genuine smile that almost seemed to be masking an apology.

Without the need for more small talk, Jackson jabbed the knife deep into Arthur's stomach, not protected by the rolls he would have if he were leaning forward. He pulled it out almost instantaneously and jabbed it back in, repeating that another time before leaving it lodged in. The blood came pouring out onto his hand and down to his wrist, soaking into the arm-hairs. He ignored them, and focused on the dying man sitting in front of him; eyes wide and quickly losing life. He didn't scream out in pain when the knife penetrated his stomach, it shocked him more than anything else.

This had actually happened.

Jackson stayed in place, still gripping the knife handle, reliving the moment the blade pierced the skin over and over again in his head. He felt like he'd just popped a balloon with a small needle; there was a lot less resistance than he thought there was going to be. He let go of the weapon and marvelled at the now-dead body.

Fascinating. His eyes followed the blood still streaming out the wound, soaking into his clothing; warm and thick like custard.

Somehow, he thought, the world had just gotten a little better.

But he didn't want to waste time staring at Arthur; there were two more people he had to talk to.

9

Arthur was slumped, eyes still open, with his arms laying palms up by his side. Jackson stood admiring from afar, leaning back on the opposite wall. He felt an unusual sense of pride sweeping over him, like he'd just achieved something special that he never thought he'd do. He relished in the feeling; closing his eyes and making the most of it.

    He was a murderer now. That was weird to say. He had actually killed someone. The strange thing was, he felt absolutely no different.

    Should he feel bad? Should he be traumatised?

    Oddly, he absolutely wasn't. He felt good. He felt alive. He'd always considered himself to be the kind of person that would wretch at the sight of blood; he never liked doing the experiments in high school biology. Never in a million years did he think he could actually take someone else's life. Sometimes he'd thought about – even sometimes dreamt – that he'd take his own life one day, back during his mid-to-late teen years when nothing ever seemed to go right for him, and especially when he was 16. But he never thought his life would come to this point.

As a cool breeze glided in from a small window in the corner, slapping him in the face and snapping him out of his disturbed day-dream, his focus shifted back to the corpse – covered satisfyingly in blood – sat in front of him. The son of his neighbour. That made it even more invigorating.

'This is odd,' he spoke softly to the body, as if he were still alive, 'I look at you and I don't see anything. I have this weird feeling going through me, but I'm not 100% certain what it is.'

He got closer to Arthur's body and looked down, admiring the flow of blood seeping from his open wounds.

'Is it remorse? Is that what I feel? Should I be sorry that you're dead? I mean, I know I took a life, but you did the same and felt nothing, so why should I? D'you think I'll feel the same about your two friends when I kill them?'

He stopped and shivered, a tingling sensation running up his spine and around his head.

'Oh, it felt nice to actually admit that. I'm going to kill two more people,' he shivered again, smiling, 'I'm going to kill your friends. My wife won't die for nothing.'

He looked down again, looking almost disappointed that Arthur wasn't replying to what he was saying or showing any change in body language. He laughed it off, realising he was being a bit too crazy.

Becoming increasingly bored of just standing, he reached down and began searching Arthur's clothes – getting blood over his hand in the process – to find his phone. He felt it in the back pocket of his jeans and pulled it out, thanking him as he did so. It was a cheap-looking Android phone, with a long crack going down the right-hand side of the screen. It still worked, which was the important thing. Surprisingly, it didn't have a password lock on it so Jackson was able to get straight in without any effort; something he was very much grateful for.

He clicked on the *Messages* icon and was planning to look through them, but there was none. Arthur had deleted them all. He'd deleted all of his other apps, too.

If he even had any, to begin with. Maybe it was a burner phone? That would explain why it looked so old and tacky.

Jackson tried a different avenue. He clicked on *Contacts* and began having a look through. Arthur hadn't erased any of them. There was few of them, to begin with; maybe he was in the process of erasing them and got caught up with something. He scrolled slowly down the page, looking for names he recognised. After passing names like *Bitch from UCI* and *Forehead*, he came the two names that he was looking for - he thought. *Jay Cobb. Sully Van.* He assumed that was Jacob Davies and Grey Sullivan. It'd sure be awkward if he was wrong and he ended up murdering the wrong people. That would be a problem that he *really* didn't want to deal with.

He stood still for a few minutes, staring at Jacob's contact info, deciding on what he was going to text him in an effort to lure him to the building. He had to pretend to be Arthur, but he didn't know how he spoke because there was no message history.

We have a problem, he texted. Simple but effective, let Jacob do most of the work.

He glanced over at Arthur and observed him while they waited for a response.

We do?, it read.

Cops came to my mom's, started asking shit about the thing that happened across the road.

Oh shit, we do have a problem.

Jackson figured he was getting somewhere; his cover was intact and Jacob had hooked on to the bait. He had to be cautious, he didn't want to seem too eager to get him there.

We need to meet. Private, he sent. He was hoping that wasn't too obvious.

Where? Not many places around, Jacob replied, still oblivious.

Abandoned building across town, usually quiet, best place I could find.

Is that not too risky? Seems a bit cliché, lol.

Jackson was becoming impatient; he needed a way to circumvent the hesitance without breaking character and seeming too eager. He decided to try a different way; use a different bait.

Dunno, but Grey's already on his way, you need to come too.

He stared at the screen for what seemed like 15 minutes without blinking. He turned to brightness down to avoid giving himself a headache, even though his vision began blurring after a while and the headache began creeping in any way.

Jacob's reply came in and his heart skipped a beat.

Dude, you never call him Grey, it read.

He didn't know what to say back, or how to react. He couldn't just not reply, that would make it even worse. His face and his hands started getting clammy, the adrenaline and all the other positive feelings that had been flowing effortlessly through his veins subsided and were replaced by anxiety and nausea – his usual combination.

The phone pinged again.

It must be serious. I'm coming, whats the address?

Like the breeze that flowed through the window not long before, a huge sigh of relief rushed through him and sent him spiralling back into reality. The anxiety was gone, but so was the adrenaline and the feeling of excitement. He felt like he'd dodged a bullet. He came to the realisation that he was in too deep, way too far from his comfort zone.

After looking up the address to make sure he was bringing Jacob to the right place, he tidied the place up a little bit and left, waiting around the corner so he could hear anyone approaching. There weren't many people around during that time of day, so if someone did pass, it would be the right person.

Hopefully.

Jackson had been standing in the shade behind the building for a good 15 – maybe 20 – minutes before he heard any noise that was worth anything. Outside of that, it was strong winds that blew leaves towards his face and made the chill of the shade a little colder. The branches above and behind him were cracking, making concerning noises and putting him on edge. Birds were angrily chirping, possibly shouting at each other from across the trees and various rooftops throughout the neighbourhood.

After getting lost in the various sounds and enjoying the calming effects they were having on his blood pressure, Jackson heard the distinct sound of shoes scraping against concrete in the distance, getting closer and closer until they stopped just outside the building. He untangled himself from the branches, keeping his sharpened breath to himself as a rogue branch scraped along the side of his neck. The footsteps walked back where they came from for a few seconds, then turned around and walked in Jackson's direction. Just in case, he flattened himself against the shadowy wall to avoid detection, like he was playing a stealth-based video game.

The footsteps stopped again and approached the entrance. He heard the clearing of a throat; a childish but smokes-20-a-day type of cough. Jackson walked a bit further along the wall, watching for anything on the ground that could give away his position. He heard a light tapping on the door of the garage. It was weak, but loud enough for anyone inside to hear it.

'Yo,' a voice muttered softly like it was whispering through the cracks in the door frame.

'Guys,' the voice said again, softly still but little more aggressive this time.

Jackson peered round and set his eyes upon Jacob Davies for the first time. He wasn't what he expected based on the things he'd heard and imagined. He was a puny looking man – or boy? Maybe he was more like a boy. He was a little on the short side, his blond hair was greased to his head and hanging roughly over his forehead, covering a minefield of acne. His face was cleaner – at the least the part he could see.

Jackson leaned back against the side wall and took a long, controlled breath, before pulling the knife out of his pocket and wrapping his clammy fingers around the chipped plastic handle. He edged around to the front of the building, slowly observing Jacob look guiltily behind him, and scratch various parts of his body as some kind of nervous tick. As Jacob stared aimlessly down the road he came from, Jackson saw an opportunity to sneak behind his oblivious prey. With an almost hunter-like precision, he whipped his left arm and placed his still-clammy hand over Jacob's mouth, who jolted on the spot like he was taking a tour through a haunted house. He mumbled something into the palm of Jackson's and tried to writhe out of the grip, but he was too weak. His frame resembled that of a pre-teen so he knew he was resigned to capture.

'Hello, Jacob,' Jackson said intimidatingly into his new victim's ear, with a delicate tone.

He swung his other arm around and held the knife up to Jacob's eye level, warning him of the danger that now faced him.

'Remember when you killed that woman?' Jackson said as if he were about to tell a funny story.

Before Jacob could respond with more mumbles, Jackson plunged the blade deep into the top of Jacob's thigh, just below his pelvic bone. The deep laceration sent blood rushing out of the wound and down his trouser leg. Jacob screamed weakly into the palm of

Jackson's hand, while his eyes rolled smoothly back and forth in his head.

Jackson immediately removed the knife from the thigh, sending more blood spitting out onto the ground in front of them, catching the bottom of the door on the way down.

Indistinct, pain-filled noises attempted to fill the dull silence, as Jackson opened the door and dragged him effortlessly inside to sit with his friend.

10

Jacob was groggy and unknowing; his butt was aching and his head was itchy, but he didn't have the energy to scratch it. He was slumped against the same wall as Arthur, unaware that anyone was actually in the room with him. When he managed to get a good look at his surroundings, he furrowed his eyebrows like he'd just woken up from an alcohol-induced coma – with the headache to match. He glanced down at his legs lay out flat on the hard floor and tried to focus his vision on the thick tourniquet that had been wrapped around his left leg. As his eyesight became clear, the pain from the wound came rushing back and he winced, jerked his leg, and jolted himself up to a straight sitting position.

He reached down and inspected the bandage, trying to feel around for the exact location of the wound. As he quickly glanced to his right, like anyone would when they're still unfamiliar with where they are, he got the shock of his life. He shrieked, quieter than he would have liked, but still noticeable. He quickly shuffled away from the body and tried to avoid throwing up.

'Art?' he said, a little more than a whisper, 'what the—? What happened?'

He stared at his friend for a while, looking him up and down to try and wrap his head around what he was actually seeing. He couldn't take it in. There were so many injuries, so much blood.

'Arthur can't help you, I'm afraid,' a voice said from the corner of the room.

Jacob looked over to where it came from, seeing only a desk full of tools and a few thick concrete pillars. After a few seconds, Jackson appeared from behind one of them, holding a small bucket in his hands and carrying a proud, wry smile on his face. He took a few steps toward Jacob and launched the contents of the bucket over him. The ice-cold water sent pulsing shivers all over his body, causing all of his muscles to tense and the pain in his leg to increase dramatically. He screamed out, in a mixture of shock and pain. He began to shiver violently, as small droplets out water flicked off him and onto the walls like he was a dog that had just come in from the rain.

'As you can see,' Jackson began as he came to a stop a few feet in front of his newest victim, 'he's pretty dead, so isn't really in a good position to answer of any your questions. By the way, I do hope they were rhetorical. If not, that makes you really stupid.'

Jacob couldn't think of anything to say in return; there were four or five other things that seemed to demand more of his attention.

After the stabbing feeling of the cold had subsided and he regained some feeling in his limbs, he wiped the excess water off his face and looked towards his kidnapper, finally taking it all in.

'Who are you?' he asked.

'Who am *I*?' Jackson replied.

Jacob coughed, releasing some more droplets of water that were still attached to his lips. 'Yeah, that's what I asked.'

Jackson smiled. 'I'm just a guy who lost his wife, looking for some answers,' he looked at Arthur, then back at Jacob, 'It's not going well so far, though.'

Jacob looked at Arthur as well, beginning to put some of the pieces together.

'You see,' Jackson began, stepping slowly closer, 'I noticed that ol' "Art" over there did a bad thing; a real bad thing. He even had a wound to show for it.'

Jackson pointed to Arthur's head and the darkening purple bruise courtesy of a baseball bat. Jacob looked and studied it with a confused look on his face.

'Now, I know that you and Grey Sullivan were the two that were with him that night. I want you to give me better answers than he did,' Jackson said, 'because you can see the consequences of a lacklustre answer.'

'Look, man, you don't have to—' Jacob began.

'No!' Jackson shouted back, his voice echoing wildly around the bare walls of the building, 'you don't *get* to say that to me. *Not again.* Your *friend* did and look what happened to him.'

His shouts were deep, and his anger was prevalent and genuine. There was a worried sparkle in Jacob's eyes as he started unknowing at the man in front of him. His personality was perplexing. One moment he was shouting at him, terrifying him to his very core, and the next he was speaking calmly but nervous, looking as if he were completely out of his depth.

Jackson sensed that and felt the need to address it.

'Look,' he said, after taking a few moments to calm himself down, 'you know I'm new to this, right?'

Jacob nodded.

'So, like I told your friend, I don't really know what is gonna happen here. I haven't planned it out like some deranged serial killer or some meticulous criminal, I'm just going with the flow, y'know?'

Jacob didn't reply, he just nodded again, which prompted a look of angry concern to evade Jackson's face.

'Now's the time to ask some questions,' Jackson said with a smile, bringing his knife out again, the blade edge covered in hardened flakes of blood.

Jacob sat up straight against the wall, trying to get as far away from it as possible. He glanced over to his friend as if he'd be able to save him from the situation. He was delusional, but he just wanted to go home.

'I want you to tell me why you did what you did, and I want you to apologise for it,' Jackson said.

'I don't know what you think I did, but I had nothing to do with it,' Jacob glanced over at Arthur again, the look on his face turning sour, 'he-he made me do it. Could you not tell that he was the *mastermind* of it all?'

'That's funny,' Jackson said with a smirk, 'that's what he said, too. He said you "paid him to go", that you had something "big" planned. Now... who am I to believe, huh?'

Jacob laughed, humoured by the seemingly made-up story.

'Did he actually tell you that? He said I *paid* him to go and *kill* someone?'

'Y'know, you seem so calm and, I don't know, down-to-earth for being in this position,' Jackson replied, 'I have a knife in my hand – which, by the way, has your friend's blood on it – and you're just casually sitting there like nothing happened. Arthur had the same care-free attitude, and look what happened to him.'

Jackson wasted no time in moving the process along, not being bothered to go through the same tedious conversations and back-and-forth that he did with Arthur. He quickly cocked his arm back and launched it into the side of Jacob's face, cracking his knuckles on his jaw, and sending droplets of saliva a few feet across the ground. Jacob hummed sharply and aggressively, trying to mask the pain that he was in. He placed his hand on his face to try and comfort himself, but it didn't last long.

Without giving him a chance to pull himself together, Jackson pressed the butt of the knife into the laceration in Jacob's leg, forcing him to forget about his jaw and scream out in pain, holding his hands above Jackson's to try and get him to stop.

'Stop! Stop, please!' Jacob pleaded.

Using his own tactics against him, Jackson just smiled. It was a 'playboy' smile, reminiscent of the ones both men had flashed at him before.

'I'm not even going to bother asking you the same questions I asked Arthur, you're just going to give the same answers.'

Jacob was breathing heavily; he couldn't focus on anything right now, other than the deep and searing pain in his leg. He kept tensing his muscles, trying to stem the pain but nothing worked. He was just forced to sit through it, unbearably. Every minute lasted what seemed like an hour.

'Where's your phone?' Jackson asked, hovering the butt of the knife over his leg just in case he needed persuading.

Jacob pointed to his right-side trouser pocket, retrieving it before he was commanded to do so. It was the same phone that his friend had, just without the crack on the screen. Maybe that was the 'burner' they all decided on, and their real phones were locked away for safekeeping.

'Password?' Jackson asked again.

'2... 1... 9... 1,' Jacob replied, having to take a deep breath between every number, even then he could only whisper.

Inputting the right numbers, Jackson began scrolling through the phone. Every now and again, he glanced down at Jacob to check on him. He was alive by definition, but there didn't look to be any life in him. His breathing was slow and meticulous. The way his lips were coming together looked like he was clenching his teeth, and he was taking long blinks. He was willing himself through the pain. The expression on his face made it look like he wanted to say something, but after a few glances over to Arthur, he realised that it wasn't worth his time; and it wasn't worth wasting the only few breathes that he thought he had left.

He stared across to the other side of the room like he was there by himself and nothing else mattered. He didn't care what Jackson was doing anymore.

But maybe he should.

After browsing through all of the menial stuff on the phone, which he didn't care about at all; texts from various take-outs being the most prominent appearance, he found the number of Grey Sullivan.

He quickly racked his brain for something to say, before sending a one-line text inviting him to the building, hoping he was as oblivious as Jacob was in his reply.

'How you feeling down there?' Jackson asked while he waited for the phone to go off.

Jacob slowly moved his head to make eye contact with his kidnapper and took a few long blinks, as if to say *'really?'*.

Jackson shrugged.

'Never... felt better,' Jacob replied after a few short minutes, 'how you feeling... up there?'

'A lot better than you, I can see that,' Jackson replied with a smile. Jacob forced a smile back, losing the hostility that he possessed previously; coming to terms with his life now.

'What made you... think that?'

Jackson laughed and shrugged again like he was doing his best to be condescending. He felt powerful and in charge; something he'd never really felt in all his years of life.

As he was about to respond, Jacob's phone vibrated in his hand and smiled.

Oh fuck, I'll be over soon, bro, the text read.

'Well,' Jackson said, 'looks like we're going to have another guest at this party.'

He threw the phone down at Jacob, hitting his stomach before bouncing onto the floor with a quiet thud, before returning to the corner of the room to wait for the knock.

11

It felt like he was dozing off. Jackson had been sitting in the corner of the room, just below a window that was slightly open, staring at the thick concrete pillar that dominated his vision. He could see two pairs of legs but nothing else. Jacob moved his pair every so often, probably about all that he could muster at that point. Every few minutes, Jackson heard a quiet wince and a soft struggle; other than that, he felt like he was alone in the room, with nothing but his thoughts.

With his feet crossed and outstretched, leaning on his heels, and his arms folded, he felt like a bored security guard in a building that would never be at risk. He sat in silence, reliving everything. He felt like he had to decide whether or not to feel bad; to feel guilty.

Shouldn't he be feeling *something*? He'd just killed someone and then stabbed someone else. He wasn't going to stop, either. That was the scariest part. He had no idea what was propelling him. Was it the adrenaline? Was it the feeling of being in charge? Or was it just revenge?

As his head began to droop and his eyelids got too heavy, he felt himself fall into a soft, relaxing slumber. But only for a few minutes.

He jolted up to the sound of a fist banging heavily on the door. It was quick and methodical, tapping to an unheard metronome. It was a constant thud in Jackson's ear that didn't stop until he got to the door. He took it slow, trying to be quiet. The door-handle creaked agonisingly as he pushed it down, opening the door just enough so that he didn't need to show his face. He felt pressure from the other side; Grey was trying to force his way in, sensing the urgency of the situation.

'Come on, Art, stop playing,' Grey said from the other side, a strong element of dominance in his voice.

With a scheming smirk coming over his face, Jackson swung the door open, grabbing Grey by the collar. The force of the movement swung Grey around in shock, to face Jackson as he stood there, in the doorway, glaring down on his potential victim.

The playboy smile reappeared, while confusion invaded Grey's young face.

Still holding his collar, he swung him across the room as hard as he could, mixing his upper body strength with the adrenaline that had been harvesting itself in his body for most of the day.

Grey was sent hurtling to the ground, a few feet in front of Jacob's outspread legs. He looked down at his friend, not surprised that the three of them were now in the same room together. He knew they'd get caught for what they did. He just didn't know the day would come so soon, and that it would be at the hands of *him*.

Grey looked up at Jackson, unsure of what to feel or how to react in the situation he currently found himself in. Before he could make any noises or look around to see where the hell he was, he felt the full force of the bottom of Jackson's shoe in his face, almost breaking his nose. His head was sent hurtling backward, smashing off the rock-hard floor. He was dazed and groggy, knowing even less about where he was. More importantly, he had no idea who'd just kicked him in the face. As he was deep in thought, he didn't notice the same foot coming back to his face a second time.

And then a third.

Jackson dragged him over towards the wall and lay him roughly next to Jacob, who looked down at his other friend with a blank look on his face, feeling no emotions towards him; just basic acceptance.

'Okay,' Jackson said, looking down at both of them, 'since we're all here, I can hopefully get a solid answer from at least one of you.' He looked towards Arthur and then back to the other two. 'Arthur was a let-down, so hopefully, the two of you can corroborate a story to help me understand this whole ordeal.'

'What do you mean?' Grey asked, finally pulling himself together, but feeling the effects of the kicks.

'What do I mean? I mean, I want an answer to the question I've been asking this entire time.' Jackson said, walking over to the other side of the room to a small sink near the end of the tool desk. He picked up a glass and filled it up halfway with water, taking small sips as he walked back over to the men.

'Forgive me for the transparency,' Grey replied, 'but, what question? I've just gotten here so I'm not exactly caught up.'

'I want to know,' Jackson took another sip, 'why my wife had to die. Hannah didn't do anything to anyone her entire life, so I want to know why she *deserved* to die. Because I've been racking my brain for a long time trying to come up with an answer and I come up blank every time.'

Jacob remained quiet, looking at Grey then looking back at Jackson, suggesting that he answer the question for the both of them. Grey laughed awkwardly, not worried about the situation.

'What's so funny?' Jackson asked, taking a step forward.

The smile vanished from Grey's face, and his eyes moved towards the floor, feeling more awkward.

'No, come on,' a hint of anger and frustration crept into Jackson's voice, 'is my wife's death funny to you? I've asked all three of you *why* she had to die, and I haven't gotten anything from any of you. What's so hard about that damn question? And what is so *damn funny*?'

Jacob stayed quiet like he was the third wheel on a romantic date. Grey laughed again, less awkwardly this time, before adjusting in place to make himself more comfortable.

'You're way out of your depth, bro,' he said, rubbing his face where he was kicked, 'You're trying to be something you're not and I can see straight through it. This isn't—'

Before he could finish his sentence, Jackson hurled his glass at the wall just above the men's heads, smashing it and sending water and large shards of glass falling over, and around, them. One shard scraped down Jacob's neck and he winced, while a few narrowly missed the side of Grey's face.

'*No!*', Jackson shouted as the glass shattered, '*you don't get to say that to me*. All three of you had told me that and it's *pissing* me off.' There was a deep anger in Jackson's voice; it sounded more gravelly and it wasn't like his usual tone. 'If this wasn't me, do you really think I'd have gone this far? Maybe it wasn't me before; I work in a coffee shop for God's sake.'

He waved the knife through the air, reminding the men that he actually had one.

'And I fully intend to hurt you for what you've done,' he finished.

Grey acted like he wasn't listening, instead of focusing on ridding his personal space from glass, throwing it to the corner of the room to his left, and wiping his hair to get rid of excess water.

Jacob looked at Jackson, readying himself to speak for the first time in what seemed like forever. He'd been slowly getting his composure back, trying to forget about his leg wound.

'Calm… down, Jordy, you'll… hurt yourself,' he said.

Jackson froze and stared down at Jacob, almost offended by what had just come out of his mouth.

'What did you just say?' he asked.

'You just need… to take it easy, man. If you keep… swinging that knife around, you'll—'

'No, no, what did you just *call* me?'

'I called you Jordy. That's your name... isn't it?'

'It's *not* my name, actually. My name is Jackson Yardley.'

Grey looked up, suddenly interested in the conversation, and stared at Jackson. He burst out laughing; not at the situation but at how awkward it currently was.

'So you're not... you're not Jordy Renalto?' Jacob asked.

After calming himself down, Grey finally spoke. 'Funny story...' he said.

'I don't think anything could possibly be funny about this,' Jackson replied, 'because I'm not even sure what the hell is going on right now.'

'Well, it turns out that we *may* have made a mistake.'

'What *kind* of mistake?' Jackson stepped forward, making sure he had a good grip on the knife handle so it was ready to use in an instant.

'Uh... well,' Grey started, beginning to fidget, 'I guess it turns out we, kinda, *may* have, gotten the wrong house. So your wife—that was an accident. We, uh, yeah, we weren't supposed to hit you, I guess that's the problem here.'

Jackson stared, wide-eyed, at Grey as each word dripped painfully off his tongue. He could see the sweat beginning to form on his face as he spoke, while Jacob was trying to pretend that he wasn't there, doing his best to fade into the background.

Jackson couldn't move, paralysed, but it felt like his hand had seized around the knife handle and he couldn't let go even if he tried. He started to tremble;

there was anger, pain, hurt, and plenty of other emotions swimming through him at that point and he didn't know which one to make the prominent one. He was confused, in every sense of the word.

'I guess,' Jacob said, quickly glancing at Grey before looking up, 'we should feel even worse that we raped her.'

12

We?! We *raped her?*

Jackson stared blankly into Jacob's eyes, not listening to whatever else that he had to say. His lips were moving but there was no noise. There was no noise from anywhere. He couldn't hear him speaking; he couldn't hear Grey coughing and shuffling along the floor; he couldn't hear the scraping of the tree branches along the glass windows along the side of the building. He heard a constant dull, squealing noise in his ear as the minutes ticked past. Grey looked at him, concerned, waving his hand in the air to get his attention but he was frozen solid.

'Shut up,' Jackson calmly whispered a few minutes later. He didn't move a muscle, he didn't move his eyes, he was still frozen.

Grey then began to talk, but Jackson didn't that either, he had still zoned them out. His brain didn't want to take in what they were saying; it was still focused on the last bit.

'I said shut up,' he whispered again, softer still. He still hadn't moved for a good ten minutes, but time didn't matter to him anymore. Nothing seemed to matter anymore.

Suddenly, the squealing stopped and all the different noises returned to his ears, seemingly crashing against his eardrums and sending an unfortunate ache through his head.

'—and you know what?' Jacob finished.

'What?' Jackson whispered again, finally looking somewhere other than straight ahead – down at Jacob.

'She probably enjoyed it,' he replied, with a wry smile.

Jackson took a step forward so that he was right in front of Jacob's legs and crouched. 'What did you just say to me?' he asked.

'What? She looked like the type to,' Jacob replied, unphased by Jackson right in front of his face, and feeling a lot cockier than he did before. Grey's presence seemed to have awakened something in him.

Without warning, Jackson lashed out and slammed the knife into the side of Jacob's stomach, slowly twisting it until he met resistance; the blade scraping against the lower part of the rib-cage. He released his grip and took his hand away, leaving the knife sticking out of Jacob's body, watching as the blood ran over the edge of the blade, and marvelling at his handy-work. Jacob looked down at the knife and tried to scream; a fragile, exhausted scream, but no sounds come out. He was left sitting in a slump, trying to comprehend what was happening to him.

He coughed in bunches, as blood began trickling out of his mouth every so often.

'She... looked,' he began, struggling to get the words out,' like... a—like... a slut.'

Overcome with rage, and as the intense adrenaline returned as quickly as it left, he grabbed Jacob's hair and ripped his head back, screaming into his face. '*No,*' he shouted, '*I said shut up.*'

As easy as he stuck it in, Jackson ripped the knife back out of Jacob's stomach with a grunt, bringing clumps of blood with it and splashing delicately onto Grey's clothes. His face twisted in disgust and he shuffled away to avoid more of it.

In one easy motion, he sliced swiftly along Jacob's neck almost from ear to ear, killing him in an instant, as the other two men were splattered with his blood. Grey shrieked as loud as he could, a new feeling of terror taking over him. He began trembling and his eyes darted around all corners of the room, not wanting to look straight at it. He didn't want to see the blood, he wanted to be as far away from it as possible.

But, if he moved, he'd probably be dead. He was never leaving that building.

Jackson didn't flinch as the blood covered his face, he just calmly closed his eyes like was falling asleep. After a few seconds, he opened his eyes and fell back into a sitting position, coolly spitting out the blood that had found a way into his mouth. It left a strong, slightly salty taste on the top of his tongue. It was as if he'd stuck a penny in his mouth and started sucking on it.

But the taste didn't last long. Soon after, he felt a burning sensation that travelled to the back of his throat.

Then, before he could stop it, a small stream of vomit burst out his mouth and onto Jacob's ankles in front of him. He let out a pained groan and slumped backward, leaning on one of the pillars and wiping his mouth.

13

Jackson sat dejected against the pillar, leaning his head back and trying to regain some composure. He began breathing heavily, closing his eyes and focusing only on himself at that point.

Inhale for a few seconds. Hold it. Exhale for a few seconds, he thought.

Inhale. Hold it. Exhale.

'Y'know,' he said softly, 'it's times like these where I understand what you've been saying this whole time.'

Another deep breath in. Hold it. Another deep breath out.

Grey tried his best to wipe the disgusted, horrified look off of his face – and the blood that was attached to it – and looked at Jackson. 'Huh?' he asked.

Jackson opened his eyes and looked back at Grey. He sat comfortably and relaxed; one leg straight and the other bent with his foot flat on the floor. He rested his wrist on his knee with the knife hung over it. Small droplets of blood were making their way from the tip of the knife to the ground between his legs.

'Well, I mean, that was probably the most disgusting thing I've ever seen in my whole life,'

Jackson said like he'd lost the hostility and was talking to him as a friend. 'I can't remember the last time I threw up. That was just... that was something else.'

Grey looked confused at Jackson. He'd seen at least three different personalities since he arrived there and he was unsure how to act, or how to respond to anything that he said. He knew he was scared, though. He didn't want to end up like Jacob, but he had a gut feeling that he was going to die at some point.

Maybe he could use his charisma and self-taught negotiation skills to his advantage.

'Look, man, I never wanted to be included in the plan,' he said. 'That's the honest truth. I feel horrible that they got the wrong person, I'm really sorry that you got caught up in it all.'

Jackson glared back at him, feeling multiple different emotions.

'So *now* you're sorry?' he replied, sensing the hostility beginning to return.

'Well, yeah—'

'It's too late to be fucking sorry, Grey. I asked for an apology from all three of you, but you kept spouting the same bullshit about thinking you know who I am and that I'm in over my head. But *now*—' he let out an offended 'pfft' and stood up '—now you feel bad for killing her, and now you're full of apologies. How *convenient* for you. I'm sure it has nothing to do with the fact that you just watched me slice your friends throat and you—'

He paused to wretch, like he was going to throw up again, then calmed down and said 'You're covered in his blood. Give over, will you?'

Jackson began getting frustrated again; his nerves had calmed and he was reminded of where he was and what he was actually doing. He started pacing slowly like he was deep in thought, leaving a small trail of blood droplets behind him as he held the knife loosely in his right hand. There was nothing on his mind, he couldn't find a train of thought, it all seemed like TV static. Shortly after, he stopped and turned to face Grey, who was still shuffling in place, not hiding how painfully uncomfortable he was.

Outside, the wind had subsided and the branches had stopped scraping ominously against the glass windows. There were a few more cars driving past than there was when he arrived, but he made sure to park his Jaguar in a different neighbourhood nearby, and out of sight. There was a dull glare forcing itself inside the building; the sun was at just the right angle in the sky to see what was happening. It was just a shame that it couldn't call the police and get Grey the hell out of there.

'Set something straight for me, please. I just can't wrap my head around this whole thing,' Jackson said.

Grey sat up straight and looked up into Jackson's eyes, trying to be serious but straining his neck in the process.

'If I tell you everything,' he started, moving slightly in place to get more comfortable, 'will you let me go?'

'That's not what I asked,' Jackson replied, lowering himself to a crouch.

'But if I tell you everything I know, will you let me go? I won't snitch or anything.'

'How in the hell did you get confused between two houses? How dumb could you possibly be? All three of you. And *then*, the stupidity doesn't end there, does it? *No*,' he stood back up and began pacing. 'You entered the house, saw a *woman*, not the man you went for, and decided to kill her even though that was *clearly* not your target and you should've known that! That makes absolutely no sense to me, and I need it to. *Somehow*.'

'Do we have a deal, then?' Grey asked, not even bothering to respond to the lecture Jackson had just given him.

Angered by the ignorance, Jackson took a threatening step towards him, making sure the knife was in a good position to do some damage.

'Okay, okay,' Grey replied, throwing his hands up in a defensive position, 'I'll tell you what I know. Just— man, just stay away from me with that damn knife.'

Jackson stopped and retreated, holding his hands behind his back and leaning on the pillar behind him.

'Jacob was the main guy behind it all,' he began, 'he's the one that called me and Arthur about the whole thing.'

Jackson scoffed, but Grey simply rolled his eyes and continued.

'It was a week or so before it happened when he called me. I was in my apartment watching random basketball highlights on YouTube; and he calls me up when it's like 11 pm, saying he's got a job. I was confused because y'know, I've already got an actual job and he's talking like we're part of some big criminal enterprise. I remember it because when he said that, I said to him "are we in a gangster movie now?"'

He quietly laughed to himself, then realised where he was, dropping his face back to the serious, try-not-to-die look.

'Anyway,' Grey said, 'he told me this guy had hired him to do this job, right? He didn't tell me who the guy was, and I didn't ask because I didn't even know what he was going on about. He went on and on about some random crap but told me that he needed to kill a guy called Jordy Renalto. Again—' he swallowed his saliva, catching his breath '—he didn't tell me much about that. But apparently, Jordy had done some real bad stuff; I'm talking, really, really bad, and there were people that wanted him dead. But that's not the best bit, oh no.

'Jacob said this guy would pay $25,000 to kill Jordy. Can you believe that? Twenty-Five Thou.' He raised his eyebrows in fake shock as if he were trying to sell the story. 'I was a bit sceptical, as you can imagine; that's a lot of cash just to kill some random guy. But, Jacob seemed convinced about it, he vouched for the whole plan, so I said "fuck it, I could use the money'.'

Jackson kept slowly pacing along the same line – roughly 10 feet either way – with his eyes closed, taking in all the information and trying to visualise the whole thing. He only opened them every so often to make sure Grey was still firmly seated on the floor. When he paused for a while, Jackson stopped and looked at him, sensing that he was getting to the important part and wanted to react accordingly.

Grey looked at Arthur and Jacob, shaking his head unpleasantly as he thought about what had happened. He shuffled along the wall a little more, feeling the sweat moving across his entire body. He felt warm but cold at the same time, and his butt was numb from sitting on the hard, damp floor for so long.

The blood that splattered on his clothes from Jacob's neck had dried and gone a darker shade of red. That would surely give him nightmares.

If he could live long enough to sleep another night.

'Carry on,' Jackson said.

'Okay, so,' Grey went on, 'Jacob had called Art, as well, and said he was fine with it. So, the way I was seeing it, was that we kill one guy – how hard could that be, right? It'd be three of us against one of him, a one-day job – then we each get $8,000 plus. That was a no brainer. You'd do that, right?'

Jackson kept quiet, trying to hide the anger he felt from that question. He glared at him, and Grey sensed the burning intent in his darkening blue eyes, so he shut himself up.

'Of course, whatever,' Grey muttered to himself before carrying on, 'Jacob said the guy had given him a brief description of his house, and he'd said it was somewhere in Irvine. Art said it sounded like the house that's opposite his mom's. Obviously, we didn't know any better because we weren't that familiar with the area, so we just went along with it.'

Grey shuffled in place again, complaining silently to himself about the comfort of his seat. He looked at Jackson as if he wanted to ask him for somewhere nicer to sit, but Jackson remained unmoved, only interested in the story he had to tell.

'Right, yeah, moving on. We got to the house, didn't see any car or anything, so we assumed it was empty. So we—'

'If you thought it was empty, why didn't you just leave?' Jackson interrupted.

'Art wanted to break in and steal stuff; y'know, as a warning or something. I don't know, man, I just went along with it.'

'Well, you shouldn't have,' Jackson said angrily, taking another step toward him. Grey threw his hands up defensively once again, knowing it would do little to deter the knife-wielding maniac.

'Do you want me to tell you everything or not?' Grey asked, getting agitated himself.

'I want you to get to the damn point, and answer my question.'

'Alright, alright.'

'Thank you,' Jackson said with an exhausted sigh.

'We got upstairs and we saw a woman and assumed it was Jordy's wife or girlfriend or something, so we were gonna use her as bait, or as leverage, whatever. But she pulls out this baseball bat and starts swinging it wildly. To be honest, I feel like it got Jacob a bit too excited. She came towards us and kept swinging it, and she smashed Art in the side of the head, he fell into the wall, pretty dazed. Jacob got angry and he stabbed her loadsa times.

'Next thing I know, she's on the floor and he drops the knife and starts pulling her trousers down, and she's too weak to stop him so he just—'

'Don't you dare finish that sentence,' Jackson said, anger swelling up inside of his body.

'Yeah,' Grey conceded, 'you get the picture.'

'I just don't get it,' Jackson shouted dejectedly, stopping to let out a confused and frustrated grunt towards the ceiling. Sadness started to creep in as he was reminded of what happened to his wife.

Grey could see the pain in his eyes; the dark red seemed to be gradually losing its colour, becoming dull and lifeless. He could sense the pain in his words; the cracking in his voice and the lightening of his tone.

'You need to admit that this isn't you,' Grey said sympathetically, hoping for a different response this time around. 'You're not the type to do stuff like this, you're a normal person. As pissed off as you get when I said that last time, it's the truth and you probably know that yourself. You just *want* to be this person because it's easier than actually dealing with your problems; it's easier than actually accepting it.'

'You don't know me,' Jackson replied, insulted, 'you don't know anything about me. There's no point in trying to play psychologist because it's not going to work.'

'But—'

'No! "But" nothing.'

'Well, yeah, because we both know I'm right. You're not listening to me.'

'Because I don't *have* to listen to you,' Jackson spoke louder, aggravated and impatient.

'Well you should, because I can see it in your face and I can hear it in your voice: this is hurting you more than helping. Killing me is just going to make you worse, and you're too new to this to know—'

'Oh yeah, and you're a seasoned expert, are you? Are you a hardened killer? A career criminal?'

'I'm much more suited to it than you.'

'Well, I can sure as hell see that from just looking at you.'

Grey was beginning to get frustrated, too. He felt like he was talking to a brick wall, and Jackson was being too immature and naïve for any negotiations to work. He felt like he could fight back if he could. There was too much weakness in his figure, and he knew that Jackson wasn't all there; he wasn't fully focused.

As the room went quiet for a few minutes, outside was still full of life. There were birds chirping happily in the trees as they watched the sun set slowly over the concrete horizon, deepening the glare coming through the windows and casting a dark orange tint on the side of Jacob's colourless face.

'Look to your right,' Jackson said, almost defensively, 'I've just killed two people out of nothing but revenge. And it felt *great*. That was a kick that I don't think I've ever experienced before, and I'm perfectly fine with feeling that a third time.'

Grey pointed at the vomit in front of, and covering, Jacob's feet. 'But you saw a load of blood and done *that*. So, which one do you think is *actually* you? What do you think Hannah would do if she walked in and saw you like this?'

Jackson burst into a small fit of rage hearing his wife's name come out of his mouth. It's like it was a trigger for a split personality. 'She can't walk in because you fucking killed her, didn't you?' he exclaimed.

Grey jerked his head back slightly, suddenly feeling a little more nervous than he did a few minutes before.

'And don't you dare even say her name. You have no right to say anything about her; you didn't *know* her. I knew her, and you and your *stupid* little friends took her away from me. *And you tell me it was a fucking accident?*

Jackson's face began to get red, and he felt like he was burning up. There didn't seem to be any control left in his body.

'Okay, calm down,' Grey replied, unapologetic.

'No, I won't calm down,' Jackson said, getting louder with every word, 'I'm sick to death of you, thinking you know what kind of person I am, and telling me—'

He walked over to Grey, gripping the knife tightly in his hand. Grey became worried and started squirming. A distinct look of worry plastered itself over his face and he felt his chest tense up. Jackson leant down and wrapped his left hand around Grey's neck, pressing tightly over his Adam's apple and digging into each side with his fingers.

'Get up,' he whispered, 'get up right now.'

'What are you—no,' Grey said, struggling for breaths as Jackson forced him up by his throat. 'You don't have to—'

'Shut your mouth,' Jackson replied, turning him around and using his forearm to press Grey's cheek against the wall.

It felt cold and dusty on his face. He tried to free himself but the force behind him was too strong.

'Look, man, you really—'

'I said shut up,' Jackson exclaimed again. Grey could smell mint on his breath as it was forced into his face; faint but strong, causing a tingly itch inside his nose.

'Do you honestly think I wasn't going to kill you before I left?' Jackson asked, pressing harder with his forearm, squishing Grey's cheek against the wall, 'Did you think your *negotiating* was gonna work? *Did you?*'

'Please. Just, please—' Grey pleaded, tears beginning to effortlessly fall down his cheek, showing his true colours.

'It's too late, I'm afraid,' Jackson replied, calmly and remorseless.

Without thinking twice, he removed his forearm from Grey's neck and straightened up. Without giving him a moment to react, Jackson stretched out his left arm and placed the palm of his hand onto the back of Grey's skull, applying more pressure, making sure his head was straight. He got a strong hold of the knife and dug the blade deep into the back of his neck, in the centre. A sharp, intense gasp shot its way out of his mouth, an involuntary spasm of pain. Jackson could feel bone on the edge of the knife, recognising the resistance as he jarred the blade back-and-forth for a few seconds, severing Grey's spinal cord in a few short, easy movements.

As the nerves were snapped and paralysis set in an instant, Jackson took his hand away and removed the knife, causing Grey's knees to immediately buckle beneath him. The rest of his body quickly followed suit. An intense snapping sound vibrated through the air, sending shivers all around Jackson's body, as Grey's ankle snapped violently from the force of gravity pulling his torso down to the ground. He folded like a play-mat, then sprawled out like a rag doll. The snapping of all of his nerves caused his eyes to quickly roll back into his head like he was deeply engrossed in a dream. The milky whites of his eyes were thick and horrifying, and he started drooling incessantly.

Jackson stared down at him, partly terrified, but enthralled. He dropped the knife; the cold steel hitting the ground startled him; he was lost in his own world, fascinated by Grey's body completely shutting itself down in front of his face.

He heard some faint choking sounds as Grey choked on his tongue, until a few minutes later, when the drooling subsided and his mouth closed.

After that, he was gone.

14

Jackson's hands were stained – figuratively and literally. He felt like Lady Macbeth as he stood over the small sink in the corner of the room, scrubbing his hands of blood. It was beyond dried; not crispy or flaking off as he scraped it, it had simply become a part of his hand. The light tan of his skin had gotten a wine-coloured tinge and he couldn't get rid of it.

He scrubbed and scrubbed, using multiple cloths – both wet and dry – to try and rid himself from it but nothing worked. The sink was fit for a prison cell; somewhere he hoped wouldn't turn out to be his permanent accommodation when all the dust had settled. He needed to be smart, he needed to be a step ahead of everyone else. He needed to accept that this was his life now; he could either embrace it so he wouldn't get caught and hopefully find another way to replicate the bursts of adrenaline that kept him going; or he could fall back into his past life, serving coffee and being scared of everything.

It wasn't a choice anymore. Prison wasn't for him. He was a killer now. He needed to act like it.

After drying his hands over the sink, he stood up and cracked his back like he was a glowstick, getting a sudden burst of energy. He turned around and looked at his victims. Puddles of blood had dried in front of them, retaining a darker red outline. Arthur's face was white, but his eyes were still slightly open. Jacob was slumped over, leaning on Arthur's arm with a deep laceration across his neck, with dried blood covering his clothes. It was like they were napping together after a long day. Grey was in a place of his own, contorted in an inhumane way against the wall, limbs going every which way.

Jackson smiled to himself, feeling oddly successful, but knew he couldn't relish in it for too long. He didn't want to spend another minute in that building, the stench of death was beginning to dominate the air and it was disturbing his nose. He started to clean up what he could, he tried to eliminate all traces of himself from every surface. He left the three men how they were; it was almost artistic how each one fit together with the backdrop of the wall.

He wiped down all of the surfaces that he remembered touching and threw some water on the floor where he'd been stepping. If he was going to be caught for anything, it wasn't going to be because the police identified his shoe print and traced it back to him. Just in case, he tried his best to wipe where he'd had his hands on the men, covering all bases.

Afterwards, he scrubbed the blade of the knife to make sure no small flakes of blood were going to drop off and sink to the bottom of his pocket. He returned it to the guard that it came in and put it back in his pocket like he'd never even used it.

He went over to the door and placed his hand on the knob, stopping and turning to check for anything he'd missed. Happy with his cleaning, he opened the door and stepped through, closing it softly behind him.

The low-hanging sun sent deep, orange rays along the road and into his eyes. The chill of the air that began circulating his body made him feel cool and refreshed. The sky was turning an attractive shade of pink, combining with the beams of the sun, making a small portion of the clear, cloudless sky a peachy colour.

He breathed it all in, comforted by the freshness. He closed his eyes and let the experience take over him; feeling the breeze lightly brush against his cheek. He felt like he'd just walked into a new, different personality. He felt like he'd just walked into a new life.

He quickly turned back to look at the building and scoffed. In a way, he was excited for someone to find the bodies; he tried to imagine how they'd feel when they discovered the massacre. It made him smile, and he enjoyed that feeling.

He walked away from the building and towards the street where he'd parked his car, straightening his clothes out as he crossed the road.

Boy, he needed a drink.

15

Jackson coughed as the third glass of neat whiskey caught the back of his throat. It used to go down so easily, but now it tasted thicker and it left a burning sensation on his tongue. He put the glass down on the coaster and shivered. He needed another one.

'I can get you something a bit easier if you want,' the bartender said as Jackson held up his glass for another. 'It looks like you're struggling with that.'

'It's just been a long day, I'm usually fine,' he replied with a cheeky smile.

The bartender stood in front of him, pouring another single measure and placing it back on the coaster. She put a few strands of light brown hair behind her ear and studied the guy getting progressively drunker in front of her eyes.

'Maybe you need a mixer,' she said, 'it'll make it easier on your head. You get a similar taste, but it feels better in the morning.'

'I don't know,' he replied, keeping his head down and focusing on his drink, 'I'm not really too worried about it being easy in the morning, y'know?'

The bartender rested her palms on the counter and looked down at him. 'Really rough day, huh?'

'Yeah, you could say that,' he forced a laugh out, but she saw straight through it.

'Okay, here,' she reached down to her soda gun and started filling his glass up with cola, 'you might not want it to be easy on your head, but this will make it easier on your wallet. Go a bit slower on this one, yeah?'

He looked up to her and nodded solemnly. She flashed him a smile and walked down the bar to serve another customer.

The bar was relatively quiet, but it seemed energetic and ready to erupt with partying at any given moment. There were a variety of different coloured lights littered around the top of the wall, with signed and framed posters of various California-based athletes beneath them. A large jukebox in the corner of the room behind a booth-seat began playing the opening drum solo of Steve Winwood's *Higher Love*. The melodies sent a calming vibe through him and he started tapping his foot on the bottom of the bar stool.

Think about it, there must be higher love, he sang quietly to himself, still with his head hung, staring into the chasm of cola in his glass.

A large group of people walked in, talking amongst each other and spoiling his enjoyment of the music, but he kept singing along in his head until the song finished.

Taking small sips of his drink, and enjoying the bleakness of his thoughts, he felt the stool next to him move. His eyes moved towards it, seeing the slim legs of a female patron sit down. She ordered a bottle of beer and looked over to him. He could feel her eyes burning a hole in the side of his head, but he didn't want to move.

He sat on his stool without moving, bent over and looking down in his glass, for what seemed like an hour, and the sensation of her burning glare never went away. His eyes darted in her direction every so often and it always seemed like she was looking at him. Something had to be done.

He turned to face her and was just about to call her out when she spoke to him instead.

'Sorry,' she said, 'I know I've been staring for a while. I was just, like, seeing how long you could stay in the same position without moving.'

Her voice was calm, relaxing, like listening to the waves of the ocean at night.

'Yeah, I—uh,' he tilted his head slightly, confused yet impressed by her intuition, 'I was just gonna ask you why I felt you staring at me ever since you came in. That's, uh, odd.'

'I can sense these things,' she replied with a smile. It was attractive and comforting.

'Oh yeah?' Jackson returned the smile, more awkward than anything else.

'Well, it's sorta what I do. I get paid to have good senses.'

'I see. So, you're one of those people that set up stalls on the side of the road and offer to tell people their future?'

'Maybe someday, I hope so, yeah,' she smiled again, 'but right now, I'm just a detective. It's not as fun.'

She took a drink of her beer, quickly turned her head to burp under her breath, then turned back to look at him.

'A detective, huh? That's a pretty big deal,' he said, straightening his back and taking a sip of his own drink.

'Yeah, I guess. I mean, I'm kinda still getting used to it. It's a different deal in California.'

'Are you not from here?'

'No, no, I just recently moved here. It was probably a few months ago now. I'm actually from Ohio.'

'You're a long way from home, then, aren't you?'

She nodded and took another drink, moving her stool a bit closer to him. As the conversation broke, Jackson managed to take in his surroundings a little more. The big group of people were still chatting like they were never going to stop and the lights were slowly changing colour like they were wrapped around a Christmas tree. The jukebox in the corner finished off the last powerful chorus of Michael Bolton's *Forever Isn't Long Enough* before moving seamlessly on to Kansas's *Carry On Wayward Son*.

'So why did you move?' Jackson asked, his eyes moving from the jukebox back to the woman.

'I guess I just wanted to go somewhere with more opportunities, more things to do. Ohio was nice and all, but I wanted out. The last case I had there dragged on for way too long, and it was only supposed to be a simple fugitive recovery. So, after that finished, I needed to change my scenery. Sorry, that was a long answer.'

'Hey, no, don't worry about it. I did ask the question; I wanted to know. It's not like I'm going anywhere. What's your name, by the way?'

'My name?'

'Yeah,' Jackson gave a friendly nod and a smile, 'you know, the thing that people call you.'

'Well if that's what we're doing, my name's Detective Harrod.'

'Okay, well, what about your birth name. What do *normal* people call you?'

'Oh, *normal people*. Well, that's easy. My name's Lily. What's yours?'

'My name's Jackson. Normal people just call me Jackson.'

She laughed and took another drink. Jackson did the same and they shared extended eye contact. Jackson could feel something that he hadn't felt in a long time, but he was just attributing that to the alcohol. It couldn't be anything else.

He hoped. It was still too soon.

'So, Lily Harrod, tell me about this case from Ohio. I'm intrigued. Why did it drag on for so long?'

'Hm,' she replied, swallowing a big gulp and wiping the excess froth from the side of her mouth, 'I'm not sure I can disclose the details.'

'Oh, come on,' Jackson said, 'it's a closed case from months and months ago. You can totally tell me everything.'

She edged a little closer and looked around the room, pretending that she was an informant giving classified information. Jackson played along and leaned in.

'So, it happened in this really small town. I'm sure only 800 people or something live there. I'm talking, really small. What was it called? Lemme think.'

She whispered to herself for a few seconds, saying different letters of the alphabet to try and trigger her memory.

'Oh yeah, okay,' she continued, 'it was called Stardew Falls. The case itself is really long, lots of details and background that I don't really want to go into. Basically, girl gets kidnapped by her own grandpa; grandpa kills the mayor, the ADA and the ADA's wife, beats one of his sons, Larry, to within an inch of his life; then puts his other son – Miles, the one with the daughter – through hell to try and get her back. Maybe he was bored, wanted to reconnect with his family, I don't know.

'Anyway, the old guy got shot by Larry and fell into a coma. That's when I got put on the case, because he got flagged on so many of our systems once he was admitted to hospital. After a few weeks, he wakes up and *somehow* manages to escape.'

Jackson sat still, engrossed by the story, and taking sips of his drink every so often.

'Then,' Lily went on, 'I get a call saying Grandpa turned up at a church in Chillicothe, a little town 90 miles away from Stardew. That also happened to be the church where Larry was getting married. I send officers down there, and they tell me there's a damn hostage situation going on. In the middle of a wedding – his *son's* wedding. Imagine that?'

She laughed, excited to be telling the story, opening up to Jackson after ordering her second beer. She took time to catch her breath as it seemed to him that she'd been telling the entire story without stopping to breathe. She was excited, like she had to get it out in a certain amount of time otherwise he'd forget the best bits, or it wouldn't be as good of a story.

She cracked her new bottle open without a thought and took a few chugs before setting it down on her coaster. A few small drops of condensation trickled down the neck of the bottle and landed on the counter.

Jackson made eye contact with the female bartender and ordered another whiskey and coke, flashing her a smile to indicate he was okay now. Then, he turned his attention back to an expectant Lily, waiting for him to look at her so she could finish her story.

'That's crazy,' Jackson muttered, not taking his eyes off her face as she told it, smiling to himself when she got excited.

'That's not even the craziest part,' she replied, 'Now, I get down there and it's a total mess. People are scared, they're gathered in the corner of the room because this *insane* old man has his son and son's fiancée at gunpoint, meanwhile, his other son is trying to talk him out of it. Then we get there and we're trying to talk him out of it as well, but it's clearly going in one ear and out the other.

'Anyway, after about an hour, we've got the Marshalls here because he's a wanted fugitive. Soon as they arrive, he starts shouting more. Before we can react or anything, he shoots the fiancée straight in the head. Obviously, somebody then shoots him multiple times. Larry starts beating the crap out of his dead body, crying more than I've ever seen someone cry. It was a carnival, it was.'

After finishing her tale, enough for a blockbuster movie, she relaxed and chugged half of her beer before ordering a third and smiling to herself; proud and happy.

Jackson took a big gulp of his newest glass, throwing half the contents of it down his throat in one swift motion. It tickled the back of his throat this time; the burning sensation had dissipated and he could taste it, and he was suddenly feeling better about himself.

As he stared at the woman sitting next to him, it dawned on him that the hours he'd been sitting at the bar with her, he'd forgotten about everything. He'd noticed the way her butterscotch hair fell over her face, and how she'd flap her hand softly at it to move it. He'd noticed the freckles on her face that seemed to vanish when she smiled, and how her gunmetal grey eyes seemed to shine as she did.

After a few hours of just talking and finally enjoying someone's company, a thought occurred to him. Maybe he wasn't okay, maybe he was troubled in ways that he'd never comprehend or manage to deal with.

But for that one night, he knew he was completely fine.

II

16

'And now, breaking news out of Irvine,' the news anchor said, trying and failing to force some emotion into his monotone voice. 'Police have tonight discovered the bodies of three men who have been brutally murdered in a small, abandoned building near Little Joaquin Valley in West Irvine. For more, we go live to Simon Morris, who is on the scene.'

The broadcast switched to a middle-aged man with a large microphone resting just under his bottom lip. The breeze and the humidity in the area made his skin look velvety and his thick black hair was windswept, going off in each different direction. His eyes were focused on the camera, waiting for his cue to start speaking. Behind him, detectives and forensic investigators were going in and out of the abandoned garage, taking plastic bags back and forth and talking amongst themselves. Inside, there were occasional bright flashes where photos were being taken of the scene. After a few seconds of looking oblivious, Simon began to speak.

'Yeah, I'm here outside the abandoned building, which we know used to be some kind of garage. The bodies of the three men, all in their late 20s, were discovered around 7 pm tonight. A runner came past and reported smelling something foul coming from the open windows at the rear, and called the police. Police entered and found what can only be described as a bloodbath.

'I'm hearing that the identities of the three men are still unknown, but we will reveal any information as soon as we get it. However, one thing we do know is that it seems to be the work of just one person and not multiple. Detectives believe that only one murder weapon was used, which is yet to be recovered. It's believed to be a knife, with a blade roughly 7 or 8 inches, from first reports. But, there are no witnesses, and from what I can see from looking behind me, no solid leads or evidence. Police also initially believe that this location was used because of the lack of activity and foot-traffic on this long stretch of road, but there is a church, and a school roughly half a mile down Orchard Hills Trail, just in front of me.

'However, even with the lack of leads and no clear suspect, detectives seem confident that they'll be able to catch whoever was responsible for this brutal attack. Only time will tell. Let's just hope they follow through on that before things spiral totally out of control, and we have ourselves *yet another* serial killer in California. For ABC7 News, in West Irvine, I'm Simon Morris.'

As the broadcast switched back to the main anchor, who proceeded to promise that they'd give updates when they received them, Jackson switched the TV off and set the remote down on the coffee table. Lily walked into the room and stood behind the sofa, kissing his head before standing up straight to fasten her shirt.

'They're not wrong,' she said, 'we have absolutely nothing on that case.'

Jackson turned his head around to look up at her, confused and slightly nervous, for some reason. '*We?*' he asked.

'Yeah,' she replied, 'I've just been assigned as lead to that case. From what I hear, and from the basic reports I've read, it is turning out to be quite a bloodbath. I'm going down there soon to start fully working on it, so I might not see you a lot.'

'You're lead? On *this* case?'

'Yeah, I actually asked for it. It's a really high profile case, and I haven't been here long so I thought it'd be a great opportunity to make a name for myself. Is that okay?'

'Uhm, yeah. I, uh—' he stood up and walked around the sofa to stand in front of her. 'I don't see why it wouldn't be.'

She smiled and kissed him on the cheek, before tying her hair up into a professional-looking ponytail. She walked over to the long-standing mirror in the corner of the room and adjusted her outfit. Jackson just watched, feeling multiple different feelings and not knowing which one to focus on.

He was happy for her; getting a big-time case so soon.

But why did it have to be that *big-time case?*

'So, can you tell me anything about it? Maybe I can help you? A fresh set of eyes, outside the case, y'know?' Jackson said.

'I'm, uh,' Lily chuckled to herself quietly, 'I'm not sure if I can disclose anything. It's an ongoing investigation. You're not part of it. I'm sorry, I can't.'

'Well if you need any help, or if you get stuck on anything—'

'Yeah, I know, I appreciate that, but I'm not sure if it's gonna work right now. Just, uh, let me see how it goes first, yeah? I haven't seen the place yet, only know what I've been told.'

'Okay, well I'm gonna head back to the motel and I'll let you get over to the scene.'

Lily turned around, happy with how she looked and ready to start her day. She had a concerned look on her face, a genuine one that comforted him.

'About that,' she said, moving to the doorway to put her shoes on, 'when are you going to find an actual place – an apartment or a house – to live rather than being in a motel? I don't imagine it's very nice, or big enough for you.'

'I know, but it'll do for now. I'm looking for new places but there's not a lot. It's a gradual process. I will find one, though.'

She smiled and kissed him softly on the cheek, indirectly ushering him out. He smiled back, taking the hint, and took a slow stroll out of the door and down the long, concrete driveway. Lily followed him, stopping at the doorway and seeing him away. Before reaching the end, he stopped and turned back to face her, catching her off-guard as he did so.

'I hope you catch whoever did it. I really do. It's a horrible tragedy,' he said with a reassuring smile.

He didn't wait around for a reaction. She would be kept busy with work and the pressure of finding leads, while he had plenty of time by himself to pursue *other, more exciting* ventures.

He got in his car and looked at her one last time before driving off. He made sure he looked at her long enough to see her smile imprinted in his brain, so he could see it whenever he closed his eyes.

He'd use it as motivation for part two.

17

Jackson woke up with a jolt, snapping out of a nightmare that had been recurring for the last few months. He could feel beads of sweat moving agonisingly slow along the small of his back and his face felt sticky. He shook his fingers a little bit to regain the movement before removing his t-shirt to get some air.

Sitting up in the bed to recover, he took a few deep breaths and closed his eyes. The clock that hung on the wall adjacent to his head ticked painfully loud. Black with a crisp marble pattern on the face with thick, gold hands, it rang in his ear like an alarm clock that wouldn't stop. It seemed to get louder as he focused on it. All the other noises in the area seemed to fade away and the slow, meticulous ticking of the second hand tortured his ears. He looked at it, bringing back into focus the other noises. It was just a hair past 11 am, the morning sun was shining through the grey curtains, creating a light yellow tinge on the dull, brown carpet.

Jackson turned to look straight ahead at the foot of the bed. He stood staring at a blank, white wall with darker patches dotted around where it looked like it had been painted over in the wrong shade. The bed was inside an alcove in the corner of the room near the door, and there was only a foot and a half gap between the bed and the wall.

He looked to his right, seeing out of the window and down the street on which the motel was located. After a few seconds of admiring the view, he turned back and Hannah had appeared in the gap. He was suddenly transported back to his dream.

Or he was hallucinating; that couldn't be ruled out at this point. His mind had been going off by itself lately and he had a constant headache.

He could feel her presence in the room. She was always in the room somewhere, following his every move and judging him every time he did something that would usually be out of character. She wasn't wearing any clothes, just a large white towel that was wrapped around her body. It looked crisp and soft, and he could smell the freshness from where he sat. She stood motionless with her thighs pressed against the bottom of the memory foam mattress, creating a small indent. Her once-mesmerising eyes had no colour and her once-fresh face was pale. As the minutes passed, colour began to return to them, but not the usual bright blue that he had loved for many years. This time it was a light pink like she'd suffered a subconjunctival haemorrhage. It began taking over the milky whites of her eye and in no time at all, her pupils were surrounded by a sea of red.

Then she glanced down as the towel began to change to the same colour as her eyes. The red was growing darker and darker the more it soaked in, but she still stood and looked at it like Jackson wasn't even in the room. Without saying a single word, she looked up towards him and let go of the towel, letting it fall to the floor with a soft thud. Her naked body was drenched as if she was fresh out of the shower. The droplets slipped down her body in formation, giving her paling body a chilling look. After a few seconds, they began to change colour. Then her wounds opened again. The thick stench of blood filled the stuffy air of the motel room, and Jackson watched in awe as the blood dropped out of the openings in her stomach and onto the end of the mattress.

Eventually, she spoke. Her voice was deeper and unfamiliar. 'I'm sorry,' she said as she looked far into his eyes. After that, her pupils were engulfed by the red sea that was flowing through her eyes. Jackson had to close his eyes as tight as possible; he didn't want to see her like that.

Then, he heard a voice again, 'Jackson, please forgive me.' It was only a whisper, but it sounded like she was right next to him. The smell of blood powered through his nostrils and attacked him.

When he opened his eyes again, she was gone. As was the blood from the mattress.

He was alone again.

The dream seemed to happen every few days and he couldn't get away from it. But for now, he had to do *something.* He shook the thought of Hannah's living corpse from his mind and got out of bed, sweating more than he was when he woke up, noticing the patch of sweat that soaked into the sheet beneath him. His knees were trembling and his ankles felt weak. He walked over to the small refrigerator in the opposite corner of the room near the kitchen area and pulled out a bottle of water, condensed and damp to the touch. After taking a few immensely refreshing gulps, feeling the feeble plastic of the bottle crunch underneath his fingers, he set the bottle down onto the makeshift desk and sat down on the most uncomfortable chair he'd ever sat on.

The window behind him was slightly open and he could feel the soft morning breeze flowing through the curtains and hitting against his back, moving up over his bare shoulders. The sun was beaming in through the window, bypassing the protective fabric that coated the room in slight darkness, bouncing off every available surface and giving a shine to some of the wood.

After taking a few minutes to reset his body, Jackson opened his laptop and grabbed a few pieces of paper from one side of the desk. There were names he had to write down, research had to be carried out and notes had to be written. It'd been three days since he'd last seen Lily, only talked to her sparingly when she had a break. She'd be deeply engrossed with trying to figure out who killed those three men and wasn't exactly available for meaningful conversation with her boyfriend, so he thought it'd be the perfect time to begin the next part.

He'd manage to search the internet for a name and jot down a few lines of notes when he heard a deep thud against the front door. Some of the decorations and ornaments shook in place, as surprised as he was by the sudden interruption. He decided to ignore it and went back to his laptop, scrolling through pages and pages of pointless information to try and get somewhere meaningful.

The door thudded again, louder and for longer. A painting on the wall to his left, hung next to the clock, rattled tenderly before coming to a stop at a mildly infuriating angle. These things had to be straight on the wall or it would put him off.

'Who is it?' he shouted from his seat.

'Irvine PD, please open the door,' a voice shouted back.

Jackson furrowed his brows and slightly titled his head. He closed his laptop and set the notes aside where they couldn't be found.

'One second,' Jackson said as he grabbed his t-shirt from the light beige rug that lay just next to the bed.

When he opened the door, a tall and slim man stood in front of him. His short black hair was spiked in a perfect line and his jaw was chiselled and noticeable. He had a small scar along the bridge of his nose that he kept scratching at. The small name badge on his left breast read 'BELL'.

'Are you Jackson Yardley?' Officer Bell asked. His tone was calm but suggested dominance.

'Well, people usually call me 'Jay',' Jackson replied.

The office stopped scratching a looked him up and down. 'So you *are* Jackson Yardley?'

'Yeah, I guess I am.'

'Can I come in?' The officer looked through Jackson and into the room behind him, trying to see if there was anything in plain sight that he could use to get in without permission.

Jackson shuffled in place. 'What's this about? How did you even know I was here?'

'Can I come in? I need to ask you some questions.' The officer was unmoved, giving Jackson a stern look while he fidgeted gently at his belt, hovering over a weapon or a notepad, it was unclear which one from the angle he was standing.

'Uh,' Jackson turned around to assess the tidiness of the place, before giving his attention back to the officer, 'yeah, sure, make yourself at home.'

'That won't be necessary, Mr. Yardley. I won't be long.'

Jackson scanned the room to make sure nothing was on show, then shut the door behind the officer as he strolled into the centre of the room and turned around. His walk was slow and calculated; he was trying to act like he had something and he was trying to act like he was the leading man in the situation.

An old trick, and Jackson wasn't buying it.

'So what is this actually about?' Jackson extended his arm, fingers together and palm up, gesturing to the laptop. 'I've got work to do,' he moved closer to the officer. Bell's cologne was strong, sprayed all over his uniform and upset Jackson's nostrils as the breeze knocked it distastefully around the room.

I'd rather smell this cheap cologne than that damn blood again, Jackson thought to himself, ignoring what the officer was telling him.

'Well?' Bell asked.

Jackson quickly shook his head, saying 'Sorry, what?'

'Where were you on the night of Thursday, May 9th?' Officer Bell repeated, hands held firmly behind his back.

'Um,' Jackson said, 'I don't really know. That was nearly, what, a month ago now? I can hardly remember where I was last week.' He smiled, trying to get a humoured response but it didn't work.

'That seems a bit convenient,' Bell replied, taking a leisurely walk around the room, roughly inspecting it. 'Don't you think?'

'Convenient for who? And, uh, *what?*'

'Convenient for you, Mr. Yardley,' Bell said, turning back around. 'Because we have a right to believe that you were the last one to see Arthur Renshaw alive. He was found murdered along with two of – we assume – his friends. They were brutally stabbed to death in an abandoned building. It's not actually too far from here, believe it or not.'

'That name sounds familiar,' Jackson replied, calm and indifferent. Rather than humour him, he returned to his desk and watched the officer walk around trying to pretend he wasn't searching the place. Bell then took out a small reporter's notepad with a blue plastic cover and flipped it over, going through the first few pages before settling on one and beginning to write a few notes. Jackson watched him with a subtle eagle-eye, making it seem like he was focused on his laptop screen.

Officer Bell finished what he was writing and looked up, catching Jackson's glaze and smiling in a friendly but intimidating manner. 'I'm sure it will sound familiar to you, Mr. Yardley.'

Jackson returned the smile he was given and leaned back in his chair. He could sense there was some kind of game going on, and he didn't want to be the one who blinked first. He needed to ride this out until the end, get the officer off his scent and plead ignorance until it proved impossible to do so.

'Any particular reason why you think that? I work at a coffee shop and live in a motel,' Jackson said, almost smug, but knowing that bragging about that was sad.

Officer Bell put his notebook away and walked closer to the desk, beginning to get impatient with the answers Jackson was giving.

'Look,' he said, placing his hands on the table palm down, just in front of the laptop, and looking down, 'I don't have time for games. I can easily take you in for obstructing an investigation. Maybe I could even take you in for murder. That'd give me 48 hours to prove that you're the one that did this, which I'm sure is plenty of time since once this case gets rolling, the evidence will coming flying in. Won't it?'

'That would be a waste of police time, and police money,' Jackson replied, 'If you arrested me for murder, it would look bad on you.'

'Oh, I'd be praised. My gut tells me you did it, I've got a feeling.'

'What would your captain think about that? You brought me in for murder based on a *feeling*, and then while you're focusing on me, more people will die. You'd be a laughing stock, wouldn't you?

Bell gave a wry smile and said, 'How do you know more people are gonna die?'

Jackson sat up and folded his arms along the table, looking up at the officer. He was close enough to smell the strong cologne that he was wearing; pungent and manly, giving off the impression that he was a 'manly man'. He could see the slight yellow tinge of his teeth as he held his mouth slightly open, and the tiny pricks of hair that were creeping their way up from inside his skin to rest on his top lip.

'I have nothing to hide,' Jackson whispered, 'ask me whatever you like.'

'Okay, then answer my first question, please, if that's not too difficult for you,' he stood up straight and got his notebook back out, ready to quickly scribble down the answers so he had plenty of material for the many reports he'd probably need to write. 'Where were you on the night of Thursday, May 9th.'

'I went for a drink with Arthur, yeah, but that's it.'

'Oh, you remember now, do you?' Officer Bell said, writing in his pad and nodding slowly, before saying, 'so what exactly happened?'

'His mom is my neighbour, and she knew about my, uh, my *situation*. She suggested I take him for drinks since she thought I needed a friend and I had nothing else to do so I just agreed to it. That's it.'

'Right, okay, where'd you go?' he refused to look up from his pad, his wrist was moving wildly trying to keep up with Jackson's answers, but he wasn't writing properly, just basic notes and trigger points. A skill he'd learned after years as a detective. To an untrained eye, the pages of his pad were stock full of random letters and out-of-place words.

'A bar, I can't remember where. We weren't really there for that long so I didn't take the time to remember the name of it.'

'Why weren't you there long?'

'Because Arthur said that something important had come up and he needed to go. I didn't exactly want to be out with him either so I didn't question it, I just let him go.'

Bell stopped writing for a second and looked up at Jackson, seemingly without lifting his hand up from the page. He was still applying pressure to the pen, creating a dot in the centre of the page. 'You just—' he waved the pen through the air, rotating his wrist, trying to follow the story '—let him go? Just like that?'

Jackson nodded and stood up, informally signalling that he was finished talking and wanted the officer to leave now.

'Did he say anything? Like, where he was going or what was so important?'

'Nope.'

Bell realised Jackson's change in body language and growing impatience, so he put his notebook away and smiled. 'Well, if I have any more questions, I'll be sure to come back.'

He turned around and walked a few steps towards the door before stopping in place and looking back over his shoulder, saying, 'Well, that's unless you haven't moved to a different motel.'

He quietly chuckled to himself and made his way towards the door again. Jackson followed him closely, ready to lock the door as soon as it shut behind him. As soon as Bell crossed back over the threshold, Jackson had his hand gripped firmly on the door handle.

'I do hope you don't waste your time and actually find who did it. I've seen it on the news. Horrible stuff,' Jackson said, 'I'd hate for you to spend all your time focusing on one person, just for the actual killer to *strike again*.' He smiled again and began to slowly shut the door. Bell turned back around with a wry smile of his own. Neither man was blinking in the game, and they both knew it.

'It's funny,' he muttered calmly, an aspect of arrogance creeping into his voice, deepening the pitch slightly and making it seem like he needed to cough. 'I do hope you're right. I hope it's not you. If it *is* you, I'm going to love coming back here and putting you in prison for the rest of your life.'

Jackson smiled again, not replying, just itching the door closed a little more. Bell leaned into him, trying to whisper something that he wanted only one person to hear, just before the door was shut in his face.

Bell got close to his ear, breathing softly and keeping his hand hovering over the weapon latched firmly to his belt. He spoke soft, too, just louder than a whisper, 'Just because you're sleeping with the lead detective, doesn't mean you can just get away with anything. She can't help you. I hope you understand that.'

The vibration of his speech rattled the inside of Jackson's ear, sending a cold shiver down his spine. He could feel a deep rage inside of him, it was burning down in his stomach and he felt the need to do something about it. He stepped back away from the door and smiled condescendingly. Bell did the same and straightened out his uniform.

Jackson remained calm. He tried hard to suppress the anger that was slowly bubbling inside of him. The adrenaline that he'd slowly begun to miss was starting to return and he couldn't do anything but smile. He had to force himself to stay focused on what he was actually supposed to be doing. Everything would fall into place if he stayed at peace.

He smiled, scratching the side of his head and taking an extended blink. 'You have a good day, officer,' he said, and gently shut the door.

18

Jackson had been leaning his head against the door for a good few minutes before he decided to open his eyes and stand up straight. He'd heard cleaners zipping back and forth between rooms, speaking amongst themselves through various open doors as they made the beds and cleared out the dirty towels. As one of them wheeled a cart past his door, the squeaking of the wheels vibrating through his head, he overheard them talking about a police officer that had been roaming the halls. Apparently, they thought he was attractive and he'd smiled at them in passing.

After the cleaners had started talking about menial, work-related issues, Jackson stopped listening and turned around. He took a deep breath, lowering his blood pressure, and ridding himself of the personality that he'd just seemingly took on. That wasn't him, was it? Was he that cold to be talking back to a police officer with such ease, such superiority? His whole body began to tremble as his nerves got the better of him. He held his hands on his hips and closed his eyes once more, this time phasing out the activity of the motel hallways behind him and trying to suppress the bad thoughts that started swimming through his head, doing lengths and widths and filling the space of his conscience.

What if he'd slipped up? What if the officer had seen right through him and gotten aggressive? What if he'd actually come through with his threat and arrested him for obstruction of justice?

Stretching his arms, feeling a faint, dull click in his right elbow, he said to himself, 'Nope. Stop.'

Jackson returned to the desk and the laptop that still sat upon it. He moved the smooth, matte touchpad and the screen awoke. The soft LED glow of the screen cast a blue shadow onto his face. The picture that he was looking at was reflecting deep into his eyes, and his vision became blurred as he focused on it. His eyes darted from side to side, up and down the page as he scrolled, clicking across various tabs on the web browser to find what he was looking for.

Across the desk, the notes that he'd previously made sat under the navy blue padded-sleeve that would house his laptop for travel. Jackson moved it out of the way and retrieved the sheets. They looked blank until he moved the sleeve, a good cover for him if Officer Bell had ventured over to his desk to snoop around.

On one sheet, he wrote names. They came pouring out of the pen, the ink absorbing itself into the paper, and it wouldn't stop. They were just coming to him without thinking. Every time he wrote one name, he remembered another one. As he heard the tip of the pen scratch gracefully against the parchment, the adrenaline began to come back. He could feel a tingling sensation travel from his head down the back of his neck and to his back. He felt like he could feel his spine gently rattle. He could only smile as a plan began to form in his head; locations, dates, and times. Jackson could see how everything was going to play out, and it felt like his brain was smiling.

On a different sheet, he wrote the rest of the plan. One by one – name by name – he wrote everything he could think of for each of them; what he initially knew about them, why they were on the list, when would be the best time to go for them, how long he'd need to wait between each one, and any other ideas that sprung to him as the minutes quickly ticked by.

With another quick glance at the clock on the wall, he noticed it was a little before 1 pm. He'd managed to phase out the incessant ticking, but it returned to haunt his eardrums the moment he set his attention upon it.

Happy with the number of names he had so far, he turned his attention back to the laptop and the research he'd need to carry out before each target. Scrolling through a few pages – pointless sites that told him to buy things and offered him the chance to work from home and early hundreds of dollars a month – he eventually stumbled upon what he was looking for. Across the top border of the page, read **Irvine Design Studios** plastered in bold, with a small logo in the left corner. He scrolled through a few pages of projects, news, and blog posts until he got to the 'Meet The Team' page. Then he put a face to the first name on his list.

The man was smiling for the photo, showing a well-kept set of pearly white teeth and small dimples on each side of his mouth. The way his smile formed made it looked like he was nibbling gently at his bottom lip. His hair was trimmed at the sides, while the top was styled back, made to give it volume and a natural 'bed-head' look.

Even looking at his face, Jackson felt something inside of him begin to ignite. He began to feel how he did when Arthur sat inside his car; he was on the edge of his seat, just waiting for what was to come. He wanted to go to great lengths to maintain the tingling that ran up and down his spine, dipping in and out of the crevices in the bone.

And hopefully, he'd be able to get an answer for what happened to his little sister.

19

Jackson's mind drifted back to 2000. He'd not long turned sixteen and he was beginning to feel like more of an adult every day. Sienna, his little sister of two years, was still quite childish and he'd always enjoyed taking care of her, keeping her out of trouble. He embraced the role of "protective older brother", cast onto him by his parents, but it was fun.

They went to the same school; always made the short walk to and from their home together. It was the best way for them to avoid the resident bullies of Sienna's class: Chase Morgen and Andre Nelcourt.

Boy, they just never let up.

She'd told him about the many occasions that they'd harassed her and sometimes assaulted her. She'd refuse to go into school some days because she didn't want to face up to them, and she was too scared to tell her teachers about it. The one time that Jackson took matters into his own hands, he'd only made it worse.

He'd approached them in the corridor one lunchtime as they were getting things out of their lockers, laughing together. He stood behind them and glanced at them with a deep look of scorn plastered on his face.

'And what do *you* want?' Andre asked, closing his locker and adjusting his glasses to sit better on his nose.

'What do you *think* I want?' Jackson stood only a couple of inches taller than both of them, but he tried to make it look like he towered over them by lifting his shoulders up straight and looking down his nose.

'Uh, sorry, we're not gay,' Chase spoke this time, laughing and showing the small dimples on each side of his cheek. 'Get lost.'

'Yeah, we're not gay like you, so get lost,' Andre repeated, clearly not the leader.

Jackson shot him a glance of embarrassment, slightly squinting his eyes and arching his left brow, before returning his attention to Chase. 'You need to stay away from my sister. This is the only time I'm gonna tell you.'

The two boys looked at each other, then Chase looked at Jackson again and gave him a scheming smile, saying, 'Who's your sis—? Oh, Sienna Yardley is your sister, huh? Ha, what a stupid cry-baby.'

Almost instinctively, Jackson grabbed Chase's jacket with both hands and pushed him forcibly back into the cold blue steel of the locker. Chase's head flung back and smacked against it, a deep clanging sound echoing through the hallway and grabbing the attention of other students, who then began to stare at the new commotion. Andre took on a guarded, defensive stance and tried to force Jackson off of his 'boss', but he was weak at heart and his efforts were wasted.

'D'you wanna say that again?' Jackson said to Chase, almost snarling in his face. Their eyes were locked together, their noses were almost close enough to touch. He could sense the fear in Chase's dark blue eyes, and his nervous, compact breathes spread across his face.

But then, Chase smiled.

Before Jackson could say anything else, two teachers came rushing through the gathering crowd of students and pulled the two boys apart. Chase flattened his uniform out and shot Andre a proud look as if the teachers were on his payroll and he knew he was untouchable in that school.

That day, they taunted Sienna for getting her big brother involved. They kept passing her handwritten notes throughout their classes containing horrible messages. She'd come home crying that day, and it broke his heart. He had tried to help, but he made it worse. He knew he couldn't stop it.

But it only got worse from there

Another day came to mind. *That* day. As they'd left the front door in the morning, the sun was bright and joyful. The sky was empty of clouds and the heat was trying to force its way under the thick fabric of their clothes and onto their young skin. By the time they'd reached the school, some 20 minutes later, the sky had darkened and the sun was hidden behind dark grey clouds that were ready to spill their contents at a moment's notice. They stood outside the school and talked for a few minutes.

It was a single-storey building in the shape of the letter L that stretched as far as a football field. The exterior walls were an old shade of yellow, dirtied by scratch marks and small graffiti markings. The windows look pristine, if not slightly dirty themselves. They were the result of recent renovation efforts that didn't last very long. In the centre of the schoolyard stood a large grass island, elevated a few feet. It was home to a large tree that protected a vast portion of the yard from rain. Jackson could barely get his arms halfway around it, but it was a place that a lot of students went to sit if they wanted to be alone.

As they walked up, the boys spotted her and laughed to themselves before going up the steps into the right side of the building – the bottom tip of the 'L'

'See?' Jackson said with a reassuring tone, 'they've gone, so you can go inside on your own. I have to go in the other way.'

He turned to face her and placed his hands on the tops of her arms, squeezing her shoulders gently together, and telling her, 'It'll be okay, okay?' He spoke soft, his voice was emotional and genuine.

She looked up at him and gave a half-smile, nodding slightly before hugging him. He stood up straight and hugged her back, feeling her squeeze with all her might. He kissed the top of her head and let her go, watching her as she walked past the tree and towards the school's entrance. She turned back just before the steps and waved at him, a blank look on her face. He waved back and then made a *shoo* motion with his hand. Turning around, she opened the doors and let the darkness of the hallway take her in.

Later that day, after he left school early since one of his teachers was sick, Jackson was lying on his back on his bed throwing a baseball up and catching it, when he heard the front door quickly open and shut. Sienna came running up the stairs, the banging of her feet was reverberating through the rest of the house and shaking his bedroom door. He held the baseball and sat up, looking towards the door and the noise that was getting louder by the second.

Jackson heard her sniffling as she reached the summit of the staircase and, like a car drifting on a wet stretch of road, turned quickly towards her bedroom, slamming the door behind her. After a few concerning seconds, he got up and left his room, walking the few feet across the hallway to his sister's room. He could feel his bare feet sinking into the carpet and the fibres creep between his toes.

Putting his ear to the door, he listened in to try and figure out what she was doing. The only noise that came through was the intermittent sniffling and the aggravated springs of the bed like she kept changing position. He lightly tapped on the door with his knuckles before putting the handle down to walk in. But it was locked.

'Sienna?' he asked. 'Can you let me in?' He put his ear back on the door. The cold wooden surface chilled the skin on his ear, but he quickly got used to it.

'Go away,' said the soft, muffled voice from the other end of the door. She was probably crying into her pillows to try and keep the volume to a minimum.

'Come on, Si, just let me in. I wanna talk,' Jackson's voice held a growing sense of worry, and he slightly raised the pitch in his voice to portray that to her.

Her voice became clear as she lifted her head up from the pillow and said, 'I said go away, I'm fine.'

Jackson lowered in his head, knowing he wasn't getting through to her, and turned around, placing his back flat against the door. He slid down to a sitting position, crossing his legs and turning his head to talk through the wood.

'You know for a fact I'm not gonna go anywhere until you let me in,' he faced forward and leant his head back, 'so you might as well just open up. I've got plenty of time to chill.'

Still holding his baseball in one hand, he began tossing it a foot or two into the air, just high enough to be eye-level. His eyes concentrated on catching the ball every time, but he managed to speak coherently at the same time.

'I tried to help. You know that, right?' he said, sadly. 'I thought when I stood up to them for you, it would just make it all go away.' He stopped tossing the ball and rested his hands back on his lap. Turning towards the door again, he continued. 'I didn't think it would make it worse. I always tried to protect you. I always *will* try.'

There was still no movement from the room, so it looked like he would be sitting there for a while. He looked down at his lap and inspected the ball that was resting in the small hole that his crossed legs had formed.

'I know I can't say a lot that will help right now,' he said. Then, quietly to himself, 'I was never bullied, so I'm not really sure what words to use here,' and then, 'but I promise I'll do my best to keep you safe. I'll try and stay close to you at school more. I'll try and keep an eye on you when we can't spend time together.'

He heard some slight movements and more sniffling from inside the room. He thought she was coming to open the door, but the noise was distant and subsided after half a minute. He didn't know what she was doing, but it wasn't letting him in, and it didn't sound like she wanted to speak to him.

Jackson looked down, a solemn look creeping onto his face, and rolled the ball back and forth between his legs. As if speaking to the ball, he said, 'I know you're gonna grow up to be something amazing one day. Maybe you'll become super successful and you can move away from here, maybe somewhere like—like Nebraska or Oklahoma. I know you like the Midwest.'

A cold silence filled the air, and he heard the intermittent chirping, or arguing, of birds just outside the open window of the bathroom in the adjacent room. Their parents were out, so the rest of the house was empty. He had thought to call them and tell them he was worried about Sienna, but he thought he was overreacting.

There's nothing to worry about.

'You know, Si,' Jackson began talking again, looking straight ahead into his own bedroom. 'One day, you're gonna be a woman with a family of your own. You're gonna be happy, surrounded by love, then Chase and—

and Andre are just gonna be bad memories. Maybe you'll have forgotten them altogether.'

He moved forward a little bit and stood up, turning to face the door again, uselessly trying the door handle to see if she'd unlocked it without him hearing.

'Sienna, please,' he muttered softly, 'can you just let me in? I just wanna give you a hug. We don't even need to talk. Please.'

His words trailed off and he rested his forehead on the door, his eyes closed and his hand still feeling the clean metal of the faux-gold handle.

'I might just barge my way in if you won't let me in. I mean it.'

He hadn't heard a noise from the room in a while, and his concern was growing. He had just assumed that she'd finally calmed herself down and was taking a nap.

He lifted his head up and took half a step back from the door. 'I'm not gonna be happy if you're sleeping,' he threatened, jokingly.

After knocking a little more forcefully and trying the handle again, with no response or stirring from the bed, he let his impatience get the better of him and turned to the side, readying his body for impact. He bent his arm in towards his stomach, lowered his right shoulder, and tilted his head away from the door.

Then he pushed.

Attempt number one was a failure. The door didn't seem to budge and a sharp pain went down his arm and up to his neck. He thought she'd at least tell him to stop trying to break the door or realise he was serious and come and open it herself. But none of those things happened.

He tried again, not giving his body – or the door – time to recover. *Thud.* Still no luck.

He took a few breaths and tried again. *Thud.* His shoulder was beginning to ache and he thought he could feel the door weakening. Either that, or he was. Even after multiple times of him crashing into the door, there was still no noise from inside the room.

'I hope I didn't just say all that nice stuff—' *Thud.* No luck, '—just to find out that you were—' *Thud. Thud.* The door swung open, '—sleeping.'

As the force of his young shoulder finally penetrated through the damaged lock on the door, sending him stumbling halfway into the room, he discovered that he wasn't actually talking to his sister.

He had been talking to a body that was swinging gently from a trembling ceiling fan.

20

Why was Chase allowed to live? Why was he allowed to make something of himself knowing he and his friend drove a 14-year-old girl to suicide? That just seems unfair. Jackson needed to know why. He needed Chase to tell him why. If nothing else, his 'adventure' would be about getting answers for all of his unanswered questions.

But nobody knew – not even him – how far he could go. It scared him.

As Jackson sat scrolling through Chase's biography on the Irvine Design Studios' website, he could feel the rays of the sun getting hotter on his back. Nearly two o'clock in the afternoon, the sun would be at its peak, and it sure felt like it. He felt like someone was holding a man-size magnifying glass to one spot on the top of his back, just between his shoulder blades.

Was it possible to be inside, fully clothed and still get sunburn?

Slightly shifting himself away from the main beam of the sun, Jackson returned his focus to the biography of his first target, scoffing as he read each paragraph.

Chase Morgen is one of the brightest, most influential people at IDS. His natural talent and innate eye for detail make him one of the most sought after people in the industry. As a Design Director, Chase believes that the key to a successful relationship between himself and clients is the building of deep trust, which can then be reflected throughout a project.

Combining a strong understanding of various effective development techniques, and a prolific understanding of the ever-changing markets, Chase represents everything that IDS stands for. He believes that a successful project is a reflection of the client, and therefore a representation of the architect and he prioritises communication in order to achieve the goals that are set for him.

Recently being assigned as project lead for a significant new building in downtown Irvine, Chase expects to make it the pinnacle of his work, using his wealth of knowledge to create a staple of the Californian horizon.

Originally from Irvine, Chase moved to Indiana to study at the prestigious School of Architecture at Notre Dame University. As part of his studies, he spent a year in Rome studying classical architecture, which he uses as inspiration for his projects. His multicultural, bilingual personality is reflected in all of his work, as is his dedication, passion, and commitment. He is a member of the AIA, LEED, and NCARB accredited.

Jackson couldn't stop shaking his head as he read through it. It didn't seem to make sense to him. How could the guy who bullied his sister so much turn out that like that?

He didn't understand it. He would probably never understand it. But he'd try.

Clicking off the biography, he looked around the web page more, studying the different architects that worked there, trying to imagine them all as childhood bullies. But he found something he wasn't expecting. A few rows up from Chase was the awfully familiar, chubby, spectacle-wearing face that belonged to Andre Nelcourt.

They succeeded together as well? Are you serious?

Underneath his name read ASSOCIATE DESIGN DIRECTOR. *Ironic*, Jackson thought. *Even after nearly 20 years, Andre is still just the follower, always behind Chase in everything. That's probably why he got into this business; because Chase did first.*

Jackson leant back in his chair, prying his eyes away from the screen after noticing he was getting closer and closer to it the more he concentrated. He gave them a rub with the tips of his fingers and sighed, before standing up to look out of the window behind him. The motel car park stretched back 50 or 60 meters, decorated with cars of various colours and a few motorcycles. The dark grey concrete that made up each parking space was beginning to crack and turn into potholes, while the white paint that marked each space was fading, turning two spaces into one. The back wall that separated the motel from the streets – thick stacks of light yellow bricks – had been damaged and partially torn down, making it easy for anyone to trespass.

The sun was still high in the sky, untainted by clouds and shining brightly down on the world. The beams bounced off the roofs of the cars, making the colours glimmer and sending a glare straight towards Jackson's eyes.

He turned around the look at his room, blotches of blue and white clouded his vision as he adjusted to the fullness of the interior. He didn't like feeling that this was his home until something else came along.

Sitting back down in the chair, Jackson turned his attention back to the laptop. He revisited Chase's biography, reading it over once more and scoffing again. He made a note of the contact number, took his phone out of his pocket and dialled the number with a wry smile on his face.

It was time to begin.

21

'Good afternoon,' a cheery voice came across the other end of the line, a deeper variant of the one he remembered from his school days, 'This is Chase Morgen, how can I be of service today?'

A chill went through Jackson's body, hearing the voice again, knowing he was so happy and so successful. But he had to remain calm and carry out the plan properly, with no slip-ups.

Putting an emphatic tone in his voice, trying to sound like a businessman himself, he replied, 'Hi, Chase, my name is Jack Harrod. I was told you were the man to contact if I needed to get myself a building in the greatest city in California.'

He could feel Chase smile on the other end, adjusting in his own desk chair, readying himself to get another project.

'Well, Mr. Harrod, I feel you've come to the right place. What can I--?'

Jackson cut him off. 'Well, my company in Maryland is looking to expand. We thought it'd be best to go out West, where you never see a bad skyline. We have a vision, and I think you're the man to help us achieve that vision.'

'Well, of course, Mr—'

'Please,' Jackson interrupted again, still emphatic, 'call me Jack.'

'Well, *Jack*, I feel like your timing might be just a little off. You see, I'm already working on a project; the scale of which is something I've never experienced before, and I feel it would be best to devote all my time to this project. I do apologise.'

Jackson adjusted his position in his chair, resting the elbow of his free arm on the table with his arm up, and rested his head on his hand. He listened with a straight, unimpressed face.

Chase continued, 'From the sound of it, you're really excited about your project, and I'm glad you already have a vision for your building. I do hope that you stick with us at Irvine Design Studios for your vision, as I'm more than confident that another member of our team can still make it a huge success for you.'

'Well, now, you see,' Jackson replied, losing some of the emphasis and turning his tone a little deeper, 'this could make you a very rich man. It would tower over the Irvine skyline and give you a legacy that you might not be able to get anywhere else.'

Chase chuckled slightly, before replying, 'As great as that sounds, Mr. Harrod, I'm afraid I am unable to take on another client of such magnitude. But I will be more than happy to send you in the direction of one of my colleagues, who are just as passionate, dedicated and skilled. If not more.'

'The vision I have for this building,' Jackson went on, completely ignoring what Chase had said, 'is to be sustainable, and a powerful symbol of Irvine. I want it to serve as a reminder to you of what you did.'

'Excuse me?' Chase stiffened in his seat.

'See, I already had a name for the building in mind. I want the letters placed just above the entranceway, in big solid letters. The Sienna Yardley Memorial Building. It's got a nice ring to it, don't you think? You know, after that girl that you killed?'

Chase gulped, trying to speak but he couldn't find the words. All that came out of his mouth was an indistinct humming.

'Come on, I'm sure you remember,' Jackson said, cheery but stern.

'I'm – uh – I'm not quite sure what you mean.'

'Well sure you do. You remember your time back in school, don't you?'

'I – uh—'

'You know,' Jackson spoke as if he was trying to remind a good friend of their good times, 'how you and your good friend Andre were the bullies? You taunted her, and insulted her?' He ironically chuckled to himself, before continuing, 'It's funny, I remember this one time when you saw her in the cafeteria and you thought it would be *funny* to pour a bottle of water over her head. It completely ruined her clothes. And do you know *why* you did that?'

'I – uh, I'm—' That seemed to be all that Chase could produce. He'd forgotten how to form words, and he could temporarily only make noises.

'It was because she was reading a book. At lunchtime. *That's it.*' Jackson raised his voice, unable to let some of the anger inside of him stay dormant. 'How funny is that?' he shouted.

'Look, I'm going to—'

'Oh no, I'm not done yet,' Jackson was raising his voice as if he were lecturing a child who'd done something unforgivable. 'How about another time when you left a $10 bill on the ground; a *fake* bill, no less. You left it on the ground in the hallway, and you waited for her – only her – to pick it up. But when she got there, she didn't even look at it, but you *still* ambushed her anyway. Do you remember what you did?'

'I-I…'

'That's right! You grabbed her and used a *god damn library stamp* to completely cover her face. She refused to go to school for nearly a week after that.'

'Don't call here again. I don't know what you're talking about,' Chase's voice was forcefully monotonous, but Jackson could detect the sadness and fear in the words.

'She killed herself, you know?' he said matter-of-factly.

Silence fell. Jackson waited for a response but he got nothing. He couldn't hear Chase's short breathes, or anything in his office. There was an eeriness about the atmosphere that he'd just created and it was slightly off-putting. He could sense that Chase's mouth was open in shock and his eyebrows were slightly raised.

'She came home one day,' Jackson went on, 'and she was crying her eyes out. She stormed up the stairs and locked herself in her bedroom.' Still leaning on his elbow, he bowed his head and placed his hand at the top of his neck, scratching his head softly. He lowered his voice when he resumed speaking, solemn and emotional, 'I tried to get her to talk to me. I sat in front of her door, just talking to her, trying to reassure her that everything was going to be okay. She kept crying, kept telling me to go away.'

Chase was still silent on the other end of the phone, and Jackson felt a solitary tear drop from the corner of his eye, and he tried to stop his voice from cracking as he spoke.

'I just sat. I got concerned so I tried to force the door open. When I eventually got in, there she was.' His lips felt wet as a few more tears passed down his cheek and over his mouth. 'She hung herself because what you and your friend did to her. You sent... You made a 14-year-old believe that—that suicide was the only answer – the only way out. *Fourteen*. I promise you,' he lifted his head back up and wiped his eyes, 'I promise to right now that her, and my, suffering will come full circle.'

The room was silent once more. Jackson composed himself, ridding his eyes and cheeks of any tears, and took a few deep breaths. Chase began breathing again, coughing quietly and trying to come up with something to say. The room was beginning to get more humid and Jackson could feel the sweat beads start to form along his forehead. The clock on the wall forcefully ticked past 2 pm.

'Don't call here again. I'll be informing the police,' Chase eventually said, surprisingly composed.

Jackson laughed out loud, a strong *HA* that bellowed through the dirty air of the motel room, then spoke again with his own intimidating composure. 'The police won't be able to help you, Chase. Don't worry, though, I'll find you.'

The second he finished his sentence, Jackson hung up and placed his phone down on the table with a light thud. Closing his laptop, he returned his attention to the sheet of paper that contained all of his notes, writing more about the phone call that he'd just had. He made notes on Chase's voice, the body language that he imagined he'd have, the way he was replying to everything he was saying, and anything else he thought to write. He was trying to get a picture of what Chase was like now, thinking of the right way to deal with him when the time came.

Sooner, rather than later.

Making sure he knew what he was doing, he slid the paper under his laptop and pulled a small reporter's notebook out of the drawer by his left knee. Putting his pen in his pocket, and his phone next to it, he got up and took another glance out of the window behind him before walking towards the door to leave.

22

In the days that followed, Jackson had been seemingly been everywhere that Irvine had to offer. From the motel after his phone call with Chase, he'd driven down to Irvine Design Studios and studied the building. It was a medium-sized, two-storey structure that looked just right for an architecture studio. It was inside a small cul-de-sac to the east of the city. Clean white brick lined the perimeter of the building's face, with long black windows in regular intervals inside an indent in the brick. There was a balcony extending out from the upper floor and stretched the length of the building. It was in a patch of land by itself, surrounded by a wide walkway that resembled the moat of a castle.

Jackson had sat in his car on the other side of the road, in a small parking lot that belonged to a Burger King. He could see the entirety of the studio from where he sat and had a view of both doors on the left and right sides. He could see anyone that entered or exited the building.

By the time that Chase had actually left for the night, the sky was glowing a deep purple and a dim moonlight was casting its shadow along the streets.

Streetlights had begun flickering on in perfect unison. Jackson had the window rolled down in his Jaguar, and the air smelled clean. There was no humidity, and a post-rain freshness lingered in his nose.

Chase left the building on his own, holding a thick black folder to his chest. Jackson had watched him get into a charcoal grey SUV, and as soon as he heard the engine rev up, he did the same with his Jaguar. After that, he followed Chase along winding roads and over highways towards his home. He made sure to keep his distance – the length of a few cars – and had his lights down to a soft glimmer to not be a distraction. When Chase turned his car into a long, paved driveway decorated with both brown and cream paving stones, Jackson continued past, making a mental note of the location. It'd taken him roughly 20 minutes to drive from the studio at a steady pace, and he made a note of the time to determine how long it would take him to get back to the motel. He had to be there in the morning to continue.

The day after, Jackson had parked his car at the bottom of Chase's street, just far enough away to be inconspicuous but close enough to have a good view of his parked car in the driveway – in the same position that he'd left it the night before. He'd made sure to get there early enough – a few ticks short of 8 am.

Throughout the day, Jackson went to Orange County Great Park and observed Chase meeting who he assumed was a client. They'd sat on a bench on a walkway under the cover of a long row of thick oak trees. Behind them, and the trees, was a carousel full of children screaming excitedly. In front of them, 40 meters away, was a hot air balloon that looked like a giant inflatable pumpkin with a smiley face on it.

Chase spoke with a middle-aged man for at least 40 minutes, exchanging laughs, documents, and ideas. From Jackson's view just behind the carousel, it seemed like it was a meaningful meeting. After it had finished, the client got up and walked away towards the balloon while Chase remained seated. He was looking through the various files, scribbling on them with a pen he'd stored in his inside pocket. He placed the documents back into the black folder he always carried and made a phone call, talking for a further ten minutes. Jackson presumed he was relaying the important information from his meeting to his superiors.

Soon after leaving the park, Chase ventured a few minutes across the street into a Costco wholesale, most likely unrelated to his work. After that, he visited Walmart on the opposite side of the road.

In the few days that Jackson had closely monitored his movement, he'd watched him go to work for hours, visit the dry cleaners, and multiple bars. He'd returned to the same park for another meeting – shorter than the first one – and Jackson was able to figure out a pattern of his activities. He always seemed to go to work at the same time every day. He left his house between 8:15 and 8:25 in the morning, depending on how congested he thought the roads might be. He stayed there most of the day, only leaving to grab lunch or have a meeting. He tended to leave around 6 pm when the sun was still subtly beaming but getting low, and darkness was ready to wrap its cold hands around the city.

For an hour or two after he'd gotten home from work, Chase would remain in the house with the lights off. There was only a faint glow peeking through the window, most likely a lamp on his desk. Jackson would need to get him during that timeframe, and he'd have to make sure he picked a day where the people were scarce and there was little activity in the area.

And so there he sat, in his Jaguar parked in the same spot at the bottom of his street. He felt like he blended in, he felt like he belonged. He was surrounded by large condos and houses that would set you back seven figures, and he felt comfortable knowing he was sitting in an expensive car.

Jackson watched Chase's house for half an hour before finally readying himself to go. He noticed the dim glow through one of the windows just past where the driveway began, knowing he was concentrating on his work. He'd found his moment.

But as he was about the pull the latch to open the door, his phone buzzed in his pocket.

What an awkward time to get a phone call.

It was Lily. They hadn't spoken the entire time he'd been following Chase, and even before that. He felt like it had been a week since he'd even looked at her. He answered the phone and heard the familiar chirping of her voice on the other end.

'Hey, Jackson, remember me?' she joked.

He smiled and returned to a comfortable position in the driver's seat. He didn't want to miss his chance to get to Chase, but he'd wanted to speak to her for a while.

'No, sorry,' he replied with a smile, 'you'll have to jog my memory.'

'This is Detective Lily Harrod, of the Irvine Police Department. I'm just calling to ask your whereabouts.' There was a cheeriness in her voice that he'd missed.

'Oh, Ms. Harrod? I think I remember you. You're that gorgeous redhead, aren't you?'

She didn't reply to his quip, but she laughed, and let her voice settle back to its regular tone. 'Shut up. Seriously, though, where've you been? It's been, what, a week since I saw you? I miss you. I mean, I know I've been super swamped with this case – which, by the way, I'm getting absolutely nowhere with – but I'd still like to see you from time to time.'

'Yeah, I'm sorry. I, just—I've been trying to sort myself out, y'know? I was looking for a new job – something that actually means something – and I've been trying to find a new apartment. I really don't want to live in that horrible motel any longer than I really have to. It's starting to creep me out.'

His mind returned to his recurring nightmare. Hannah, standing over his bed. Her blood dripping on to the sheets and through to the mattress. *Why was she always apologising?*

'Jackson?' Lily asked. He noticed that he'd zoned out for a few minutes and ignored what she said.

'Sorry, sorry, I was in my own little world. What did you say?'

'I said, I was really proud of you for trying to get your life together again. I know it's been really tough the last few months. I'm really glad you're getting back on your feet and not letting it get to you.'

'Oh, believe me, it's getting to me.'

'Oh.'

A moment of silence made the conversation awkward, but he passed over it and kept talking.

'I do appreciate the sentiment, though. I'm glad I found you. It's made the 'healing process' a little bit easier.'

Jackson lay his head on to the steering wheel and closed his eyes, taking a few quiet breaths before talking again. 'I'm sorry if I seem distant sometimes,' he started, 'it's just... Hannah's death—' he stopped at the sound her name coming out of his mouth, taking a few more breathes to compose himself '—Hannah's death hit me so hard. Sometimes I feel guilty for being with someone so soon, or even at all, and I have to really try to be positive about myself.'

Lily made quiet humming noises, listening intently. After another few seconds of eerie silence, she cleared her throat and spoke; her tone was lower and she didn't seem as chirpy as she was.

'I understand how you feel, Jackson, I do,' she said, 'when my husband left me, I didn't really know what to do with myself. I felt like I was in a sort of limbo where I didn't know how to act, or what was appropriate. I mean—' she coughed again '—I know he didn't die. He stayed in Ohio when I moved out here, and we couldn't make it work, but I sort of understand. Does that make sense?'

Jackson smiled, still with his head of the steering wheel, and nodded slightly – less of a nod, more like he was itching his forehead.

'Yeah, he replied, I get you. And thank you, that means a lot. I'd be a lot worse if I was alone. I'm really glad I'm not alone.'

He could feel her return the smile, hearing her hum happily under her breath. 'Of course, I'll always make sure you're not alone. I know we haven't seen each other much lately, but I'm always here for you. There's not a thing you could do where I wouldn't be with you.'

Jackson lifted his head up and looked towards Chase's house, a nervousness building up inside him. 'I'll hold you to that,' he said.

They said goodbye, planning to see each other soon – Lily informed him that she was in desperate need of a break – and hung up. Jackson sat holding his phone for a few minutes, processing all of the information.

Will she stick by me when this is all over? Is she really going to still love me?

He placed his phone into the glovebox, where no one would expect it to be, and collected the rest of his things. He picked up the bible that was resting on the passenger seat – one he'd borrowed from the motel room – and exited the car. He crossed the road with haste, not bothering to look left and right to check for oncoming traffic. He'd carried out enough research and studied enough to know that there was very little activity in the area at that time of the day.

The paved driveway he walked up, past the grey SUV, led to a closed garage – a light brick structure with dark orange tiles on the roof. The white garage door had small arched windows lining the top, but it too dark to see in. The garage top extended further right than the actual building, forming a roofed walkway towards the front door. Jackson felt shadowed and protected from the outside world as he approached the light cream door.

He took a few breaths to collect his thoughts, double-checking to make sure he had everything he needed to carry on.

Jackson tapped lightly on the door and took a step back. The wood felt cold against his knuckle – the roof of the garage prevented the sun from reaching this part of the property. After a few seconds of no response, Jackson knocked again, a little louder. After another few seconds, the light was coming through the door from the back of the house was covered by a dark shadow, getting bigger as it approached the door.

Chase answered with a defensive look on his face, never expecting visitors, and never appreciated it when he actually got them. Unplanned guests were the worst.

'Can I help you?' he said.

Chase's averagely-built frame was sporting a loose-fitting black sweater that went over a slightly lighter black shirt. The collar flapped generously over the neck – he'd probably have at least three buttons undone since he was off the clock for the day. His sleeves had been rolled up a little, showing off the beginning of a tattoo, and letting a two-tone metal watch hang loosely over his wrist.

'Hi,' Jackson said, as cheery as he could force himself to be. Pretending to be a door-to-door salesman, he held the Bible out in front of him. 'Can I perhaps have a minute of your time to talk about our Lord?'

Chase laughed – a hearty laugh from the pit of his stomach – and replied, 'No, thanks,' before shutting the door.

Before he could, Jackson stuck out his leg and trapped his foot between the door and its frame. All of the cheeriness escaped his body in one motion and he placed his hand on the wood, slowly pushing it back open. Chase's face dropped.

'I think I'm gonna take it anyway,' Jackson said and forced himself inside.

23

The motel room still had a faint stench of blood – it was something Jackson just couldn't get away from. No matter how many times he sprayed cologne on himself, or sprayed the room with air freshener, the smell never fully went away. He'd felt like the more times he had the nightmare about Hannah, the stronger the smell would get. It was thick in his nostrils, like the smell of rusted iron. Maybe one day he'd wake up and there would actually be droplets on the end of his mattress.

Or maybe he was crazy.

Outside, the sun was dim and weak, and the rays that extended into the room didn't quite reach the bed. It was a cool day; there was a slight breeze flowing around the room through the open window and it brought with it a sense of relaxation.

Jackson lay on his back on the bed – one arm bent behind his head and the other resting on his chest – staring up at the ceiling. It was a dull shade of white that had been painted over way too many times. But his face was just as plain.

After going to Chase's house a few days before, he'd been riding a high ever since, feeling like he wanted to keep going but having to stop himself from getting too carried away. It was an intense feeling that he didn't quite know how to describe, he just knew that he wanted more of it and needed to keep working his way down his list if he wanted to make sure the high kept returning.

But, lying on the bed with a blank stare, he'd lost it for the time being. He hadn't moved in an hour, just listening to the generic noises of people going about their lives outside, and the ticking of the clock behind his head. It had become a relaxing metronome; a calming device that he was taking advantage of while he still could. With his eyes closed, he could hear his breaths as they slowly came out of his nose.

This was when he was most at peace.

Suddenly, that was disturbed when another thudding noise rattled through the door. The knocks were loud and quick, clearly someone was in a hurry to be seen to. Jackson got up from the bed as slowly and as calculated as the ticking of the clock and approached the door, shouting for the visitor to identify themselves.

'It's Lily,' the voice from the other end shouted. It was muffled through the wood, but she didn't sound too happy.

Jackson opened the door and Lily couldn't get in quick enough. She looked upset and dejected; something was clearly bothering her which then began to bother him.

Had they found new evidence in the abandoned garage? Was there an actual suspect now? Was he it? Is that why she looked so sad?

He kept a straight face and didn't let his growing nervousness affect his body language.

'What's wrong?' he asked as he closed the door.

She stopped in the centre of the room and turned to look at him. Her face was a lot paler than it was the last time he saw her and her light orange hair was becoming a light brown on her roots.

'It's this—' she let out an aggravated *ugh* '—this stupid case. I just don't know what to do. I really, really don't.' She combed her hands through hair, clearly stressed, and impatiently circled in place.

Jackson moved towards her and put his hands softly on her hips, feeling the soft fabric of her sweater and keeping her still. There were minute streaks of red journeying through the whites of her eyes, like attractive forks of lightning tearing through a cloudless sky. It looked like she hadn't slept since she took on the case, and it was slowly tearing away at her.

Jackson felt torn; different feelings were fighting to be at the forefront of his brain and it was giving him a headache. He didn't like seeing what it was doing to her – his actions seemed to be well on their way to ruining her life – but he figured that he'd be proud of what he'd been doing if *anyone else* was the lead detective. He knew he had to keep going, no matter what. Then he could help her solve it.

'Calm down, calm down,' Jackson said to her, a little more than a whisper, 'tell me what's wrong.'

Even though he'd stopped her from circling, Lily was still fidgety. Her breaths were sharp and quick. 'It's this—this—What do I *do*?'

'What do you mean?'

'I need *help*,' a tear formed in the corner of her left eye, growing redder by the minute, 'please help me.'

'I'd love to help,' Jackson muttered, wiping away the tear with his thumb, 'but you need to tell me what the problem is.'

She took a few breaths to compose herself, wiping her eyes with the heel of her palms and took a step back. She said 'okay' to herself a few times as she tried to figure out what to tell him, still not wanting to reveal too much about an ongoing investigation.

But it was slowly driving her crazy and she needed help.

'Okay,' she said, out loud this time, 'I'm just not getting anywhere with any of it.'

'Any of what?' Jackson replied, his tone sympathetic.

'Just... any of it. We've spent days combing through that garage place in the valley where those three guys were killed, and do you know what we found? Absolutely nothing. I don't get it.'

'So the guy cleaned up after himself?'

'You could say that, yeah,' Lily combed her right hand through her hair, scratching her head on the way. 'There's absolutely no traces of anything – no signs that anyone has been there. We couldn't find any witnesses since it was so out of the way, and there were no cameras either. We might as well just rule them all to be suicides.'

She let out another *ugh* – under her breath this time – and took a minute to calm herself down.

'So,' Jackson began as he walked towards the refrigerator, 'have you found of the cause of death for them all?'

'Yep, stab wounds. Really bad ones, too.'

Jackson got a bottle of water from the fridge and walked back over to her, saying 'Oh, really?' as he handed her it.

She quickly thanked him and opened it, twisting off the cap with a *click*. She took a few gulps and continued. 'And the third guy – Grey Sullivan,' she wiped her mouth with the back of her hand and set the bottle down onto the desk behind her, 'he died from asphyxiation. He choked on his own tongue.'

Jackson's eyes widened. 'How do you choke on your own tongue if you got stabbed?'

'I think we're dealing with a professional,' Lily remarked as she took another small sip from her bottle.

Trying to hide the smirk from his face, and the sudden sense pride that he was feeling, he sat down the edge of his bed without breaking eye contact with her. 'Really? What makes you think that?'

'Well, this kind of attack, with this kind of precision, you don't see that with someone who hasn't killed before. Grey's spinal cord was completely severed from his head – with almost perfect technique.'

A look of disgust came briefly across Jackson's face, and Lily nodded in agreement before continuing. 'The killer stuck the blade in his neck at just the right place with no mess, or mistakes. From what I saw from the state of the wound, it was quickly in – then jiggled around a bit – then quickly taken out. He was paralysed pretty much straight away, and completely lost all of his nerves. So his tongue just fell to the back of his throat and then, bang, he was dead.'

'That's brutal.'

'Tell me about it. And then, what makes it worse, is that we couldn't find any clues or any evidence that could lead us anywhere, and more keep piling on.'

Jackson furrowed his brows and leant over, resting his forearms along the length of his thighs, and said, 'What do you mean, "more keep piling on"?'

Lily turned around and walked around the edge of the desk to sit in Jackson's chair. His body tensed up, knowing she was so close to all of his notes and his list of names. She glanced over the desk, only taking in the messy state of it, and looked back over to him.

'Well, we've found another body.'

Jackson's eyes widened again, lifting his eyebrows to a symmetrical arc. Every so often, he glanced at the laptop in front of her, the protective sleeve to her left and the few pieces of paper that were housed safely underneath it. He felt like he'd be tense until she left, but he tried his best to keep his poker face.

'You have?' he said, concerned.

'Yeah, across town. I think it's—' she stopped to scratch something off Jackson's desk, before wiping her hand on her trousers and looking back at him '—I think it's related to the other three murders. That's what the reports are telling me, at least.'

'What makes you so sure?'

'Well when the coroner first got to the body, his initial thought was that it was the same knife. He said it looked to be the same dimensions; same width, same thickness, and the same size blade – eight inches. We haven't confirmed anything yet, so this is just my impressions. And nobody has to know that I told you. It's confidential, and my job would be in jeopardy.'

Jackson nodded firmly, then mimicked zipping his mouth shut and throwing the key to the floor.

'Well, the house that the body was found in belonged to a—' she awkwardly positioned herself on the chair and took a small notebook from her trouser pocket and flipped a few pages in '—Chase Morgen. He was an architect at a big firm called—' she looked at her notes again '—Irvine Design Studios. He'd recently been commissioned to lead the design of a huge office tower. I'm not really sure on the motive, and how they're connected other than the murder weapon, but it's still early days yet.'

Jackson stood up to stretch his legs and walked over to the desk – maybe trying to make sure she didn't snoop. He leaned over and placed his palms on the edge of the dirty brown wood and spoke again, asking, 'So have you found more evidence this time? Or did he clean up?'

'We found *some*, but I think most of it is unimportant, or stuff we can't follow up on.'

Jackson tilted his head slightly.

'Well, there was a bible,' Lily carried on, 'we found it on the floor near the body, but that doesn't mean anything. There must have been a struggle since there was an upturned table near and some books were thrown about. The bible must have fallen off the shelf or something. I'm not 100% on the particulars, but you get the basic idea.

'Then, we have a witness that said she saw the same car parked at the bottom of the street every day, but she's quite an old woman, so all she told me was that it was usually far away and that it was white. But, I mean, it could just be a car that belonged to someone down the street and they'd recently bought it. Who knows? But, we'll try and find camera footage of the area to see if we can track it, though, just in case.'

Jackson could feel the dampness of sweat on his face, but not letting it show. His mouth was starting to get dry, and he moved his tongue along his gums between his teeth and bottom lip.

'Well, that's good. It's a start, isn't it?' he said, trying his best to sound supportive.

She nodded, taking a drink of her water while he spoke. She swallowed and wiped her mouth.

'Uh-huh, but there's more. It gets really confusing. So, basically, the guy was brutally murdered. And I mean, brutally. So he's face down on the floor when we find him, and there's a small piece of paper – a note – just lying on the top of his head as if it were nothing. It's really bizarre.'

'A note?'

'Yeah, I wrote down what it said,' she looked at her notes again, scanning the pages for a few seconds before looking back up to him, 'It read 'Her blood is on his hands. This is not murder'. What could that even *mean*?'

Jackson shrugged, and said, 'That's pretty cryptic – kinda eerie.'

'Yeah, I'm stuck on a few things. First, I have *no idea* who the 'her' in the situation is. Secondly, that last sentence is really off-putting. How could it not be a murder? That doesn't make sense, does it?'

Jackson shook his head, pretending to rack his head for thoughts and ideas. He could feel a multitude of emotions swirling up inside of him. He felt that familiar rush of adrenaline that had been fuelling him – but this time it was a different variation. It was like he was watching a movie that was keeping on him on the edge of his seat and he really wanted to know what was going to happen. He also felt sympathetic to her, she was clearly having a tough time and he felt like he would eventually start to really hurt her. He was starting to believe that he had different personalities depending on the situation he was in.

Something like that.

Lily turned around to glance out the window, holding her hand up to her face to shield her eyes from the sun. It had gotten strong since Jackson had been lying down, and was beating down on her back and making her sweat, giving her face a light glow. She stood up and walked around the desk and over towards the bed where Jackson had been sitting, murmuring to herself that it was way too hot and she couldn't handle it. Jackson breathed a sigh of her relief, quietly, and turned around to watch her walk away.

'I guess there is one positive about it,' she said softly as she slumped into her seat on the edge of the bed.

'What's that?' Jackson asked, moving over to stand in front of her.

She looked up, her eyes still red and the colour in her pupils beginning to discolour.

'There was a fingerprint on the note.'

24

As silence took over the room, and the breeze stiffened, bringing with it a tense chill, Jackson's mind wandered back to that night, only a few days before.

Chase had stumbled into the entrance hallway of his house as Jackson pushed himself in, smiling as he shut the door behind him. Chase looked scared and confused. The man that had just broken into his home was clearly not wanting to talk about anything religious, and he was angry at himself that he'd fell so easily for it. But it was an honest mistake.

'Wh-what do you w-want?' Chase asked as he backed himself up against the wall nearest the living room door. He narrowly avoided knocking over a small potted plant that was placed carefully in the centre of a washed-oak end table.

'I want you to go and have seat,' Jackson replied calmly, gesturing towards the open door next to Chase, 'That's not too scary, is it?'

Chase strongly shook his head, showing the growing terror in his eyes. He slid along the wall, trying not to turn his back on Jackson, and quickly entered the room. Still holding the Bible in his hand, close to his

chest with the cover facing out, Jackso[n]
and observed him take a seat on his s[ofa,]
leather 3-seater with a dirty brown f[inish. It]
fit well with the rest of the room; full of d[ark]
colours. Chase leant back in the sofa, adjusting to a
comfortable position, and trying to get as far away
from Jackson as possible.

'Comfortable?' Jackson asked, 'okay.'

He flipped open the bible, glancing up to Chase
every now and again to make sure he wasn't moving.
He made understanding humming noises as he quickly
flicked through the pages, pretending like he knew
what he was reading – or even knew what he was
actually looking for.

'Okay,' Jackson said, slamming the bible shut with
one hand and tossing it onto the floor to his left, 'full
disclosure: I'm not actually religious. You might have
known that already, what with me breaking into your
house and everything, but I wanted to be honest and
open with you.' Jackson leant over and placed his hand
on Chase's left knee, softly saying, 'If there's no trust,
what else is there, y'know?'

Chase stared up at him with wide, scared eyes and
nodded slowly, pretending to understand. Jackson then
stood back up and pulled out his knife from the back of
his trouser waistband. At the sight of it, Chase's eyes
grew wider and he began to squirm, twitching his neck
and wiping his sweaty palms on his jeans.

Jackson looked down to study the bible on the
floor. It had landed in front of a tall, wooden bookcase
that didn't look sturdy enough to hold the books and
ornaments that populated it. Looking back to Chase,

gesturing towards the book with his knife, he said, 'That seemed to be the easiest way to get you to answer the door. I couldn't really think of another plan, and there was one in my motel, so here we are.'

'O-o-okay,' Chase replied, his gaze still firmly held on the knife.

'You sound scared. Are you scared?'

'W-well, yeah. I mean, you just b-broke into my house and you have a-a knife. You're crazy.'

Jackson took a step forward – startling Chase – and smiled, 'Sometimes I don't feel crazy, but then things happen and it makes you change. You understand? I used to be normal – at least I think I did. And then, you know, circumstances change and so, too, do people.'

Jackson turned around, seeing a small coffee table the same colour as the bookcase. In the centre of it, a fruit bowl was full of bananas, apples, and oranges. Around it, a couple of dirty plates and a glass that was half full of soda.

'Do you not like cleaning up after yourself?' Jackson asked, turning his head to look at Chase.

'Those are—'

Jackson held up the knife, hushing him, 'Doesn't matter, not important.'

He pulled the coffee table closer to the couch, moving the bowl and plates back to create a space for him to sit down.

'Okay, where was I?' he asked as he sat down, 'Oh yeah, right. Basically, you calling me crazy is unfair, you see? Because, in a way, you're one of the reasons why I am.'

A confused look came over Chase's face. It was fresh-looking and his usually-styled hair was losing its volume and beginning to drop down to hang over his forehead. He flicked his head to get it away, stopping it from tickling his eyebrows.

'Let me tell you a story,' Jackson said, tapping the side of the blade against Chase's leg, 'You remember seeing that thing on the news about the three guys who were found dead in an abandoned garage up in—in Little Joaquin Valley?'

Chase nodded.

'Well, that was me. And there's a really good reason for it. Just like there's a good reason that I'm sitting in front of you. They, unfortunately, were 'Patient Zero', so to speak. I was normal, I work – or worked – in a little coffee shop and I watched sports. I like reading non-fiction books; learning about new things to impress my friends with. Stuff like that, yeah? So then those three guys come along. They break into my house while I'm at work, and they go and rape my wife. Can you *imagine* what that would do to a person? And that's not even all of it. After they rape her, they repeatedly stab her, then just leave. Just like that. Nobody could remain normal after that, don't you think?'

Chase shuffled again, watching as Jackson effortlessly waved the knife through the air he told his story. 'W-why are you telling me this?'

'Now, now, I'm getting to that. Anyway, long story short, I got my revenge and I killed them all,' Jackson leant in, trying to keep his voice low, 'Don't worry, I didn't rape them, too.'

He leaned back again and straightened his body, knowing his posture was lacklustre, and feeling a slight crack in his shoulders and letting out a relaxed *ahh*.

'I felt so good doing that,' he continued, 'that I wanted to do more. I wanted to keep *feeling* that. It was exhilarating; something that I'm sure you'll never get to experience. So this brings me back to you.'

'Why me, though? What did I do?' Chase replied, his voice breaking.

Jackson laughed, just as heartily as Chase did when he answered the door, and said, 'What? Have you forgotten already?'

'Forgotten what?'

'The little phone call we had the other day. Do you not recognise the voice of your future business partner?'

'That was—'

'Yes, that was me,' Jackson exclaimed, almost excitedly, 'but I think there's more to say.'

'But—'

'Well, I wanted to hear your side of the story. I want to hear you say the words,' Jackson stood up and started slowly walking in circles around the living room. He passed Chase's desk near the bookcase – less of a desk, more of a plain black tabletop with legs – that looked like it was straight from IKEA. His laptop was shut and there were scatterings of notes and sketches around it.

'What do you want me to tell you?' Chase pleaded.

Jackson stopped in front of the small electrical fireplace on the wall and turned to face him, 'I want you to tell me why you bullied her. I want an explanation.'

'I don't have one, man. I was – I don't know – I was a stupid, dumb, kid that thought I was above everyone. I-I thought I was a big shot. I'm-I'm sorry, okay? I never meant for her to go and do... that.'

Jackson stepped forward and held his arms out, palms up, '"That?" You can say the words, Chase. You don't have to tip-toe around it. She killed herself. She—'

He stopped for a second and turned to face the wall, sadness beginning to creep into his system but he tried his best to quash it straight away. He put his head down and to the side so that he could still see Chase from the corner of his eye. When he spoke again, it was softer.

'She hung herself from the ceiling fan in her bedroom,' he finished.

'I-I-I'm really sor—'

'While I *sat outside the fucking door*,' Jackson picked up one of the plates from the coffee tabled and launched it at the wall next to the front window. It shattered on impact, sending shards of all sizes flying through the space around it. The sound was deafening. Chase looked in horror, jumping in place as the plate hit the wall, but Jackson stayed still and calm, without a reaction. He stood breathing heavily looking at where he threw; the brief sadness being quickly replaced by deep anger.

Still looking at the wall himself, Chase started talking again, 'I'm different now. I promise. I-I was only 14 when it happened. I didn't know what I was doing.'

Jackson turned around, glaring at Chase with hatred burning through his eyes, 'Of course you knew what you were doing,' he shouted. 'You might have only been 14, but you knew *exactly* what you were doing to her. The things you did, they were calculated, planned out. It wasn't just name-calling or anything like that; you actually sought her out. She was your target.'

'I regret who I used to be. I was a horrible person. You have to believe me!' Chase kept pleading but it didn't seem to be doing him any favours.

'That doesn't help now, does it?' Jackson kept his voice raised, not being able to stop his rage from boiling over. 'You took it *too* far. You should have seen what you were doing to her. She saw her cry many times, and you kept going. And when I tried to stop you – when I grabbed you in the hallway, you had the guts—' he gripped the knife as hard as he could, ready to strike at any moment '—to stand there and *smile at me.*'

'Please, just listen to me,' Chase held his hands up, just about ready to jump onto the floor and beg for mercy, 'I'm a good person now. I'm not that person anymore. Please, don't hurt me. I'm sorry for what I did to your sister, but I promise—'

'Say her name,' Jackson interrupted, suddenly calm. His tone was soft again.

'W-what?' Chase replied, caught off guard.

'Say her name!' Jackson shouted as loud as he could. In the same motion, he placed his free hand on the underside of the coffee table and hurled it across the room, smashing it against the bookcase and knocking everything off the shelves, chipping different parts of the wood and making a dent in the wall next to it. '*Say it,*' he repeated.

'Sienna! It was Sienna!' Chase cried out.

Then, in one swift manoeuvre, Jackson cocked his right arm backward and slung it forward with immense force. Like he was sticking a fork into a cake, the entirety of the blade effortlessly penetrated the underside of Chase's chin, slightly above his Adam's apple, and disappeared into his head. Chase's mouth fell open and Jackson could see the knife passing straight through his tongue and into the roof of his mouth. Blood began filling it up and dripped onto his teeth, along his gums, and travelled slowly down the back of his throat. Chase's eyes froze, looking straight forward. From the power that it had been thrust inwards, the blade had completely severed his optic nerve, snapping the surrounding tissue and almost making his eyes tumble out of the sockets.

He was dead in a flash.

More blood came trickling out the bottom of Chase's neck and onto Jackson's hand. It was thick and warm, like honey, but smelled like a rotting piece of metal. In another swift motion, he pulled the knife out and Chase toppled forward; the momentum making him fall off the sofa and onto the floor in a heap.

Jackson stood over him, mouth slightly open in the shape of an *O* and exhaling sharply. His whole body felt tense, and he could feel the veins slightly bulging out of his arms. His right hand had gone red from gripping the knife so tightly.

Suddenly, he screamed. He felt the adrenaline surge through his body and revitalise him. He felt like a basketball player after hitting a game-winning shot. An exciting rush came over him and he didn't know how to cope with it, so it forced its way out through his mouth.

As Jackson moved, Chase fell forward slightly. He was resting on his knees, which were brought all the way up to his chest. His arms were limp and placed him behind – his palms were facing up and next to his feet. His head was down, touching his knees, hiding the damage that had just been inflicted on him.

Jackson looked around the room before walking through to the kitchen. On top of a black marble counter with faint white glimmer spots, just next to the refrigerator, was a small notepad and a couple of pens. He'd probably used it to write down his shopping lists.

He took one of the pens and turned the pad sideways, writing a message across the lines of the paper, in bold letters. After finishing it, and stashing the pen in his pocket, he tore off the page and took it back into the living room, smiling the moment he laid eyes on Chase again.

He was proud.

Crouching down just in front of him, Jackson placed the note on top of his head so that it was clearly visible to anyone that discovered him. With another smile – he was beaming with pride – he stood back up and began wiping down all of the surfaces he'd remembered touching, using a cloth he'd brought from the motel room.

After five or ten minutes, and going over things a few times to make sure there was no trace of him, he was happy.

Boy, was he happy.

As easily as he entered, he left the house and into the cool breeze of the night. The clouds formed a protective cover over the dim glow of the moon, which itself was quite low in the sky. He stood on Chase's driveway for a few minutes, listening to the relaxing noise of distant car engines zipping along the highway, and the barking of dogs along the street. A small drop of rain splashed against his cheek, followed by a few more. The light drizzle that followed was soothing. He looked up with squinted eyes, letting the drops hit his face and drip down to his chin.

With another smile, one of content, he walked down the driveway and across the road towards where his car was parked, still not bothering to look both ways.

25

Shortly after Lily had mentioned the fingerprint, she'd received a phone call that got her either excited or riled up, Jackson couldn't tell which one it was. It hadn't been a long call, and she didn't say much, just the occasional 'okay', 'yeah' and 'ooh'.

After putting her phone away, she'd abruptly left Jackson's room, exclaiming that she had a plan, and didn't make any contact with him until a few days after.

'Jackson, Jackson, you need to come over,' she'd told him over the phone. He was sitting at his desk again, going over the notes he had for Chase and crossing his name off the list he always kept with him. He'd begun to briefly look into the next one when she'd called.

'You sound happy,' he replied, putting the phone on speaker and laying on the desk next to him. He was trying to concentrate on writing notes and clicking through pages on his laptop.

'Oh, I am,' she said, 'I think I'm getting somewhere. You need to come see this. I need a different pair of eyes on all this.'

'Well, yeah, just let me—'

'And, and, if I don't talk about it with someone then I'm gonna go crazy.'

'Okay, I'll stop by when I fin—'

'Great, see you soon.'

The phone clicked off without him being able to reply. He looked at the screen for a few seconds with a confused smile on his face, before putting the phone in his front pocket. After quickly scanning through the webpage he was looking at, he closed his laptop, hid the notes, and picked up his car keys.

When he arrived at Lily's house some thirty minutes later – he hated rush hour traffic – she was busy talking to herself holding two different sheets of paper. The room was flooded with different documents and files. On the back wall, near the door to the kitchen, she had a medium-sized dining table that was covered in sheets of paper. Only tiny spots of wood came through. Just to the right of the table, placed on a sleek, varnished oak unit was a large flat-screen TV, which Lily was standing a few feet in front of.

A news broadcast was playing, showing a familiar face. Next to the makeup-covered, shiny face of the female news reporter was an overlay that showed the same photo of Chase Morgen that Jackson had discovered on the design studio's website. At the bottom of the picture, a headline in big bold letters read: **LEAD DESIGNER OF NEW MARITECH OFFICE TOWER FOUND DEAD AT HIS HOME**.

MariTech? Why would a Fortune 500 company like them want to build a new headquarters in Irvine? Supposedly the CEO was a real hard-ass.

Jackson lowered his brows and watched intently as the broadcast played. The reporter interviewed a witness and then spoke to a detective, but the volume was low so he couldn't make out what they were saying.

The broadcast went off as Lily turned around, seeing him the doorway and smiling excitedly. Without letting go of the papers in her hand, she quickly waved him over.

'Come here, quick. I think I'm starting to link it together,' she said proudly.

He gave her a smile and walked over to the dining-table-turned-desk. There were various crime scene reports – all of which had been scribbled over and annotated – and photos of all the scenes. There was also a photo of the exterior of the abandoned garage that she'd drawn circles on with red marker, highlighting various points of the area. There was a separate picture of the interior. It had been taken from the centre of the room, facing the wall where Jacob, Grey, and Arthur had all died. More red circles decorated it, along with handwritten questions stemming from some of them.

Why were they all killed differently?

Arthur simple, Jacob brutal, Grey calculated and methodical.

This patch isn't blood. Forensics seems to think it's vomit. Could be killer's?

Weird mark/scratch on wall here, something might have been thrown.

On the other side of the table were pictures of Chase's house, inside and out. The memory of it was still fresh in Jackson's memory. His body had been moved for the picture, but the mess from the bookshelf and the table remained.

'What's all this?' he asked as he finished his examination of the documents.

Lily saw where he was looking, nodded, and said, 'Oh, that. Well, yeah, that's my-my—' she waved her hands around like she was searching for the words '—my mood board... something like that, yeah.'

'So what is it that you need to show me, or tell me?' he asked, still studying the documents, trying to gauge where she was in the investigation.

'Okay, well, I think I'm starting to get a theory, and starting to get an idea of what kind of person the guy I'm looking for is – his personality, his history, and so on.'

He looked up at her with faint question, and asked, 'How do you know it's a 'he'?'

She considered the possibility for a short while, briefly looking over the notes she had in her hand, and the crime scene photos on the table, and shook her head.

'I guess I don't, for sure,' she began, before picking up the photo of the interior of Chase's house, 'but I'm taking an educated guess. This scene, this... guy, just the way he was killed – it was... brutal.'

Jackson nodded in understanding.

'I just...' she continued, 'I think with how professional all these deaths looked, and how much force was put behind the knife, I think my safest bet is to assume it's a guy, and then if it turns out to be a woman, I'll hold my hands up and apologise for being a little bit sexist.' She flashed him a smile, 'Deal?'

He returned the smile and nodded, then turned his attention back to the table. 'So what is your theory? I'm intrigued.'

'Okay, sit down,' she gestured towards the couch that was a few feet away from the table and picked up a few sheets of paper. He obliged, leaning back to get comfortable, and looked up at her.

'Okay, where do I begin?' she asked, scanning the pages.

'I don't know—'

'Oh, oh, the fingerprint, yes,' she was getting excited, but calmed her tone down to talk to him properly. 'So the fingerprint we found on the note didn't lead us anywhere. I had it tested and everything, and I thought it might give us a suspect – maybe even an arrest – but no dice. Turns out it wasn't Chase's, which was a good start, but it's an outlier. There's no record of that print on our system, which – again – I thought was kinda odd.'

Jackson nodded slowly as she spoke; her hands were doing various random gestures and she was pacing back and forth.

'Because, okay,' she continued, 'these murders are so impressive in terms of planning, execution and cleaning up – yet somehow we're possibly dealing with a first-time offender? I'm not sure about that. And the Bible, too. We found a print on that which matched the one on the note. I had this weird thought that the guy was religious, and maybe he was reading Chase his 'last rights' before he killed him, or something, I don't know.' She paused in place, then, speaking to herself, 'That'd be kinda weird.'

She shook her head to erase the train of thought and walked over to the table to exchange sheets. Jackson watched her for a second then turned his head to look out of the window. The sky was dull; grey clouds formed together and spread themselves over the horizon. Patches of blue broke through but were quickly neutralised.

'Right, next,' Lily said with her back toward Jackson. She gathered some more pages and then turned around. 'The note itself was really bugging me.'

Jackson tilted his head as if to say '*how?*' and shuffled in place.

'Well the message didn't quite make sense, did it? "Her blood is on his hands"? Who is the "her"? So, I think that maybe Chase did something bad to a girl from the killer's life or past. I assume, since he says blood, that Chase hurt – or killed – some girl and the police didn't catch the guy. Then, that would give the killer a motive to do something. Which would be a good place to start – since it's always good to have a motive – but that doesn't explain the other three.'

'Because you think they're linked?' Jackson was calm, sitting with his arms up and spread along the top of the cushions either side of him. His right leg was crossed over his left, at a right angle, with the side of his foot resting on his knee.

'Oh, I don't *think* they're linked. I *know* they're linked,' Lily replied.

'Why? Because of the knife?'

'Yes, because of the knife. It's the same size blade, it's a similar MO, all four cases are really brutal slayings. I just have a feeling that they're connected. I just *really* don't know how.'

Jackson switched his legs around, crossing his left over his right, and said, 'Well have you asked around? Maybe they know the same people. Maybe they both know – or knew – the killer at some point in their lives.'

'I did that,' Lily said. She put the paper back on the table and got her small notebook from her front trouser pocket, flicking through it and looking up at Jackson every so often. Her face was beginning to get a shine, most likely from sweat, and her hair was falling strand-by-strand out of the tight ponytail she'd wrapped it up in.

She pulled the sleeves of her crisp white shirt up further than they were, stopping them just above her elbows. Her long, slim-fit dress pants looked like they were sticking to her leg, which looked uncomfortable, but she seemed too focused to notice.

'I talked to some people at Irvine Design Studios yesterday,' she continued, making strong eye contact with Jackson. The stress was showing in her eyes, but her body remained focused and energetic. 'Most people didn't seem to notice anything different. There were a few people that only found out he'd actually died when I asked them if they knew anything about it. That was an awkward moment for me. Then I spoke to a guy named Andre, who was apparently his best friend since they were kids.

'Now, Andre said that he'd noticed Chase was acting a little off since receiving a strange phone call.

Chase didn't tell him any details of the call, but it had really shaken him up and he had wanted to go to the cops about it. I tried to trace the call, but the killer blocked his number so that was *another* dead-end.'

Lily pulled a chair out from underneath the table and placed it in front of the sofa. She sat down and stretched her entire body, then got to a comfortable position and looked Jackson deep in the eyes.

'After hearing all of that... got any ideas? I'm stumped,' her voice was low, the emotion coursing through the words was genuine. She might have had a theory, and been excited about moving from the starting line, but she was stuck and still needed help.

Jackson mulled over her question, on the fence about which direction to send her. He leaned forward himself, resting his forearms across his knees, and spoke as softly as she did as if they were trying to avoid anyone eavesdropping.

'What if it is actually what you originally thought it was?' Jackson asked.

Lily pursed her lips and lowered her brows, confused.

'Well, you said it looked like a professional, right?' he asked again.

She nodded, slowly.

'Well, what if that's actually what it is?'

'I still don't follow.'

Jackson looked over to the table of photos and documents, then looked back at her. 'You've gone through all that, studied all of those things, and you've made theories about motive and what kind of guy you think could have done all of that, but maybe you're looking in the wrong place. You said it was looked like a professional job, so maybe it actually was,' Jackson leaned back again, letting his arms fall loosely either side of him. 'It might be that you haven't found a link between the dead guys, because there isn't one. Or if there is, then you might be looking in the wrong place.'

Lily got up from her chair – which looked rather uncomfortable – and sat down on the sofa next to Jackson. She turned to look at him, putting her hand gently on his thigh, and asked, 'So what is it that you're *actually* saying?'

He put both of his hands on top of hers and continued speaking, 'I'm saying that they could be contract killings. You're looking for the link between four guys, and the guy that killed them. Maybe they're just part of a hit-list. It could be random, it could be planned. But there might be more than one guy that you need to look for.'

Lily sat still for a few minutes, frozen to the soft fabric of the sofa. She blinked sparingly and moisture began to soak into her eyes from staring into space for so long.

'Or, I could just be talking crap. I'm not a detective,' Jackson said, snapping her out of her daze.

'Sorry, no, I understand what you're saying. I'm just stumped. This case is really starting to get to me,' she replied, still straight-faced. She stood up and walked through into the kitchen. Jackson got up a few seconds later and followed her in. She stood in front of the sink, leaning her hands on the clean, oak finish of the bench and stared out of the kitchen window.

'Didn't you have trouble with that case in Ohio? You managed there, didn't you?' he asked, standing in the doorway.

'Yeah, but—' she leant over and splashed her face with some water, then dried herself up with a small towel that had been neatly folded by the sink '—the worst I saw there was a gunshot wound. Now, I've got knives being thrust into people's heads and spinal cords being severed.' She shivered with a grimace and passed by Jackson to return to the living room.

Jackson turned around to watch her, noticing the stress in her body. It looked like she hadn't slept in days. The skin under her eyes was puffy and her lips looked dry and damaged. He sighed, feeling more sympathetic towards her every time he saw her face.

'You need some rest, Lily. You look drained,' he muttered as she walked over to the chair in the centre of the floor and sat down.

'I need to get a suspect,' she replied, leaning her head back and exhaling sharply.

'No, you need some rest. You need to freshen up, take a break, then come back to it with healthy eyes and a healthy mind. I'll help you.'

She straightened her head up and looked at him as he walked slowly into the living room and stood behind the couch.

'Look,' he continued, 'I have an apartment viewing in about—' he checked his watch '—an hour or so. It shouldn't take too long. After that, I'll get us some food and a couple of drinks, and I'll come back and go through it with you. But first—' he walked around the sofa to her and placed a kiss softly on her forehead '—

you need to rest. Go upstairs and take a nap. I'll come back later.'

She took a long inhalation, held it for a while, then let it out, saying, 'Yeah, okay,' as the breath escaped her mouth.

'Good,' he replied, smiling and kissing her again.

Lily stood up and they shared an embrace. Some of her hair flopped into Jackson's face as they came together and he gently spat it out. The faint aroma of watermelon floated into his nose and he smiled; it was a familiar scent that always made him feel more comfortable. It was something he never thought he'd experience again.

Somehow, his mind always went back to Hannah. He loved Lily, and he was glad that he met her. He *wanted* to be happy with her. But Hannah always crept her way into his conscience.

And the dream.

A few minutes later, after supervising her going upstairs to make sure she was going to rest, he left. The afternoon was still young, but it gave off the impression of night. The dull clouds that overlooked the neighbourhood had gotten darker and a light mist had begun to make its way down to the ground. There was still a warm breeze, sweeping its way through the gaps in his clothes and circulating around the hairs on his body.

A dog barked in a distant garden, echoing through the leaves of trees that lined the roads. The common sound of car engines passing around the city still rung through his ears, but he'd learned to tune it out.

He didn't lie when he told Lily he had to go view an apartment – he always tried to be honest with her when he could – but he had other things he needed to as well. He said he'd help her with her case, and he'd follow through on that. He didn't know how accurate it would turn out to be, though.

As soon as that was done, he had more work to do.

26

Jackson returned to the motel after leaving Lily's house to grab a few things for his viewing. When he turned the corner into the parking lot, he noticed a police car parked in a space in the corner. It didn't look like anyone was in the car, and it was putting him on edge. Maybe he had no reason to be suspicious over everything, but that wasn't new; he'd been like that his whole life.

He quickly got out of his Jaguar and ran up to his room, grabbing a few bits of paper and running back down. When he exited the back door – not five minutes after he'd entered – there was someone peeking into the windows of his car. A police officer – a familiar one.

Jackson chuckled quietly when the man stood up and looked in his direction.

'Mr. Yardley,' Officer Bell said as Jackson approached.

'Officer,' he replied with a sigh, 'You wanna tell me why you're looking in my car window? I don't think you're allowed to do that.'

'Going anywhere nice? You only got here a few minutes ago,' Bell said, still playing his game.

'I have an apartment viewing actually, I just came back to grab a few things.'

'Oh really? Where?'

'That's not exactly your business, is it?'

'I could make it my business.'

Jackson pushed past Bell and grabbed the handle of the driver-side door, showing his impatience. The officer stepped back and looked over the car. Jackson was about to open the door when Bell spoke again.

'I have a question,' he said, tilting his head a little to the side, 'It'll be quick, I promise.'

Jackson sighed and rolled his eyes, then said, 'Oh yeah? What's your question?'

Bell leaned on the front of the car to look into Jackson's eyes. 'Why did you lie to my face?'

'What did I lie to you about?'

'Pretty much everything you told me, actually,' Bell folded his arms and crossed his feet, making himself comfortable.

'Is that right?' he replied with another sigh, checking his watch.

'Yuh-huh. You see, I checked your story, and it turns out you didn't go anywhere with Arthur.'

'I did, I went to a bar and he—'

'Don't bullshit me, Yardley,' Bell said sternly, 'I followed your car on all the traffic cameras I could find, and it was heading up to Little Joaquin Valley at roughly 6 pm. I checked the bars in the area, and only one person – a bartender – remembers seeing you. But, she didn't see you with Arthur, she saw you with Lily. She said you came in between 8 pm and 9 pm. So what happened in those few hours, huh? Because the way I see it; you don't *actually* have an alibi and you lied about where you were.'

Jackson smiled dryly, and coughed, before replying. 'I didn't go to Little Joaquin with Arthur. We went somewhere else. I *wanted* to go up there, sure, because there was a bar up there that I wanted to go to because it was quiet and out of the way. But, on the way, we passed a place that Arthur said he goes to every time he's in town. He said he'd be more comfortable there, so we went there.'

Bell was watching him with stern, sceptical eyes. 'And later?'

'When Arthur left, the place we were at was getting too crowded and noisy so I went to where I originally wanted to go. And that was the night I met Lily,' he flashed a genuine smile, 'Romantic, don't you think?'

Bell stood up straight and looked around the parking lot before leaning in to get a little closer, so he could whisper, 'You're not fooling anyone, you know?'

Jackson pulled on the handle of the door and opened it, then leaned towards Bell. 'I don't need to, you've got nothing on me,' he said softly, 'and your threats aren't working. You're the only one in the precinct that knows my name, and you're out here investigating your own, personal lead when you should really be doing whatever your boss tells you.'

'Regardless of whether this is in my free time or not—'

'What's your reason? Do you want Lily for yourself? Is that it? Because it seems to me—' Jackson stuck out a finger and disrespectfully poked the officer's chest '— that you're only looking into me because I'm with Lily, and you just can't handle seeing her with someone other than you. Am I right?'

Bell took another step back and sighed, then hummed contently. 'I'll be there when you slip up, *believe me*. I'll be the first face you see.'

Jackson chuckled quietly again. 'Good day, Officer. Good luck with your investigation,' he said as he got into his car.

He switched the engine on and quickly reversed out of his parking spot, turning around and driving away as quick as he could. He could see Bell staring at him through the rear-view mirror. When he turned the corner, going away from the motel, he took a few deep breaths and tried to relax, resisting the urge to scream and bang at the steering wheel.

27

On his way to his viewing of a spacious, one-bedroom apartment in the heart of the city, Jackson had accidentally passed the building that he'd been trying to find. Only a few blocks away from the motel was a small, one-story shop with a black sign above the door that read **RENALTO RENOVATIONS**. Jackson drove slowly past on his way downtown, inspecting the interior through the windows. He saw the shadowy outline of a figure sitting at a desk, grasping an old landline receiver to his ear. On the windows were various signs – paper that had been printed out and stuck to the glass – advertising different deals, and photos of finished renovations. It seemed to be an easy target as it was quite a small building, but it sat on a long street that was densely populated with similar shops, making it tough to follow Jordy away without being noticed. And he had to park somewhere to wait, but there was little to no space anywhere along the street.

One step forward, one step back, it seemed.

A few days later, after the apartment viewing and after his cosy night in with Lily discussing the ins-and-outs of her investigation, Jackson was back at his makeshift desk in the motel room that grew duller by the day. He thought he'd have gotten used to it eventually, but the drab colour of the walls and the basic décor never sat right with him. He figured it might be better to change them to padded walls; maybe that might be a little bit more comfortable.

Maybe then he'd stop having those damn nightmares.

Phasing out his surroundings, and putting his previous meeting with Officer Bell far out of his mind, Jackson got back to work. His laptop was always active and his desk was now covered in different pieces of paper – all of which had ramblings and notes on that he didn't want to forget. But now, he always kept the list of names on him at all times.

Was it security reasons? I don't know. It was something.

Already knowing where Jordy's business was, Jackson didn't need to do as much research as he originally thought. After finishing off some notes, he took his car keys and set off downtown, knowing that Lily was too preoccupied to call him. He didn't need the distraction this time.

He needed the adrenaline. And badly.

He arrived at Jordy's shop fifteen minutes later. It was a brisk, refreshing drive. He hadn't encountered much traffic and the roads were clear and dry. The sun had been beating down onto the glimmering metal of his Jaguar and all four windows had been rolled marginally down to allow the wind to properly circulate.

It was a good day to be alive.

Pulling up on the side of the road, mounting the sidewalk, he switched off the engine and exited the car. He needed to make sure he was targeting the right person, without blowing his cover. That is if he even had a cover in the first place.

He quickly rushed across the road towards the shop, looking around for anyone that was watching him. Cars were scarce, which was a plus, but he needed to be quick.

He reached the door and pushed it open, triggering a soft ringing noise above his head that alerted the shadowy figure that he'd saw in the window. The man was sat typing on a large computer, writing some notes with a pencil every so often.

'Hi there,' the man said, placing the pencil behind his ear and leaning back in his chair.

'Hi,' Jackson replied softly, without looking at the man, and making sure the door was firmly closed behind him. He looked around the rest of the shop to see if there was anyone else there. It wasn't a big place, roughly the size of his motel room. Opposite the occupied desk was another identical set-up of a PC, notepads with pencils, and various framed photos. At the back of the room was a large whiteboard that had names of clients on them, the work that needed doing, and the date that work would be completed. In the back corner of the room was a small, black two-seater sofa with a black coffee table in front of it. The rest of the room was empty and, other than a framed certificate behind the man's head, the walls were bare –

the subtle but attractive yellow paint was enough to give the room life.

'Can I help you, sir?' the man said, leaning slightly forward, getting Jackson's attention.

'Oh, yeah, sorry,' Jackson said as he escaped from his own world, 'Are you Jordy Renalto?'

Jordy leaned back and smiled, 'That's me. How can I help you?'

'That's great, thanks,' Jackson replied, flashing a smile of his own and leaving.

Jordy called out to him as he left the shop, following him with his eyes as he walked back down the street towards his car. A confused look came over Jordy's face, but he shrugged it off and continue making his notes.

Jackson got back to his car and got into a comfortable spot, turning the seat-warmer on slightly. Then, he just waited.

About an hour later, in which Jackson had sat playing a puzzle arcade game on his phone and getting frustrated that there were so many adverts, he spotted Jordy leaving his shop and locking the door behind him. The sun was still hanging high in the sky, its vast orange rays shining blisteringly down to the ground, bouncing off every surface and reflecting off the different metals that surrounding him.

As Jordy turned to walk down the opposite side of the street, in the direction of Jackson's car, he had to hold his hand up to his face to protect himself from the beams of sunshine that were attacking him. Jackson calmly waited, trying to hide himself as best he could so that Jordy wouldn't recognise his face if he looked that way.

Jordy passed a few buildings that housed various small shops – one of which looked like it hadn't had any customers in a long time and got to a junction at the end of the street. He didn't move for a while. He stood leaning on a streetlamp and kept checking his watch every few minutes. Jackson watched him through his driver-side wing mirror with confused, narrow eyes.

A short while later, a taxi pulled up next to him and he got in. The driver took a left at the junction and started driving, going away from Jackson. Not wanting to lose him, he quickly put his seatbelt on, turned on the engine and turned the car around, making sure there were no cars approaching to crash into him. He sped up slightly to catch up to the taxi but kept a respectable distance as he followed.

He drove slowly, always making sure he kept his distance behind the taxi. A car cut in between them as he drove along Turtle Rock Drive and passed the campus of Concordia University, making him strain his neck as he looked in the distance to make sure he could still see where they were headed. After circling around the roads for fifteen minutes – according to the digital clock inside his car – the taxi finally came to a stop inside of a small cul-de-sac. It was a long street of single-story houses with garages that were almost as wide as the houses themselves.

In the distance, the hills of Turtle Ridge towered over the neighbourhood, stretching the width of the horizon. The summit of the vibrant green hills was lined with thick, fresh pine trees, following the natural shape of the Earth. It almost resembled the screensaver of old Window's PCs that he used to own. To his right was a small park that separated two streets. A winding concrete walkway lined with benches stretched from one side to the other, and a child's obstacle course stood in the centre.

As the taxi stopped and Jordy exited the car, Jackson continued on down the road and pulled up a few houses down, on the park side of the road.

He watched as Jordy walked up a driveway and entered a house that, now that he saw it, did look awfully familiar to his own house across town. He seemed to finally understand the confusion.

But that didn't make it any better.

Jackson turned his engine off and sat still for a while. He closed his eyes and went over the plan in his head, miming to himself the things that he was going to say. Checking his coat to make sure everything was there, he released the latch to open the door. As the door clicked open and the air started flowing in the through the small crack, he noticed something in his rear-view mirror. Jordy's door open and someone walked out – a woman. She shouted something into the house behind her and shut the door, climbing into the car that was in the driveway and setting off. She passed Jackson's dormant Jaguar on her way out of the street but didn't look his way.

After waiting a few minutes to make sure she was clear of the neighbourhood, Jackson got out of the car. He glanced around. There was a woman and small child playing on the obstacle course in the centre of the park and another man – in his late teens – walking a dog along the walkway. On the other side, two old men were talking at the base of a driveway as one held a car door open, itching to get away from whatever conversation they were having. But there was no-one on his side of the road, which was great news.

That woman didn't lock the front door. How careless.

He smiled to himself and hurried across the road, holding his coat closed with his forearm to make sure it didn't fly open. He had private things in his pockets that people weren't supposed to see.

He reached the top of the driveway and took a few deeps breaths, realising how unfit he was. He looked around to make sure none of the people were looking his way, then let himself in. The door opened to a well-lit hallway with stairs leading up on one side. The walls were a dark purple colour and were decorated with small picture frames of family and friends. Immediately to his right as he lightly swung the front door closed was another stained oak door that was slightly ajar, leading to the living room. Jackson heard the noise that was coming from the TV go silent, and there was a quiet rustling coming from the sofa, followed by the loud scuffling off thick socks against the carpet.

'What did you forget?' Jordy said from the living room as he approached the door. Jackson stayed quiet and stood in the doorway waiting for him.

'Honey?' Jordy asked again as the door opened. His face dropped when he set his eyes upon Jackson. The colour seemed to drain from his eyes like he'd seen the ghost of a dead relative.

'Wh-wh-wh—' Jordy muttered, trying to swing the door shut and stumbling back into the room. Jackson held his arm on the bevelled wood and pushed back before entering the room.

'I didn't forget anything, Jordy, my dear,' Jackson replied mockingly, 'but I sure would love to have a chat. Have a seat.'

28

Jordy did as instructed and slumped onto the sofa – a hard-looking two-seater that was a horrible beige colour. The room itself was wide, with high ceilings. There was a large light pink rug dominating most of the floor space, with the walls being taken up by various posters of TV shows. Next to the flat-screen TV that was stood upon a long wooden unit the same colour as the door, was a bookcase that wasn't home to any actual books. The top two shelves had photo frames and a variety of fake flowers, while the lower two shelves had small copper ornaments and a stuffed pig toy.

'Y'know,' Jackson said, watching as Jordy picked up a glass of water from a side table and, with his hands trembling, slowly brought it to his lips, 'you should really lock your door when someone leaves because anyone could just waltz in – could be a deranged axe-murderer.'

Jordy didn't reply, he kept trembling, holding the glass of water up to his chest. Jackson stood in front of him and crouched, looking almost sympathetic at Jordy for being in that predicament.

'You should feel lucky that it's not some psycho; it's just me, and I just wanna have a talk about something,' Jackson said, softly.

'You-you were at my work earlier. Wh-who *are* you?' Jordy replied. His voice was shaky, but somehow he didn't seem nervous. Jackson thought it was odd, but didn't pay much attention to it.

'Oh, who I am doesn't matter, Jordy. It's what I *want* that should be your main concern.'

'What do you—do you want, then?'

'I've just told you. I want to have a chat.'

'Well, I want you to-to leave now. I've-I've learned my lesson, and I'll make sure to-to lock the door. So can you go now, please?'

Jackson smiled and stood back up, looking down with deep, mahogany eyes that seemed to house years of pent-up aggression.

'You're so polite,' he said. He took his coat off and threw it over an armchair that stood behind him, just in front of the living room window. 'But—' he reached back into the inside pocket of the coat and retrieved his favourite knife '—I'll have to decline. You see, I can't leave until I've said my peace. That would just be a waste of my time, wouldn't it? I didn't wanna come *all* the way here, just to leave because you asked me to.' He crouched again. 'You can understand that, can't you, Jordy?'

Jordy stared at him with bewilderment, his hands quivering more and more. Jackson noticed and began to chuckle under his breath, as he watched Jordy waver between fear and what seemed to be bravery.

'I'm just gonna take that from you,' he said, grabbing the glass from Jordy's grasp and setting it on the floor beside him, 'don't want you spilling it all over your nice outfit.'

Jordy followed the glass with his eyes then, when it was on the floor, returned his gaze to Jackson and the knife he was brandishing so effortlessly.

'Okay, so...' Jackson began, 'I have a query. I want to understand something; *really* understand it.'

'O-o-okay?' Jordy replied, beginning to tremble a little less.

'Can you think of a reason—' he moved his hands outwardly in a circle '—*any reason at all*, why someone would want to have you killed?'

Jordy furrowed his brows, really confused by the unexpected question. 'What?' he asked after a few seconds of silence.

'Oh, come on, you've got to know something,' Jackson replied, speaking in a firmer, but soft tone.

'I-I really don't know what you're talking about. I renovate people's homes; w-why would anyone want to kill me?'

Jackson edged a bit closer and held the blade of the knife to Jordy's knee. 'I know you're lying to me, Jordy. I know at least one person that wants to – and has the resources to do it. So... try again.'

Jordy shook his head again, closing his eyes, and trying to wrap his head around the situation. 'Is it you? Are *you* here to kill me?'

Jackson laughed and stood up, turning to face the TV for a few seconds before returning his eyes to Jordy, and saying, 'I don't think I should answer that right now. I don't think you *want* me to answer that right now.'

'But I haven't done anything, so why would someone wanna kill me?' Jordy was beginning to get frustrated, and the trembling seemed to be subsiding.

'Why do you keep lying to me, Jordy?' Jackson asked, frustration beginning to build up inside of him too, and the volume of his words reflected that.

'I'm not!' Jordy shouted.

'*Liar!*' Jackson bellowed, his deep voice echoed across the walls of the living room and sent a cold chill down Jordy's spine.

His expression froze and he started to tremble again. Jackson stood in place and took a few breaths, calming himself down so the adrenaline didn't take over him too early. The answers to his questions were more important.

'Now,' Jackson said, softly again, 'I wasn't hired to kill you, but I know three other people who were.'

'W-what? Who? Why?' Jordy began to get worried, but still had a clear look of confusion all over his face.

'Arthur Renshaw. Jacob Davies. Grey Sullivan. Do those names mean anything to you?'

'N-no. I've never heard them before.'

'Well, those are the three men who were going to come to your house and kill you. Maybe your wife, too.'

'What?' there was a genuine shock in Jordy's voice, and he adjusted himself on the sofa, clearly showing how uncomfortable he was. 'Why would they wanna do that?'

'That's what I'm here to find out,' Jackson replied. He moved quickly over to the sofa and crouched just in front of Jordy's knees, whispering, 'They were coming to get you for something you did, and I wanna know what it is.'

'I really, really don't know. Why would anyone try to kill me? I don't know what you *want* from me,' Jordy shouted, emotion creeping into his voice and raising the tone slightly. Either he was a fantastic actor, or he really didn't know what Jackson was going on about.

'I guess it's okay now because those men aren't gonna come for you anymore,' Jackson said, looking at his knife. He did his best to clean it, but the constant work it was getting had stained the steel a faint, dark red. Speckles of dried blood remained in various patches along the black handle.

'They're not?'

'Nope, they're not. You wanna know why?'

Jordy didn't speak, but he nodded slightly, the colour still not returning to his eyes.

'Because they're all dead.'

Jordy pointed at the knife, seeing the red hue that covered the edge of the blade, and raised his eyebrows a little. Jackson followed his gaze and nodded himself.

'Yep, this is why,' he said, holding up the knife like it was a prized artefact going up for auction.

Jackson looked behind him at the armchair that held his coat. Returning his gaze to Jordy, he pointed back and said, 'you mind if I move that over here? My legs are *aching*,'

'Um, I—I—,'

'Great, thanks,' Jackson interrupted.

He gave a sigh of relief, muttering indistinctly under his breath and pulled the chair towards the centre of the room. Throwing his coat across the floor, he sat back into the chair and exhaled with deep comfort. He stared at Jordy with a happy grin, positioned like he was a psychiatrist and Jordy was his client.

'That's so much better,' he exclaimed, before crossing his legs and continuing, 'Okay, so… I'm sure you know by now that I killed those three men. But I find it hard to believe that you don't know why they were hired to kill you and your wife, because whatever you did sure as hell ruined my life, and Jordy—' he leaned forward, clasping his hands close to his chest '— my dear friend, I just can't forgive you for that.'

'I-I still don't understand. Why—? What—? I just—'

'Let's start from the beginning, shall we? You did something that upset someone with a lot of money, and it must have been *really* bad. They hired three men to kill you, telling them he'd pay them $25,000 if they did it. D'you believe that? Somebody was willing to pay *twenty-five thousand* for you to die? Boy, that's pretty bad.'

Jackson leaned back in the chair again, using different hand gestures as he told the story, swinging the knife like it was nothing.

'So, from what the guys told me before I killed them – horrible, horrible deaths – they said that this… this guy had given them a rough description of your house and told them to just have at it. *But* – and here's where it gets really weird – they didn't really know the area and one of the guys thought it sounded like a house close to his mom's house, which happens – well, happened – to be my house. They didn't know any different, so when they got to my house, they broke in and, who did they find waiting upstairs? My wife.'

'N-no…' Jordy said, the shock had completely taken over his face and he couldn't find any words to speak. His eyebrows were raised and he looked like he was just about ready to cry; his lips pursed and his eyes were beginning to get a sad glow.

'Oh yeah,' Jackson continued, 'she tried to attack them with my baseball bat. I told her to hide. I told her to call the police. I told her that it wasn't worth it – that I'd be home soon and everything would be okay. But… but…' he was trying his best to contain his own emotion, reliving the day in his head and having all the feelings come flooding back, surging through his body and eliminating any adrenaline that was building up.

'But, they got to her first,' he slowly went on, 'they r-r-raped her. They raped her in the god damn hallway of our house. All three of them! And then they stabbed her. Repeatedly. By the time I got home, she was taking her last breaths. And you know the worst part?'

He stood up and crouched down in front of Jordy again, sniffling and wiping his nose with the back of the hand that wasn't holding the knife. He looked down at the blade and took a few breaths, before finishing his story.

'The worst part,' he said, with a calm and monotonous voice, 'is that they had the wrong person and they didn't even know until I killed them. They thought they killed *your* wife, but they got mine when I didn't even do anything. So, Jordy—' he moved the knife towards Jordy's stomach, following the blade with his eyes '—you need to stop lying to me. Because I have no qualms about killing you, too'

'Look, man, I told—'

'No, no, I said stop lying, because if you—'

Jackson couldn't finish his sentence. Before the words could escape his mouth, the front door clicked open and shut and his eyes widened, as did Jordy's. They both looked towards the entrance and waited in limbo for what seemed like an eternity.

A few short seconds later, the living room door swung open, and Jordy's wife – tall with an athlete's figure – walked in with a smile plastered on her face.

But not a second later, her face dropped along with the bag she was holding in her hand.

Then, she just froze.

29

Jackson watched as the contents of the woman's bag rolled out onto the carpet. Her eyes filled with terror as she saw the knife in his hand, stained a burgundy colour that could only belong to one thing. She couldn't seem to move.

Jackson and Jordy shot each other a glance, and Jackson jumped up from the chair and pounced on her, covering her mouth with his free hand just as the shriek was creeping its way out of her mouth. He could feel the soundwaves vibrate the palm of his hand, and it sent a weird shiver through his forearm. He held the knife in front of her face, like a reminder, and directed her to the sofa to sit next to her husband.

'Scream again, and I'll kill you both. Okay?' Jackson said as he returned to his seat in front of them.

She nodded and then glanced at Jordy and said, 'What's happening?'

Jackson looked at him with a face that said *'so you haven't told her either, huh?'*.

'Well,' he said to her, 'your precious husband has done some very bad things. He won't tell me what those things are, and he's really testing my patience because I've asked *so* many times. Is he always this stubborn with you? I couldn't handle being with someone like that, personally.'

She looked scared and confused, not knowing who to give her attention to. Jordy was feeling exactly the way she was – or maybe he just wanted her to think that. Jackson had intent in his eyes; she could tell he was there for a reason, and that he didn't seem to want to leave until he got everything that he wanted.

'Sorry, what's your name?' Jackson said to her, calmly, as if they were talking at a work-related gathering.

'Um, it's-it's…' She couldn't seem to get the words out, not wanting to look away from her husband.

'Well…?' he asked again.

She finally looked at him, the terror still in her eyes. 'It's Dana,' she said.

'Hm, odd,' he replied, slightly raising his bottom lip, and shaking his head to get back to his train of thought. 'Anyway… I know you're scared. Boy, I would be if I was in your position.' He leant forward with his arms together as if he were trying to keep the pee in, 'I think I'd also be scared of—' he pointed the knife towards Jordy '—him, because he's done a terrible thing. You know someone wanted to pay someone else to kill him? $25,000. Insane.' He leaned back again.

'They *what*?' Dana asked, directed towards both men.

Jackson held his hands up, palms out, and raised his eyebrows like he was saying '*hey, don't look at me. Ask him.*'

She turned to her husband and stared at him, waiting for an answer that was never going to come.

'I don't know what you want me to say,' Jordy said, 'I'm just as in the dark as you are, sweetie.'

Jackson stood up and swapped the knife to his left hand. He towered over them; he had quite a lean frame – not exactly a fan of the gym – but he was tall and had broad shoulders. He used the power he had behind his arms and punched Jordy in the side of the face. His cheekbone shattered against the weight of Jackson's knuckles and his nose rattled as the hand followed through. Jordy's head was flung harshly backward, nearly ripping the tendons in his neck. The whiplash was almost instantaneous and blood started dripping from the left nostril.

'You're lying again!' Jackson shouted as Jordy cried out in pain, not knowing what part of his face to hold on to. It felt like he'd ran into a brick wall; his teeth were loose on that side and his head was suddenly pounding.

'What are you doing?' Dana cried, still unaware of what was really going on in her house.

Jackson glared at her and she thought she could see the flames behind his eyes. He was damaged in ways she couldn't imagine and she sensed the pent-up emotion that was bubbling inside of him – and she thought he had no way of releasing it.

Jackson told her what he'd described to Jordy about the plan. He described how Hannah was raped and stabbed, how the three men had mistakenly gotten the wrong house and it had broken his life into a million pieces, and why he wants to rectify the situation by making sure Jordy is dealt with properly.

She sat there, devastated. The rest of the room had faded away and there was no noise other than Jackson's voice. She was engrossed in the story as if it were a one-man play.

'I'm... I'm so sorry,' Dana said when he finished. He'd sat back down in the chair halfway through, checking on Jordy every so often – who looked lost in his own world.

'*You're* sorry?' Jackson replied, 'Oh no, I have no intention of accepting your apology, Dana, because you're actually rather innocent here, aren't you?' He turned to Jordy. 'What about you, huh? Are you gonna spill your dark secret yet?'

Jordy didn't respond, and Dana looked at him with judging eyes. Jackson looked back at her, and asked, 'Do you want to know what I did to those three men? Do you want to know how I killed them? Do you want to know how I got my revenge for doing those things to my wife? Maybe you'll rethink your apology.' There was a brashness in his voice; he was smug and he had no problems with showing it.

'I-I don't really—' Dana said.

'Doesn't matter, I'm gonna tell you, anyway,' Jackson interrupted.

He sat back, rested the knife across his lap, and started massaging the hand that had punched Jordy. There was a light red patch forming across the knuckles of his index and middle fingers, that he knew were going to bruise. Then, he started the explanation as if he were simply telling someone about his day.

'Arthur was the first,' he began, 'I was still learning at that point and I didn't really know what to do. I had this *big* knife but didn't know how to use it. So I stabbed him in the stomach. It was like... it was like popping a balloon with a small pin. The way the blade just sank into his fat—' he shivered, but kept a wry smile on his face '—it was such a bizarre feeling. After that, was Jacob. He was a little bitch. I hate him. With him, I cut a long, gaping line across his neck – from ear to ear – and it just opened up. The blood keep squirting and pouring out of his neck, I've never seen anything like it in my life. It was so—' he held a closed fist over his mouth to stop himself from throwing up; closing his eyes and lightly shaking his head a few times.

Jordy and Dana sat still on the sofa, traumatised. Jordy had managed to stop the bleeding from his nose, but his hand was still holding his cheek. Outside, two dogs parked at each other as the crossed the other side of the road near the park. Jackson could hear cars driving up and down the street, feeling glad that everyone who walked by did so on the other side of the sidewalk.

When Jackson had calmed himself down and put the reminders of throwing up in front of Jacob's dead body out of his mind, he carried on his story with a faint smile. Throughout the whole thing, his eyes had always been fixated on Dana – as if Jordy wasn't there.

'Grey was probably the most fun to watch. So, I'd saw this martial arts blog online and it said if you dig a knife into someone's neck, just underneath the C3 vertebrae, which is about—' he turned his head and placed a finger in the centre of his neck, where his hair formed a point '—here, you could do some real damage. And wow, it wasn't wrong. You should have seen the spasms and involuntary reflexes his body was doing. He actually swallowed his own tongue.'

'You... you're...' Dana started.

'Oh, I'm disgusting, I know,' Jackson finished her sentence for her.

'That was—that was gruesome,' she turned her face up at him, squirming in her seat, knowing now what he was capable of. 'How was it so easy for you to recite that?'

Jackson grabbed the knife from his lap and leaned forward again, muttering, 'Here's the thing... I'm not really sure who I am anymore. It was 'easy' because it was *fun.* Do you understand that? So *you*—' he turned to Jordy and pointed at him with the blade '—need to stop *wasting* my *damn* time.'

Silence. Again. He seemed to have forgotten how to talk – or he didn't want to so he didn't incriminate himself. But he didn't want to die.

Jackson noticed the silence and looked down, almost defeated, with a smile and whispered, 'okay', to himself. Then, he stood up and pushed the armchair back with calves in one quick movement. The chair toppled backward from the force and rattled against the TV, which wobbled but remained standing. He stood right in front of Dana and got back into his crouch, gripping the knife tightly in his hand.

'Wh-what are you doing?' Jordy finally said, if only to remind himself what his voice sounded like. It was relatively high-pitched, suited for a salesman, with a stiff California accent where the vowels were more pronounced in his speech.

Jackson glanced at him and smiled affectionately. He held the knife up straight and rested the tip on Dana's thigh. She tensed and looked down at it, unsure of what to do. He pressed down gently and her breathing started to quicken.

'Right now,' Jackson said to Jordy, 'it'll feel like she's getting a needle in her thigh. So… what did you do?'

'J-Jordy, t-t-tell him whatever he wants to know,' she couldn't keep her eyes off the blade; her whole body was tense and it was making her shake.

'I don't know what I need to tell you,' Jordy pleaded.

Unhappy with the response, Jackson pressed down harder, sending an inch of the blade into Dana's thigh. She let out a whimper and started to lightly cry, squeezing her eyes shut to try and stem the pain.

'J-J-Jordy…' she said again, her voice breaking.

'Yeah, Jordy, listen to your wife. What did you do?' Jackson repeated.

He remained silent, staring at the knife. His mouth was open and his lips were moving slightly – he looked like he wanted to say something but he didn't know how to use his words. After another few seconds of silence, Jackson dug the knife in deeper. Half of the blade had vanished into her leg and thick, maroon patches of blood began seeping through the tiny gaps. She screamed softly, trying to stem the noise by covering her mouth with her other hand.

'Stop! Please stop!' Jordy cried, tears rolling down his cheek.

'Jordy!' Dana whimpered.

'Do what she says!' Jackson shouted as he pushed the knife in as far as it would go.

She couldn't hold the pain in any longer. She screamed as loud as her small mouth would allow her, then clenched her teeth. Her body was trembling which made the knife jiggle in her muscle. The pain was unbearable, but it wasn't like she'd imagined. It was a strong, underlying ache in her muscle and she could feel the burning wrapping around the entirety of her thigh. The ache shot up and down her leg, but she couldn't move it.

'J-Jordy!' she shouted again, eyes squeezed shut like she was calling out to the room.

'Yes, Jordy,' Jackson said again, 'What did you do?'

Jordy cried and pleaded for him to stop, not listening to either person that was calling for him; only focusing on the knife sticking out of his wife's thigh.

Then, without warning, Jackson ripped the knife out, bringing a thin trail of blood with it and stared into Dana's eyes as they opened. They were full of tears which completely covered the light brown colour, turning them black.

Jackson looked back at Jordy, 'What... did... you... *do?*'

As the last word echoed from his dry lips, he thrust the knife forcefully into Dana's other thigh. Her head cocked back and she screamed out in anguish. Muscles and tendons ripped apart and the blood came pouring out of her leg, swimming down the side of her trousers and onto the carpet beneath. He flicked his wrist, sending the blade along her leg and tearing the muscles further. Her head shot up and a blood-curdling scream erupted from her mouth.

'Alright, fine!' Jordy screamed, 'I give up.'

'What did you do, Jordy?!' Jackson replied, his eyes still locked on Dana.

'I raped a little girl!' he shouted, and slumped back into the sofa cushions. Then, he wept.

30

Dana sobbed – both at what had just spilled out of Jordy's mouth and the excruciating ache in both of her thighs. She didn't feel like she'd be able to walk again, there was always going to be a dull ache shooting up and down her legs and would never go away.

If she wasn't murdered, there, in her own house.

She didn't know what secret he was hiding, and why the deranged man had stabbed her for it, but she wasn't expecting *that*.

'You… you…' Dana tried to say through her sharp breaths, but the words wouldn't come out. The pain was taking over her, and she couldn't think straight. Blood was trickling down her pant leg and wrapping itself around her exposed ankle. It felt warm, like syrup, and it created a foul smell in the air around her.

Jackson held his hand up to stop her from speaking again, leaving the knife firmly implanted in her thigh and stood up, staring down at Jordy with his own look of disbelief. But when he spoke, it was calm and unmoving.

'What?' he said sharply, slightly louder than a whisper.

Jordy sniffled a few times and wiped his eyes with the back of his hand and looked up at Jackson, who was combing his right hand through the bed-head look of his light brown hair.

'I-I-I don't know how it happened,' Jordy said, still snivelling.

'Bullshit,' Jackson replied, calmer still.

'It's t-true,' he continued, doing his best to talk through the tears that wouldn't stop dripping from the corner of his eye, 'I bl-blacked out as I was doing it, and I-I don't remember all of it. I think I was d-drunk, too drunk, and I saw her walking by herself, and I... I... I don't know what happened, okay?'

Dana sat in disbelief, managing to turn her head to look at him as he told the story. She could feel the colour fading ever-so-slowly from her face as blood continued to trickle out her wounds and onto the floor, staining its way through the carpet and into the underlay.

Jackson stood with the same look on his face. He hadn't moved or blinked as Jordy spoke; his eyes were fixated on the embarrassing shell of a man beneath him. He couldn't look away even if he tried. It was like he was taking part in a high-stakes poker tournament and he had a winning hand.

'Next thing I knew,' Jordy continued, looking down at his lap, a little more composed, 'it was over, and she was crying. I think I'd s-sobered up by then because the look on her face... I'll always be haunted by it.'

'Where did it happen?' Jackson asked.

'On... on the side of the road. Th-there was a big set of b-bushes, and I just snapped and it happened in there. I begged her not to tell anyone; I begged and begged. She kept c-crying, and it was getting louder, so I... so I put my hands over her mouth to stop the noise. I was still a bit—' he sighed deeply, wiping his eyes '—a bit drunk, so the noise was hurting my head.'

Jackson stared down at him, eyes getting wider as the story getting on. Just like Dana, he didn't expect that kind of secret. He shot her a quick glance and saw she was about to speak. He held up a hand to shut her up, before speaking himself, 'Did you kill her?'

Jordy looked up at him, almost shocked by the question. 'No, no, no, of course not.'

'Well, then, what?'

'She was just... unconscious. I think. When she stopped moving, I-I ran. I didn't want to be anywhere near there in case she woke up. I... I've... I've regretted it ever since. I'm not that person. I promise I'm—'

He turned to Dana to plead with her, but she wasn't looking at him. He blanking eyes were stuck looking straight ahead, unaware of her surroundings. Her right hand was placed tightly over the gash in his right leg and blood was soaking through the webs in her fingers. The knife was still protruding from her left thigh, and every so often her eyes darted towards it, almost wondering if it was still there.

Jackson remained still, staring at the wall behind Jordy's head.

Deep breath in. Hold it. Deep breath out.

He put his palms to his face, taking a long breath in. He moved his hands through his head and rubbed the back of his head a few times.

'Hannah died for this?' he asked himself quietly, but directing the question to Jordy at the same time, 'Three different men raped my wife because of *this*?'

He took a couple of steps to his left and crouched in front of Dana, ducking his head slightly to look into her eyes, which were aimed at the floor in the corner of the room near the window. She was in her own world. Jackson placed the side of his index finger under her chin and lifted it slightly. Her eyes moved slowly towards his, pale and almost lifeless, and her face was slimy from the sweat.

'I'm sorry I had to involve you in this,' he whispered, a small hint of genuineness in his voice, 'It almost seemed like you were on my side.'

He gave her a quick, small smile and looked down at the knife. Then, he grabbed the smooth black handle and started removing the blade from her leg. The life shot back into her face as the pain surged through her body, lighting up her eyes and shooting trapped breaths forcefully out of her mouth. She screamed again, getting louder as more of the knife came out of her thigh. Jackson wiped each side of the blade on her leg, cleaning it of excess blood, with a worrying sense of calm. His gaze was fixed on the radiant steel the entire time; the sun that was forcing its way through the window was bouncing off it and giving the ceiling a faintly red hue.

Still crouched, he turned his attention to Jordy, who was still trying to stop himself from crying.

'You should be sorry, too,' he muttered, 'because this is all your fault.'

'I—I—I—'

Without letting Jordy reply, Jackson spun the knife around in his hand, making sure he had a tight grip on it. He looked Jordy dead in the eyes and forcefully stood up. Using his momentum, he powerfully thrust his left arm forward, burying the entirety of the blade into the base of Dana's neck. The small dip between her collarbones was ripped apart and blood came squirting out, decorating the centre of the room with luminous red dots and covering Jackson's arm.

The knife vanished, tearing straight through the muscles in her neck and almost coming out the other side. She let out a few involuntary choking sounds and then the life in her eyes disappeared again.

Jackson's hand remained firmly on the knife-handle for a few seconds after Dana died. Jordy stared, distraught and terrified, at his wife's neck. He wished it was all a horrible nightmare, and that he'd wake up soon. He squeezed his eyes shut, hoping it would all be gone when he opened them again.

But when he did, Jackson was still there, staring down at him with eyes the colour of aged blood, and burning with indignation.

And even as he almost ripped Dana's neck in half, he never broke eye contact.

31

Dana's head rolled back to rest on the cushion and the knife stuck out of her neck at a 45-degree angle. Blood was slowly dribbling out of the wound and down onto her chest, soaking into the top of her low-cut t-shirt. She would soon be covered in it, but Jackson had no intention of cleaning it up.

Jordy sat with an open mouth, not knowing what to do or what to say. All he could do was stare at her neck. His wife was dead. She was actually dead.

'Now *you* know how it feels to see your wife—' Jackson ripped the knife out her neck, tearing the skin more and sending another stream of blood gushing onto her trousers and the now-red carpet beneath her '—die in front of your eyes. In your own house, too. It's almost poetic.'

'Why are you doing this?' Jordy cried out, grabbing his wife's hand and squeezing it as hard as he could, 'I made a mistake and she didn't do anything.'

'Well neither did Hannah,' Jackson yelled back, almost slicing Jordy's throat open as he slung his arm around, 'and look what happened!'

'But it's not my fault that those guys got the wrong house. Why are you doing this to me?'

'I don't care! *You* were supposed to die in the first place. *You* attacked a little girl. You traumatised her for the rest of her life – if she can even have one now. You're a sick, *sick,* scum of a man and you deserve everything you're getting.'

'But, that—'

'No, Jordy, no!' Jackson's shouting was getting progressively more aggressive and it was becoming frightening, '*you* were the one that was supposed to die, not *my wife*. She'd done nothing to anyone her entire life. It's *unfair.*'

He pulled his right arm back and swung it round again, connecting with the side of Jordy's head and smashing his jaw into pieces. The crunching underneath his knuckles sent a twinge up his forearm and made his elbow ache. Jordy cried out, still feeling the effects of the first punch.

'She had so much ahead of her!' Jackson shouted again. His fist swung round again, connecting with the side of Jordy's head just below his left eye. It felt like his eye had burst under the pressure, but his cheek had just shattered a little more. The tears had dried up and were replaced with blood, coming from a newly-opened gash just below his eye.

'They raped her! They stabbed her! She died in front of me, because of what *you* did!'

Another blow to Jordy's face came with every sentence. His eye was black and deeply bruised. The gash under his eye was wide and blood was quickly falling out in different streams, going in multiple directions across and down his face. Jordy couldn't speak anymore; his face was battered and he no longer had the strength to cry or plead.

Jackson stood up and stretched – lifting his arms into the air and putting his shoulders back. He rolled his wrists around and cracked his fingers.

'That's much better,' he said to himself with a deep sigh.

Then, without warning, he launched his right arm forward again. The whole of his fist smashed against Jordy's nose, crushing the bones beneath it with relative ease and sending a jolt of pain around his head. A thick stream of blood immediately came out of his nose and he cried out again; he cried like he was begging Jackson to stop but couldn't get the words out. The tears that were painfully rolling down both of his cheeks were seeping into the open wounds, searing through him like an electric shock. He was helpless, and he knew it. But he just wanted it to stop.

One way or the other.

Jackson swapped the knife to his right hand, showing Jordy the blood that was covering nearly every inch of it. The blade-edge was discoloured, not shining as much as it had when he'd first picked it up. Some of the blood had dripped to the handle and created small dry spots that seemed to stick to his palm when he gripped it tightly.

Jackson reached forward with his left arm and wrapped his hand around Jordy's neck, forcing his head back. He dug his thumb just under the jawline, feeling how quick Jordy's pulse was beating. He seemed to sense what was about to happen.

'P-please... don't... do... this...' he pleaded, doing his best to get his words out, fighting relentlessly to catch a breath. Jackson applied more pressure, mesmerised as the blood rushed to Jordy's head and his head turned a light shade of plum.

'I'm... sorry. Please... don't. I'm... sorry... for... what... I... did... but—'

Jackson pressed his hand in harder, stopping Jordy's sentence short and making him almost choke on his own tongue. He felt like he only had a limited number of breaths left, and his worst nightmare was being slowly realised. If he had to be killed, he'd prefer to be quick and relatively painless. Being strangled, and drowning were his worst fears. And it was so much worse than he could have imagined. The entirety of his face was numb and burning, blood was dripping into his eyes from a small cut on his forehead, and into his mouth from the various cuts along his cheek and nose.

'It...... was... a long... time... ago. I'll... give... you... all... the... money that I... have, please... just... let... me live.'

Suddenly, Jackson let go and Jordy inhaled sharply, trying to get as much oxygen to his brain as possible. He held his hands around his neck and took quick breaths.

Jackson looked at him, almost offended, and said, 'Is *that* what you think this is about?'

Jordy looked blankly at him. 'I-I—'

'You think this is about *money*? This is about so much more than that, Jordy, don't you get that?'

Jackson leaned forward again and pressed his palm down on Jordy's sternum, putting all of his weight behind him, standing strong on his feet. Jordy looked down at the hand and then back up into Jackson's face, which was now only a few inches from his own. He could smell the weak stench of his breath – like old toothpaste.

'I've already killed—' Jackson quickly glanced at Dana's corpse before looking back at Jordy '—five people. It was never about money. You can repent and-and regret all you want, but it won't change the fact you raped a little girl.'

Jordy just stared, frozen in place, in a terrified, trance-like state.

'And Hannah was the one who paid the price for it,' when Jackson spoke again, his tone was softer, 'do you see how little *sense* that makes?'

Keeping his hand pressed firmly on Jordy's chest, Jackson quietly inserted the knife into his side and immediately pulled it out – almost like he was a boxer giving his opponent a jab.

And again.

Jordy looked down at the two new open wounds in his side and stomach tense up. The burning sensation was like nothing he'd ever felt – and the weird thing was, he could barely feel it. If he hadn't looked down, he could have assumed he'd been bitten by a bug.

Jackson took his hand off his chest and gave Jordy a few quick slaps to the cheek.

'Nope, Jordy, up this way, come on,' he muttered as Jordy lifted his head back.

He was dazed, staring straight through him. There was colour in his eyes but very little life left.

'You need to see this,' Jackson whispered.

Then, without warning and without moving his head, Jackson's arm came spinning round and the knife slammed into the side of Jordy's neck – some of it went all the way through and out the other side – wholly severing both of his carotid arteries and chipping some of his spine on the way in. At least a litre of blood shot around the room, splattering against the walls and covering Jackson's face, going down his throat as his mouth dropped open in disbelief.

As he ripped the knife out and Jordy's corpse toppled over to the side, all the blood that would have been pumping around Jordy's body began gushing out of his neck and onto the sofa. His skin was completely dyed and Jackson just stood and stared with wide eyes, breathing heavily.

He released his grip on the knife and it tumbled to the floor. He took a few steps back and pulled the armchair up from its rested position on the TV screen, not speaking or reacting in any way. With a disturbing sense of calm, he took a seat and leaned forward, wiping most of the blood off his face with one hand. He spat out the excess from his mouth onto the floor and sighed deeply.

Then he just sat and watched as the minutes ticked slowly by, beginning to wonder if he'd gone too far.

32

Jackson couldn't get the image of Jordy's living room out of his head. All he could see every time he closed his eyes was blood; he felt like when he looked in the mirror, his entire face was covered in it, and when he looked down to his hands, they were soaked and it just wouldn't wash off.

And now Hannah was doing it, too. His nightmare was beginning to change. She still stood at the foot of the bed, watching over him with her cold eyes. She turned her head to look through the window, and the blood started dripping out of her neck. When she turned back to face him, he saw that it was slowly dribbling out of both sides, onto her shoulders and down her arms, soaking into the towel that she was still wearing.

His last words to Jordy would haunt him forever.

'You need to see this, Jay,' Hannah whispered with a casual smile.

She lifted up her arm and she was holding a long kitchen knife, the same size as Jackson's. She was about to stick it into her own neck, but he always woke up right before she did it. Not even his own brain could bear to see that.

He shot up in his bed sweating more than he would with the previous nightmare. He could feel the droplets travelling down his face and dripping off the end of his chin. He didn't wear a t-shirt to go to sleep anymore – he knew that it would be drenched and ruined as soon as he woke up.

He couldn't remember the last time he had a peaceful night's sleep, but now maybe he didn't deserve one. It seemed as though every minute of the day was spent with his mind elsewhere. He couldn't concentrate anymore – on anything. All he could see was Jordy's and Dana's face, staring up at him with disappointed, lifeless eyes.

The life he'd chosen for himself was slowly becoming too much for him to handle.

A few days – and many nightmares – later, Jackson found himself at the gates of a familiar cemetery. Somewhere beyond the towering presence of the arched entrance – old grey concrete decorated with various cracks and holes – was his wife. She was still at peace, lying comfortably in that green dress, not fazed by her wooden bed and the splinters she'd be getting.

Being careful not to step into anyone's personal space, Jackson navigated his way through the oddly inviting confines of the graveyard, walking past gravestones that had been there since the 1700s. It always made him think about what life would have been like back then.

After getting lost a few times trying to remember where he was, he eventually found Hannah's grave. It was still fresh; the marble effect on the stone was still glowing and the gold inscription was still clean and tidy. Her name radiated in the afternoon radiance of the sun.

Jackson lowered his tinted black, circle-rimmed sunglasses and inspected the area, checking for any other activity other than his, then returned his attention to his wife's resting spot.

'I brought a coffee for you,' he said, holding out the plastic cup in his hand, then setting it down on the grass next to the small bouquet of flowers at the base of the headstone, 'exactly one and a half sachets of white sugar – just how you like it.'

He adjusted his trouser legs and then sat down next to her gravestone, making sure not to sit on the patch that the coffin had been lowered into. He didn't mind about the grass stains he'd get; those were the least of his concerns.

'I'm sorry, Hannah,' he muttered softly, looking up into the sun and taking in the clean air, 'I've done some bad things since you left. I don't even feel like me anymore. I don't think you'd recognise me, and that's what really hurts. I've… I've hurt some people – I can't even bring myself to say it properly.'

He turned his head to look at the stone's face, closely inspecting her date of death and sighing.

'It's been nearly five months now, and it doesn't seem to be getting any easier. Every day I see your face – I see it in my nightmares. You're bleeding… you're bleeding all over my mattress, my-my sheets. It's—'

Jackson stopped before he teared up, looking down to the freshly trimmed grass between his legs and sighed – one that was full of loss, disappointment, and shame.

'I need to tell you what I did because it's killing me. I have all these secrets, and I don't know what to do anymore.'

He adjusted his position so he was facing the headstone and looked it up and down. He took a few breaths and began his confession.

'Those three guys that hurt you,' he said, maintaining his slow and composed breathing pattern, 'I killed them. I couldn't bear to see them get away so easily. I didn't mean to kill them, I promise. I kidnapped Arthur – the guy you hit with my bat – and tried to get an apology out of him, and an explanation. But… I don't know, something just kind of… triggered inside of me and I felt so powerful.

'So I killed him. Then, I killed the other two. It was so violent - God, it was so violent. There was blood… everywhere. It didn't seem like me, but I loved how it made me feel. And… I didn't stop there. I kept going. There are so many bad people in the world, Hannah. There are so many bad people that are still succeeding in life when they shouldn't be. Chase, and-and Jordy, and Andre – they were living their lives, and they were happy, while you and Sienna weren't allowed to.'

He could feel a tear forming in the corner of his eye, ready to fall off the edge of his eyelid and roll down his cheek. He blinked to get rid of it and wiped his nose the back of his hand.

'It's unfair, Hannah,' he said quietly, his head hung low.

'I killed the *right* people, didn't I?' he continued, looking back at her name, 'Would you say that I did? I killed the people that *deserved* it. I felt like I wanted – no, I needed – to right some of the wrongs in the world – in *my* world. You were just an accident, weren't you? But you didn't deserve that. Why can't I just get over it?'

He lifted his knees up to his ears and buried his head between them, surrounding himself in darkness as he closed his eyes and sat with his thoughts for a few minutes. He could feel more teardrops creeping their way to the edges of his eyelids, hanging on to his lashes for their lives.

The gentle breeze that floated through the cemetery combed its way through his hair and along the top of his ear. It was a chilly wind, eerily appropriate for where he was, but it didn't affect him. The sun was at its highest point in the sky, sending a thick beam of heat cascading down onto the back of his neck and shoulders, burning through the t-shirt he was wearing.

After taking a deep sigh, he lifted his head back up and lowered his eyes, taking off his sunglasses and setting them on the grass next to him.

'But nothing's changed, has it?' he murmured, dejectedly, 'even after doing all of this, nothing's changed.' He stared at the small bouquet of flowers at the base of the headstone, reading the message that was handwritten on a small card on the packet – his mom's handwriting.

'You're still dead,' he whispered, not being able to stop the small tear droplets from squeezing their way out of his eye, paving the way for more to quickly follow. 'You're always gonna be dead. And it's always gonna hurt. I can't change that, can I? I can't ch—' he lowered to his tone to slightly above a mime, and dropped his head back to the ground '—man, I wish I could change that.'

As a solitary tear followed gravity and dripped from the end of his nose and onto a thin blade of grass below, his emotions got the better of him. His eyes welled up and this time he couldn't prevent the flood from coming.

'I miss you, Hannah. I can't stop myself from missing you, and it hurts to even think about it. I know I should—' he exhaled sharply and wiped his eyes '—I know I should be okay; I have Lily and she's so great, but I just... can't get over the fact that you're really gone.'

He lifted his right knee up rested his elbow on it, tilting his head slightly and placing his hand on the top of it – resisting the severe urge to rip his hair out handful by handful.

With eyes closed tightly to stem the flow of tears – and failing to do so – he rubbed his head softly a few times before speaking, 'I just want you to come home. Why do you have to be gone?'

He slowly moved his hand through his hair and towards the front of his head, going down his forehead and then rubbing his eyes with his thumb and forefinger to dry the tears up. He had always tried to be the strong one. He didn't want to show that he was weak, because then maybe people would look at him differently – he was scared he'd be seen as less of a man if he cried in front of someone, especially his wife.

He sat, for a few long, silent minutes, just staring at the forest beyond the perimeter of the graveyard. The trees were fighting for space along the thick metal fence; the thinner ones seemed to be swaying gently from side to side and the vast collection of leaves and branches were fighting as the breeze swept through them. Jackson could feel his vision blurring as he stared off into space – he was in his own world with only white noise buzzing through his mind. He felt like he was in limbo, and he didn't have the strength to shake himself out of it. He felt his head slightly swaying, and even after he tried to stop himself, the tears continued to creep out of his eyes. The only thing he could feel was his eyes moving – looking left, looking right, looking down, but not *seeing* anything.

He didn't know how many minutes passed while he was in that spot, but the sun was still blaring down on his body when he felt himself move, so it couldn't have been that long. He slowly moved his head down and into the soft, warm embrace of his hands, seeing the faint blue-green shadow of the trees in the backs of his eyelids when he closed his eyes. The only sound he could hear was his own deep breath.

Until he started sobbing.

33

The powerful surges of adrenaline that used to transform Jackson's body had now been replaced with intense vulnerability and weakness. He felt helpless, but for some reason, felt like it wasn't over yet. There was more to do, and he felt compelled to complete the plan that he'd originally set out. But he had to make a few changes. Maybe he'd turn himself in when he was at peace, but he couldn't involve the police yet.

And Lily. She couldn't know it was him.

Wiping the tears that were travelling along the curvature of his nose, like tiny ski jumpers, he eventually sat up straight and took his phone from his pocket. He dialled the only number that came to his head.

'Hello?' a soft, high, and croaky voice came through from the other end of the line.

'Mom?' Jackson replied, rubbing his eyes again.

'Oh, Jackson, what's wrong? You sound upset.'

The more he thought about what he was going to say to her, the more upset he could feel himself becoming. He'd be able to hide his emotions talking to anyone else, but the familiar tones of his mom's voice were too much.

'Mom, I'm… I'm not okay,' he said, bursting out into tears again. He could almost hear her heart break through the phone, 'I'm-I'm a horrible person, and I don't deserve happiness.'

'Come on, Jackson, that's crazy. How are you a horrible person?'

'I'm just—' he sniffled a few times and rubbed the back of his head with his palm '—I'm just a horrible person. I've hurt so many people. I don't even recognise myself anymore.'

'Where is this coming from, honey? You're definitely not a horrible person. I gave birth to you, I raised you; you're a wonderful man, Jackson.' The emotion was beginning to form in her voice, but she knew she had to be strong for him. She cleared her throat to compose herself.

'You're gonna hate me,' Jackson said sadly.

'Jackson,' her voice was soft, but stern, 'you're my son. I could never hate you.'

He took a few breaths and closed his eyes. The soothing tone of her words was comforting, but he couldn't get rid of the thoughts that were harshly swimming around his mind and bouncing off the walls of his skull, giving him a dull headache. The sun didn't help either.

'Do you… do you promise?' he cried.

'What's going on, honey?' she replied.

'I just miss her so much.'

'Oh…' his mom softly sighing through the phone, in a comforting way. 'Jackson, where are you right now?'

'I'm sat in front of her gravestone. I can't stop staring at her name. Why does it hurt so much, mom?'

'I don't know, dear. I guess when you love someone that much, you get the idea in your head that they'll never be taken away from you. You take for granted the time that you spend with them because you're so young, you think you won't have to worry about this type of thing for years. And then—' she sniffled a little bit and took a deep breath '—then when it happens, you feel empty, you feel lost. You spent all your time in love with them – and being with them – that you completely forgot to prepare for what life would be like if they weren't there.

'There's a hole in your chest that you thought you'd never have to fill. And as much as you try, nothing will ever fit.'

Jackson sat still with eyes lightly shut, listening to her voice and trying to relax. His sobbing had stopped, but his eyes were still wet and he couldn't see properly.

'I just…,' he said with a deep, exhausted sigh, 'I just wanna hug her. I wanna ask her about her day. I want to see her laugh again just once. But I can't… and that hurts too much.' He could feel the pain in his voice, and the raw emotion. 'I don't wanna do this anymore, mom. It's too hard.'

'Do what, honey?' she asked.

'*This. Life.* I'm exhausted and… I just don't wanna—'

'Don't finish that sentence, please.'

He sighed again, rubbing the tears – that refused to stop coming – out of his eyes.

'Okay,' he whispered, 'I'm sorry.'

'I don't want to hear my son saying stuff like that,' his mom replied, trying to stop herself from crying.

'Sorry, I'm just—I'm just tired,'

'It's okay for you to be sad, honey, and it's okay for you to cry about it, but you have to be strong for everyone in your life now. Your dad and I... we loved Hannah, and we were devastated when she died, but you can't have that be the only memory you have of her, y'know?'

Jackson sighed, knowing his mom was right. She was always right; he hated that sometimes.

'And I don't wanna—' she tried to continue, but she couldn't seem to say the words. She breathed slowly through her nose and lightly coughed, pushing through the tears that had begun to slowly roll down her cheek. After a few slow seconds, she managed to finish her sentence.

'And I don't want to have to bury my own son.'

As the sound of the words echoed from her mouth – and taking in what she'd actually said – she started softly weeping.

Almost by design, the clouds that were forming in the sky above him eclipsed the light of the sun and turned the world dull. Jackson looked up and watched the clear patches of blue being invaded by a deep grey. He could sense that there was a storm on the horizon – in more ways than just the weather.

After sighing loudly into the air above him – becoming chillier by the minute – he looked back down at the ground and said, 'I'm sorry, mom. Please don't cry. I'll be okay, I promise.'

His mom sniffled and wiped her eyes and made an almost silent humming noise as she forced a smile through her tear-soaked lips.

'Are you sure? I need you to be sure. I know things are hard, Jackson, but please believe me that you'll get through it eventually. It might not be straight away, and it might hurt for a *long* time – I can't tell you that it won't – but you have people in your life that can help you, and support you.'

'I guess…' Jackson replied, losing all emotion and tone in his voice. He stared at Hannah's name until his vision blurred and he couldn't make the letters out anymore. All he could see was a gold and grey concoction of colours.

'I don't want you to always keep it to yourself, either,' his mom continued. 'Will you be okay? For the sake of yourself and everyone who loves you.'

He sighed, mulling over the question and refocusing his eyes. 'I'll be okay,' he said.

But he didn't know for sure. He couldn't be sure of anything anymore, and he couldn't guarantee that he'd be able to keep his promise, either. But he needed his mom to think he'd be okay – if nothing else, to stop her from worrying.

Or maybe he would be okay, after all.

They said their goodbyes, making sure that no more tears were shed, and he put his phone back in his pocket. He stood and wiped the excess grass and small lumps of dirty from the back of his legs.

Looking down at the grave one last time, he allowed himself a smile – more of reminiscence than anything else.

'Enjoy the coffee, Han,' he said, then turned around and left the graveyard, just as the clouds slowly passed over and the sky began to brighten up again.

34

'I think I've found my new apartment, y'know?' Jackson said as he sat on the sofa, mindlessly staring at whatever daytime TV show was playing.

Lily was sat at the dining table she'd been using as a desk, making notes on some of her reports, trying to pay attention to that while also trying not to ignore the presence of her boyfriend. She had wanted to be nice and let him come over, but in reality she was too busy to do anything other than her work. It was nice to have the company sometimes, though.

Jackson knew she felt like that on numerous occasions, but he didn't mention anything to her.

'Oh yeah?' she responded, head still buried in the pages.

'It's a little pricey, but I think I'll just be able to afford it and not worry about my money, I have another viewing in a couple days. Hopefully, I'll be able to get somewhere with it after that. The sooner I can get out of that motel, the better. I'm going crazy in that hole.'

He saw her cheeks tense as she smiled down into the paper, writing what seemed like pages and pages without stopping to rest, or drink the orange juice that was sitting on a small marble coaster next to her elbow.

'Do you think this case needs a name? Y'know, for the media and everything,' she said, finally stopping and looking up at him.

He turned the TV off and adjusted himself on the sofa. He rested his knee sideways on the seat cushion and turned to face her.

'Huh?' he said.

'Well—' she lay her pen down and took a sip of her drink '—do you know how Richard Ramirez was 'The Night Stalker' and Denis Rader was 'The BTK Killer'? Do you think this guy I'm dealing with needs a nickname? Because right now, we're calling him – or her – 'The Irvine Impaler'.'

Jackson stared at her, both confused and mesmerised at the same time.

'Uhm…' he muttered. No other words seemed to come to him.

'I mean, for the sake of alliteration, I'm a fan,' Lily continued, 'but it's not *that* catchy. You know?'

'I'm – uh – I'm not really sure I follow your train of thought,' Jackson said with a grin.

Mid-drink, Lily shook her and then, after wiping her mouth quickly, said, 'Oh, no, I'm not going anywhere with this; it was just a thought I had that I wanted to get out there.'

She laughed to herself and finished her drink, before letting out a satisfied and refreshed *ahhh* noise. Before she could pick up her pen to continue with her notes, her phone began to vibrate and sent a deep buzzing noise through the table. She glanced towards the screen with a raised eyebrow before putting the phone to her ear.

'Yeah, Harrod,' she said, in her deeper, professional tone of voice.

Jackson watched her as she stared aimlessly in front of her, listening to whoever was on the other end of the line. Most of her responses were short, but they gave away what she was actually hearing.

'Oh, hey... Yeah... Really? Another one? We haven't finished with the first two yet, what's this guy even doing?... A *double*? What's that now? Six?... Wow, that much?... That's disgusting, do I really have to come and see it?... Okay, if you say so, what's the address?'

As she stood up to go get her coat, she froze and the expression on her face turned back and lifeless.

'W-what?' she said, walking slowly to the door like she was going along a tightrope.

A deep look of worry plastered itself over her face and her bottom lip began to quiver gently. She repeated the address to whoever was on the other side, making sure she heard it right and hung her head after hearing it get confirmed.

'What are the victims' names?' she asked, tears forming in her eyes.

As she heard the two names, she couldn't stop the tears. She tried to mask the sadness in her voice, but Jackson could see the sparkling droplets falling down her cheeks. Grabbing her coat – but not even bothering to waste time in putting it on – she hung up the phone and slid her shoes onto her feet.

'What's wrong?' Jackson asked, concerned.

Lily didn't look at him. Her face had gone pale and remained blank.

'I gotta go,' she whispered as she opened the door.

'Lily? What's—'

Before he could finish, the door slammed shut and the noise reverberated through the walls of the living room. He stared out of the window and saw her getting into her car, wiping the tears from her eyes. Watching her jet black Lexus slowly reverse out of the drive, he couldn't help but worry. But he was also confused because he knew where she was going.

And now, there were no traces of adrenaline left in his body.

35

Jackson had been staring out of the window for a long ten minutes before eventually prying his tired eyes away. He'd watched cars go by in both directions, passing through his line of sight with a blur. People had walked by, too. Some were softly pulling dogs along behind them, while a few more let their dogs pull them.

Two people walked by having a pleasant-looking conversation, laughing amongst themselves, and he saw them stare back at him through the window. They smiled to each other in awkward recognition and quickened their pace to get themselves out of his view.

In a way, he'd hoped that Lily would have come back, or at least phone him to give him any sort of an update but the house remained silent and he was left listening to his own breaths and the occasional rattling of a fence behind the house. As he looked around the sudden brightness of the living room, every time he blinked he could see the shadowy outline of the houses from across the road – thick, yellow blotches – in the back of his eyelids.

He tried to rack his brain for a reason why Lily would have gotten so upset over knowing who the victims were and where they lived; she had no connection to them. She'd never mentioned any friends – mostly because she hadn't had time to make any since moving from Ohio. Regardless, he began growing increasingly concerned for her, and the two people that he'd murdered.

Stuck for any other ideas, and not wanting to stew in his own thoughts and scenarios until Lily finally returned – whenever that would be – he decided to go to the house. He already knew the address, but he figured he'd tell her that he only knew it because she repeated it over the phone.

Smart.

He got up and adjusted his clothes, straightening them out after they'd gotten creased from his constant turning-in-place on the sofa. He went to the kitchen to get a glass of water and threw it down his throat in two deep gulps. As he glanced out the kitchen window, he noticed that the clouds were hanging intimidatingly low and the sun seemed timid.

It always seems as though the world is trying to tell me something, Jackson thought as he walked back into the living room and picked his keys up from Lily's makeshift desk.

He arrived in Jordy's neighbourhood twenty minutes later, feeling like he hadn't breathed or blinked throughout the entire drive. The dim glow of the sun through the overcast sky was giving him a faint headache, but he didn't have the strength or the wherewithal to pull down the visor. The street that he'd parked on his first time there had been cordoned off with yellow police tape, wrapping around some of the trees of the park. Officers were telling anyone who went through the park or into the assault course in the centre that they had to move from the area.

Jackson parked on the opposite side of the park, able to see the house and the commotion of officers through the thin veil of trees. Five police officers guarded the area at intervals along the edge of the tape, staring outward into their designated section of the neighbourhood. He half expected to see Bell as one of the guards, but he was nowhere to be seen.

Inside the cordon, several plain-clothes detectives were going in and out of the house making notes and taking photos, while CSI's in white coveralls took samples of everything they could find. One of them came out of the doorway and onto the driveway shaking his head, clearly disgusted by whatever he'd just laid eyes on. Just outside the police tape on either side, two empty police cruisers sat dormant with their lights flashing, blinding the neighbours if they dared to look out of their window. The commotion had attracted a crowd on Jackson's side of the street – mostly passers-by that were too nosey to walk full speed, so they paused for a while on their travels.

He quickly scanned the area and eventually locked on to Lily. She was sitting on the curb with her head between her knees. Even without seeing her face, or knowing what was being said around her, Jackson knew that something was terribly wrong.

An elderly gentleman came out of the house, pulling a packet of cigarettes from the inside pocket of his coat and placing one between his wrinkled lips. A detective approached and spoke something into his ear as he lit his cigarette before he nodded and blew a thick line of smoke into the air. The man stopped behind Lily and placed a hand on her shoulder, looking sympathetically down at her. Jackson saw her shake her head, prompting the man to turn around and walk back towards the house.

Turning the car off and rubbing his face with the palm of his hands, Jackson got out and took a slow walk into the park and towards the scene. A couple of the officers spotted him approaching and gathered themselves together.

'Sir… sir, you can't be here. You need to find another way around to go wherever it is that you're going,' one of the officers said sternly.

'I'm – uh – I'm here to see Detective Harrod. She's—' he pointed to the curb where Lily was sat '—right over there. Can you get her for me, please?'

The officer that had come over when Jackson was walking towards them decided that it wasn't worth it and turned back to return to his post. Jackson shot him a quick glance then returned his attention to the officer he'd been talking to – his name badge read HILSON.

'Can you get her? Please?' Jackson asked again.

Hilson moved his eyes around his head, considering the proposition, then nodded slightly before spinning around and shouting Lily's name. Her head moved up lazily and she looked their way with dazed eyes. Upon spotting Jackson, she furrowed her eyebrows and stood up – taking three attempts to do so. She wiped the dirt from her pants and wiped her eyes, hurrying over to the barrier and Officer Hilson, who seemed to wait for an explanation.

'Jackson?' she asked, disorderly.

'Hey, Lily, I had to come down to see if you were okay,' he replied.

She ushered Hilson away, asking him to give them a minute, and kissed Jackson softly as she reached the tape.

'How did you know where I was?' she asked.

'You said the address over the phone, remember?'

Lily tilted her mouth back with her mouth slightly opening – like she was saying *ahhh* – then nodded.

'So, uhm,' Jackson began, looking around the entire area, 'what's happening? Who was that old guy?'

'What old guy?' she replied, giving him a confused frown, before realising, 'Oh, him, that's Benji, my boss.'

'Your boss? This must be serious; there seem to be a lot more people here than usual.'

'Don't even get me started. I've been crying since I got here.'

'Wh-why?' Jackson asked.

Lily sighed, taking a deep breath and looking away to quickly wipe another tear from her eye, before saying, 'This is probably the most disgusting scene I've ever witnessed in my entire life. You wouldn't believe how much—' she squeezed her eyes shut and rattled her head, shaking off the emotion '—how much blood there was in there.'

'Is it really that bad? Is that why you've been crying?'

'Christ, no. The blood is the least of my problems.'

'So what is it?' his tone was low and calming, and he was slowly rubbing his hand up and down her arm, 'I got so worried when you bolted from the house so suddenly; I didn't know why you were so upset and I got really concerned.'

'Do you really want to know?'

Jackson nodded, letting out a slight *mhm* that vibrated his lips.

She sighed deeply, saying, 'okay,' as the breath exited her mouth. She ducked under the tape and directed him to a small swing set on the outskirts of the obstacle course. The frame was copper, with patches of rust dotted around the top and the chain that held was seat looked flimsy. The seat itself was old plastic that didn't look at all comfortable for even a child.

Lily sat on one and shuffled her feet a little, letting the wind take her back and forth a few inches. Jackson chose to stand in front of her with his arms crossed, watching the expression on her face as she spoke.

'Okay, so, we think it's the same guy again. He's getting progressively more violent and we have no idea why. The entire thing is still a mystery to me.'

'Okay,' Jackson replied, putting a long emphasis on the Y to show his confusion at where she was going with her statement.

'There were two victims,' Lily continued, 'their names were… their names were Jordan Renalto – but he went by Jordy – and his wife, Dana. I-I didn't want to believe it, but I got here and there they were,'

Her expression was blank as she stared straight ahead, looking like she was mesmerised by Jackson's stomach.

'Okay, I still don't follow,' he replied.

'That bastard killed—' she tried to say, but couldn't get the words to come out of her mouth.

'That bastard—' she tried again, but with no luck. She took a long breath, and Jackson crouched down to look into her eyes, but she was frozen, and staring straight through.

Her eyes went to the ground, studying the specks of dirt that were kicking themselves onto her shoes as she swayed back and forth on the swing.

'Okay... okay,' she started again after a long silence, 'When I got divorced, I just kept my husband's name because it was on all of my records and it was too much of a hassle to go back.'

'Uh-huh...'

'My maiden name is... is Renalto.'

Jackson's eyebrows shot up. Lily pulled her head back up and looked him in the eyes, with tears slowly rolling down her cheek.

'That bastard killed my brother,' she finally said.

36

Suddenly, Jackson felt like he'd been transported to another world. His expression froze just like Lily's had, and he had no idea how to deal with it.

The noises of the cars in the distance, the detectives talking amongst themselves, and the general commotion of the crime scene had disappeared and the only sound that was left was the gently scratching of Lily's shoe against the dirt beneath her. He could feel his eyeballs moving aimlessly but he couldn't take in anything he was seeing. His mouth was open slightly and his lips were getting drier by the second. He wet his lips with his tongue every so often and tried to swallow the saliva that was bringing itself up, but he couldn't stop the back of his throat from becoming irritated.

He didn't know how to process the information Lily had just given to him. He'd rolled a few scenarios around in his head on the drive, but he never planned for *that*.

He was "that bastard".

A mixture of different emotions was flowing through him and he didn't know which one to focus his attention on – or which was the one that he was *actually* feeling. Everything felt off, and he hated it. Then, he felt guilt slowly begin to creep its way into his system, It felt awkward. He just wanted to blurt out the truth to Lily right there, but something stopped him.

Common sense, probably.

Everything he'd done since kidnapping Arthur outside his own house began to replay in his head; his life – the *new* life – was flashing before his eyes and it was horrifying to watch. He began to realise what it was he was actually doing. Lily's confession of Jordy being her brother had almost snapped him out of the new personality and he'd begun to understand the consequences of his actions. She was distraught over Jordy's death, and Jackson started to wonder how the relatives of the other victims had reacted.

His thoughts immediately shifted to his neighbour, Ms. Renshaw. Arthur was the only thing that she had left and he'd taken it away from her so cruelly. She opened up to him about her husband's death and her close relationship with her son, and he'd snatched that from right underneath her – and destroyed the last bit of happiness she felt with her life – solely based on revenge. It was justified when he started, but maybe now it was just wrong.

'Jeez, Lily, I, uh...' Jackson said, still not knowing how to process the information.

She looked at him with a smile – fake, but still a smile – that she hoped would reassure him that she'd come to terms with it.

'I'm so sorry,' Jackson said again, moving a bit closer and placing his chin on the top of her head. Her hair was soft and rich, and the aroma of her mango shampoo floated into his nostrils.

Lily pulled her head from under his and glanced up at him – her eyes full of compassion – and smiled.

'Thank you,' she whispered, 'but it's not your fault. It wasn't you who killed them.'

A nervous tension rushed through Jackson's stomach and he could feel burning at the bottom of his throat.

'I know,' he replied, 'but I promise we're gonna find out who it was. I know I've said that before, and it seems a little cliché, but I'm *really* gonna help you this time.'

'Thanks,' she whispered again, almost as if it were a reflex.

'It's gonna be okay, and I mean that. Do you believe me?'

'Yeah, yeah... I think. I'm really sure what to think right now if I'm honest.'

He placed his hand on hers and patted it lightly. 'I swear we'll find him, and put him away. It's gonna be okay.'

Jackson spoke his assurances with a calm tone but there was emphasis behind the words. He knew it might have been an empty consolation based on the situation, but it was a consolation nonetheless.

But he didn't know if it *would* be okay. He wanted to convince himself more than he did her.

Across the park and up the driveway, an exhausted-looking Benji left Jordy's house once again and immediately lit up another cigarette. His eyes closed as he inhaled and exhaled the sweet taste of smoke –

really try to appreciate the nicotine filtering into his lungs.

'Those things will kill you, you know?' one of the uniformed police officers said from the bottom of the driveway – Hamasaki, according to his badge.

'I'm old, Hama,' Benji replied, taking another deep puff of the cigarette and decorating the warm air with another cloud of smoke. 'I'm probably gonna die soon, anyway, so I might as well enjoy myself.'

As Hamasaki began to walk back up the driveway towards the house's entrance, Benji lightly grabbed his arm and stopped him, letting the cigarette dangle out of the corner of his mouth.

'Have you seen Lily?' he asked, taking a drag of the cigarette with his free hand.

'She's over there—' he pointed towards the swing set '—with that man.'

Benji nodded and turned around, seeing Lily with her head down and Jackson sitting on the swing next to her. He was looking at her and was softly stroking her hair, tucking strands behind her ear when they fell. Benji walked in their direction, holding his cigarette loosely between his lips as he lifted the yellow tape above his head and ducked underneath it.

'Lily,' he mumbled. She and Jackson both turned around, slightly startled.

'Uh-huh?' she replied quietly.

'Can I ask you a question?'

'Sure, what?'

'Why did you move out here?'

'What d'you mean?'

'Well, I know you moved from Ohio to come out here, and Irvine is a really specific place to move to, especially since it's in California.'

'What's your point here, sir?'

'Did you know your brother lived here? Is that why you moved?'

Lily considered the question for a little bit, then looked at Jackson and nodded.

'I guess so,' she said, looking back to Benji. 'I was always planning on moving out west, but when I spoke to Jordy he said Irvine was an amazing place to live so I decided to come here. Why?'

'Well, I was just wondering because—' he took a last, long smoke of his cigarette and threw the stub to the grass behind him, exhaling as he did so '—we found these in Jordy's bedroom.'

Jackson looked at Lily with an intrigued look on his face; his eyes moving between the two of them as they had their conversation. He felt like an intruder but it would have been too awkward to just stand up and leave, so he just stayed quiet.

Benji reached into the back pocket of his jeans and pulled out two small items. One looked like a photo of some kind and the other was a small, yellow piece of lined paper with scribbling on it. He handed the paper to Lily and she studied it.

'That's your address, isn't it?' he asked.

Her eyes scanned over the lines and she nodded after reaching the bottom.

'Yeah, it is,' she replied, handing the note back to him. 'I called him not long after I settled into my new house and gave him it just in case he wanted to visit.'

'How long ago was that?'

'God, I don' t know, probably…'

'Okay, not important, anyway. That then brings me to this,' he handed her the photo and took a small step forward and looked over her shoulder as she took a look at it.

Lily looked it over for a few seconds and then turned to look up at him, asking, 'Is this supposed to some kind of sick joke?'

'Afraid not.'

Jackson glanced over at what it was and his eyebrows shot up in an instant. Straight away, he could feel the sweat beads forming in the cracks in his forehead and dripping through the hairs in his brow. He looked at her, and her reaction then mimed 'fuck' to himself.

'Turn it over,' Benji told Lily.

She did as she was told and twirled the photo in her fingers. There were a few words on the back written wildly in a blue ballpoint pen.

'Is that Jordy's handwriting?' Benji asked.

A tear formed in the corner of her eye as she read it, before nodding with a slight smile on her face as she reminisced.

'I used to be the only person who could read his writing. Not even our parents understood it. I had to read stuff *to* them,' she replied.

'You know what it says?'

She let out a deep, exhausted sigh. 'Yeah, I do.'

'Well?'

Fighting back the tears, Lily squeezed her eyes shut for a few seconds, then handed the photo back to Benji without looking at him.

'It says "Dana's first scan"', she said, slowly and sadly.

Jackson turned away briefly, fighting back his own tears – and the guilt that kept piling itself onto his conscience.

'Jesus,' Benji said, looking over the photo again. 'Well, from the date stamp in the corner, it looks as though she was—' he bobbed his head from side to side lightly, doing the math '—about 14 or 15 weeks along when she died.'

He returned the items back to his pocket and turned around to walk away. He retrieved another cigarette from his pocket and stuck it between his dry lips. Pulling a lighter from his jeans pockets, he held it up to his face but stopped before sparking it up. He turned back around and looked at Lily with the deepest sympathies.

'I'm sorry, Lily.'

Spinning back around, he lit up the cigarette and blew the initial puff of smoke into the air.

'We all are,' he said, as he slowly walked back towards the crime scene.

37

Some time to think was what Lily really needed. And, to be alone.

A few days later, she found herself standing in a tranquil park with the sun beating down on her back. She was stood on a wooden pier that overlooked a small body of water that was populated by a few ducks. A few swam slowly around the water, while another one stood atop a huge rock like it was the supervisor. The pier she was standing on was made of basic, dark brown lengths of wood that had been dirtied by age and grass stains. Above her was a structure that resembled the entrance of an old Japanese temple, and it cast a long shadow across the water, creating a hiding spot for the ducks that didn't want to be in the sun.

A vast circular field opened out in front of her, on the other side of the water. Around the perimeter at specific intervals were small wooden benches that had been worn away by rain over the years. A few trees gave sun protection to the benches on the far half of the field, but they were small enough to still see through to the horizon.

Lily was leaning on the wooden barrier of the pier, taking in the open view with a content smile – as she did every time she visited – and watched the ducks go about their day. The duck that had been standing on the rock decided to fly across the field and over the trees in the distance.

Suddenly, her peaceful silence was disturbed with the sound of planks creaking loudly behind her, getting louder as they approached. Then, she heard a deep, croaky cough that could only belong to one man; the only man she knew that couldn't go ten minutes without lighting a cigarette.

'Hey, Benji,' she said, still studying the water.

Benji appeared beside her and looked out onto the field, a proud smile forming on his face.

'Lily,' he replied, turning his head to look at her.

Her eyes were slightly less red than when he'd last seen her, but she was still showing signs that she'd been crying earlier that day. The skin on her lips was cracked and there were small bags underneath her eyes.

'You always seem to know when it's me,' he said.

She nodded and turned her head to look back to him. 'That's because you can smell the smoke from the other side of the field.'

Benji laughed and leaned on the wood railings.

'And you should go see someone about that cough,' she said softly, 'it's bad.'

'How are you?' Benji asked.

Looking back at him and tenderly shaking her head, she said, 'I've been better if I'm honest,' as if it were obvious.

She returned her attention to the ducks and squinted, blocking out the sun that was being reflected into her eyes.

'I've got some news,' Benji said, also looking towards the ducks.

'He hasn't killed again, has he?'

'No, no, he hasn't. For once, it's good news.'

'Oh, yeah?' she turned to face him. 'What is it?'

Benji cleared his throat, then scratched his bottom lip with this thumbnail, before saying, 'I think we found our guy.'

Lily's expression turned to happy shock. 'You're *shitting* me,' she said as she looked out onto the field with a smile.

'Nope, we actually have a suspect,' Benji replied, scratching his lip again.

'How the hell did that happen? We didn't have any good leads, did we?'

'We didn't, but I dug deeper into the older ones.'

Lily turned back to him and said, 'What do you mean?'

Benji stood up straight and turned, leaning sideways on the top of the barrier and crossing his leg so his right foot was stood up on his toes.

'You know how the guy called Chase?' he asked.

'Yeah? I tried to trace the call but the number had been blocked.'

'Maybe not. I went further than just trying to trace the number, and checking Chase's phone records. I pinged the cell towers. The length of the call was just long enough to narrow it down to a very small location. There were a few places inside that radius that jumped out to me as possible locations that the guy could be hiding. Following me so far?'

She nodded.

'God, I need a smoke,' Benji said, out of the blue, 'my lip always gets so itchy when I haven't had one in a while.'

Lily's brows snapped together and she shot him a disapproving look.

'Yeah, whatever, unimportant,' he said, waving his hand in front of his face. 'Anyway, there was a couple of motels, an internet café – I think – and a small office block in the area. So, I had a look into all of them for any suspicious activity, or anything that jumped out to me – which, believe me, took *too* long,'

'And did anything jump out?'

'Well, I wouldn't be here if it didn't. I noticed something in one of the security tapes that I recognised. I didn't really know where from, but it triggered something in the back of my mind. Don't worry, I'm nearly at the main point.'

Lily smiled and looked out onto the field again, scanning for any human activity.

'Remember that witness that said they always saw the same car parked in the same spot down the road from Chase's house?'

'I do. But that was nothing. She was an old woman, and I'm pretty sure the car was just owned by someone down the street.'

'Wrong,' he said with a smile, 'That same car is also on CCTV multiple days pulling into the parking lot of the motel. I tried to run him through facial recognition but, just like with the fingerprint on the note, nothing came up because he's not on our system.'

'But...?'

Benji smiled and held up an index finger. 'Of course, you knew there was a 'but'', he smiled happily.

'And what is the "but"?' Lily asked.

'I got a clear view of the license plate of the car and managed to trace it back to the owner. Now, said owner is our prime suspect and we can go bring him in for questioning. It might not lead to much, but at least it's a start.'

Lily turned her body to face him, making sure she was at an angle where the sun wasn't blinding her. 'Who is he?' she asked.

'Well, the car was a white Jaguar XE, and it's registered to a Mr. Jackson Arron Yardley. He's actually the husband of the—'

'Yeah, I know,' Lily whispered, her face losing all of its colour. She felt her knees lose all solidity, trembling beneath her. She grabbed onto the wooden barrier for support, using the entirety of her upper body strength to stop from tumbling to the ground – or falling between the planks that made up the barrier and descending into the water.

Benji reacted quickly, holding out his arms to keep her up, helping her back to a standing position again.

'Lily, what's wrong? Are you okay?' he asked.

She regained most of her stability and stood up straight, still holding onto Benji's outstretched arm. Taking a few slow breaths, she hung her head again and looked to the floor.

'Are you okay?' Benji asked again.

Lily closed her eyes and exhaled sharply, trying her hardest not the throw up all over his shoes. 'I guess, other than the fact that I don't think my life can get *any* worse.'

38

It was all getting to be too much for Jackson, so he didn't dare to think what it was doing to Lily. She said she needed time to think and to be alone, and he had respected that.

Over the few days that it'd been since they last saw each other – or even spoken – he'd managed to set up different appointments for apartment viewings and meetings with landlords. He'd settled on one, near the heart of downtown, and he had a move-in date. He couldn't wait to sleep in a bed that was *his* and one that Hannah didn't stand over every night bleeding on to.

Throughout the days, the guilt began to pile up on his conscience. Every time he thought of Lily, and her reactions to the news she was getting, he felt a little bit worse. He had constant pain in his stomach and a constant headache, that he couldn't seem to get rid of no matter what he did. And he couldn't stop thinking about Ms. Renshaw, and the pain that he'd put her through. She didn't deserve that. She was also so nice to him and, although her son was a horrible monster and deserved to die, the pain of knowing how badly he was murdered must have crushed her.

After sorting out some of the paperwork for his new apartment, and mulling over the life he was living – and its tragedies – he decided that he had to apologise. His conscience was weighing too heavily on him and he couldn't take it anymore. He hadn't felt a pinch of adrenaline in over a week, and he didn't even miss it. He didn't have the strength to miss it.

Taking his car keys from their home on a table in his motel room, he left the room in a hurry, leaving all of his notes – and the list of names – in his desk drawer. He used to like to keep it on him at all times, but he didn't want to keep thinking about it. He had a new path and he needed to focus on that.

He arrived at his old neighbourhood a short while later. He parked on the pavement just in front of his old house. It had been restored to its previous look; there was no police tape covering the door and it looked fresh, ready for someone new to move in and begin their life.

As Jackson exited his car, he looked up at the window that Hannah had been staring out of. It was still slightly open and the curtains were blowing delicately as the wind snuck in through the gaps. He looked over the house, and he didn't feel like he was going to throw up anymore. He didn't have his 'x-ray vision', and he couldn't see her through the walls anymore. Now, it was just a house. Nothing more, nothing less.

He turned around, locking his car behind him, and walked towards his neighbour's house. He didn't even know if she was going to be home, but he figured she might have taken Arthur's death really hard and would have become home-bound for the time being. Maybe that's what he should have done.

He rapped lightly on the door and took a step back. When the door opened half a minute later, he found that his thoughts had been confirmed. She'd really let herself go since her son's death.

Julia Renshaw stood in front of him, looking like she hadn't showered in days. Her hair was tied back in a loose ponytail, with strands coming off every which way like she'd just rubbed a helium balloon all over her head. A pair of thick-rimmed reading glasses rested on her nose in an attempt to hide the bags under her eyes that looked like she'd been punched repeatedly in the face. Her lips were dry and cracking, and her cheeks were red and worn out.

When she saw Jackson's face, her eyes brightened and she cracked a smile – probably the first time she'd done that in months.

'Oh, Jackson,' she beamed, pushing her glasses back up her nose so she could see probably.

He smiled back, sympathetically. 'Hey, Ms. Renshaw. Are you okay?'

She grabbed him and pulled him into a deep embrace, feeling her raw emotion in the pressure she was applying to the hug.

'Please, just call me Julia. Formalities are so tiring. But, I'm so happy to see a friendly, familiar face,' she said, genuine happiness in her voice. 'Come in for a drink?'

Jackson nodded in agreement and stepped over the threshold into her house. From the first impression he got, he wouldn't have been able to tell that her son had just died. The house smelled of a fresh, lavender fragrance that tickled his nose as it swam around the air. Every surface looked sparkling and there didn't seem to be any dust on any pieces of furniture. In the living room, two turquoise armchairs sat at a diagonal on either side of a long glass coffee table. Everything on the table was at a proper right angle, and nothing looked out of place.

Laid out on the glass were different photos of Arthur, from when he was a young kid to his most current photos. It seemed to Jackson as if she spent some of her day staring at the photos, and the rest she spent giving the house a deep clean. It looked like a brand new showroom.

'I've been keeping myself busy,' she said, following his eyes as they scanned the room.

'Uh, yeah, I can—I can see that,' he sounded almost impressed.

'So what brings you by?' she asked as she took a seat in one of the armchairs.

'Um, I just came to have a quick chat with you, but I can't stay long.'

She tilted her head with a slightly confused look on her face.

'Hold on, let me get those drinks. Please—' she gestured at the empty armchair with an extended arm, palm up '—have a seat, make yourself comfortable.'

Jackson nodded and she stood up and went into the kitchen. He took a seat, sinking down into the soft cushion of the chair. It was low to the ground, and he doubted that he'd have the strength to stand back up.

A few minutes later, Julia returned to the living room with two medium-sized glasses filled almost to the brim with what looked like orange soda. The bubbles fizzled gently to the surface, getting aggressive when she wiggled the glasses trying to set them down on two coasters that were on either side of the table.

'Thanks,' Jackson said, taking a long gulp, downing half of the glass before his host could sit back down on her seat.

'So what did you want to talk about?' she asked, taking a small sip of her own drink, feeling the cracks of her lips with her index finger after setting the glass back down.

'Well, uh…,' Jackson shuffled in his seat, trying to summon the courage.

'I guess I should start with an apology,' he continued, 'I'm really sorry for your loss. I know you and Arthur were really close, and when I found out, I thought about how you would take it and it really pained me.'

'Well thank you, I appreciate that,' she replied with a smile.

'It seems like you're taking it a lot easier than I imagined.'

'How so?'

'Well, when Hannah died, I was an absolute wreck and I didn't know what to do with myself. It's been months and I still can't come to terms with it.'

Julia took another sip of her drink, while Jackson took another small gulp of his.

She chuckled quietly, saying, 'That's because you didn't see me during the days straight after.'

He smiled back and shuffled in his seat again. 'Okay, if I don't get this out now, I won't be able to get it out at all.'

'Alright,' she replied, almost like a question.

'Okay, promise me you won't say *anything* until I'm finished.'

'Sure, I promise. What is it?'

Jackson shuffled in his seat once more, then exhaled quickly and sharply.

'Okay. Here goes…'

39

'When Hannah was killed,' Jackson began, talking slow and calculated breaths to make sure he didn't stutter or miss anything, 'I took it harder than anyone thinks. I wasn't just sad – devastated, rather – it completely ripped me apart. When her funeral came around, and I saw her getting lowered into the ground, it set something off inside me that I can't really describe. I guess it was anger – a deep, deep rage – and I just wanted to get revenge; I wanted to hurt whoever did that to her.'

His nervousness was making his mouth dry, and it was getting drier every time he spoke another sentence. He took a small sip of his soda and swallowed hard, settling his nerves, before continuing.

'Three months or so after she died, I found someone else. I felt ashamed about it when it happened, because it had been so soon, but it just kinda… happened. I really like her, I really do. I don't really show it off very often so it might not seem like I even like her, but I do. I'm just still hung up on Hannah.'

Julia opened her mouth as if she were about to ask him a question but he stuck his hand out, palm out, to stop her.

'I went to her grave not long ago,' he continued, 'and I completely broke down on the ground in front of it. I called my mom as I sat on the grass and I broke down more to her. Even after this long, it still gets to me. It *really* gets to me. So, what I came to tell you, is that—'

He formed his lips into a circle and then exhaled sharply, quickly composing himself.

'—*I* killed Arthur. He'd been hired by someone – who was gonna pay $25,000 – to kill a guy called Jordy. But he went to the wrong house, and I knew from the second I saw him that he was the one who killed Hannah, because of the bruise on the side of his head. I kidnapped him, interrogated him, then killed him in that garage up in Little Joaquin.'

Another sharp exhalation.

'I also killed his two friends – Jacob and Grey – because they were in on it. They all raped her, Julia,' he said, with a few tears forming in his eyes.

He could see the shock on Julia's face, and her eyes welling up, but she was keeping her promise of not talking until he was finished – which seemed incredibly difficult.

'After that happened, I couldn't stop myself. I was on this—this strange high that I couldn't come down from – that I didn't *want* to come down from – and so I kept going. I stalked, tortured and killed the guy who drove my little sister to suicide when I was 16. I killed

Jordy, and his wife because she walked in at the wrong time.

'But... I went too far. After that was said and done, I looked around the room and all I could see was—was blood. It was covered, and I sort of... snapped out of it – whatever 'it' was. And then I—' He wiped the corner of his right eye with the back of his index finger '—I found out that Jordy's wife was pregnant when I killed her and I... couldn't deal with it anymore. Now, I feel guilty *all* the time. It feels like I'm carrying an atlas stone on my shoulders every minute of the day. I have a *constant* headache, and I don't know how to get rid of it.'

He rubbed his eyes with the index and middle finger of each hand to get rid of the tears that were coming, and because he was tired. His body was tired.

He looked at Julia when he opened his eyes again, and whispered, 'I'm sorry.'

Her face looked blank and emotionless. She was staring at the fireplace on the other side of the coffee table, with tears crawling down her cheek and leaving a trail behind them. She didn't react, didn't wipe them; she just let them fall.

Calmly, but still staring at the fireplace, she reached forward and grabbed her glass, taking another small sip. She looked at Jackson with a blank, almost angry stare and, after bringing the glass down from her lips, launched it towards him. Without time to react, he couldn't move out of the way. The glass shattered into large pieces against the side of his face, with some of the smaller bits of debris lodging themselves in his head. The soda that had remained in the glass spilled over his shoulders and into his t-shirt, making it smell strongly of oranges.

He groaned as blood began pouring from the gash on his temple and he had to close his right eye to stop it from seeping in. His face felt numb and a dull, burning sensation was going through his head. He was too dazed to move, and blood had begun working its way through the cracks in the side of his mouth.

'I don't accept your apology,' Julia whispered as she calmly stood up and went into the kitchen, wiping her tears as she did so.

Jackson watched her with intrigue, dabbing at his wound and wincing. He wiped some of the blood up with his hand and studied it, rubbing between his thumb and forefingers. His headache intensified and he almost forgot where he was. The blood was thick to touch, like a smooth red paste, and it was trickling along the creases in his fingers and down into the webs.

A few moments later, he heard close footsteps and he looked up to find that Julia had returned from the kitchen. Her face was both angry and grief-stricken, and her skin was an unflattering crimson. And, she was brandishing a knife. Her frail fingers were wrapped tightly around the handle and her hands were trembling. She was holding it like she was ready to jab at him at a moment's notice.

Jackson got quickly up out of the chair and retreated a little towards the living room window, holding his hands up as a plea – realising the irony of the situation.

'Uh, Ms—Ms. Renshaw, w-what are you doing?' he asked, eyes slightly closed.

'Get out,' she whispered as she took a slow step towards him.

'What?'

'Get out!' she yelled, jabbing the knife through the air in his direction.

'No, c-come on, now. I want to talk about this. Can you just talk to—'

'You've said what you needed to say, Jackson! Now get the *hell* out of my house!'

'Please, Julia. Are you gonna go to the police? Are you gonna hand me in?'

As she took slow steps towards him, he started dizzily backing up towards the door, unable to see out of his right eye because of the blood and struggling to comprehend the world from the pounding headache the glass had given him. His clothes were soaked in blood and orange soda, and it was all over his hand and dripping down his shoulder.

She lunged forward with surprising grace and quickness for a woman her age, startling Jackson and forcing him to stumble back. His head jolted and knocked off the wall and deepening the pain in his head. He thought he could feel some of the glass that was lodged in his head loosen and tumble to the floor.

'You're a monster, you know that?' Julia said, gripping the knife so hard that it nearly turned her hand purple from suffocation.

'I-I know I am, and I'm sorry. I don't know what else to do,' Jackson pleaded, painfully holding his hands up again.

'Do you think you're the only one that hurts? *Do you?*' she yelled in anguish.

'I... I—'

'No, no, come on. *Do you?* Do you think that you're the only one that's *allowed* to feel pain; to feel loss? Do you think that because you feel grief over your wife, that it's okay to take that pain out on other people and there won't be any consequences – because they deserve it? Because the world doesn't work like that, Jackson! The world doesn't *owe* you anything!'

Her voice was getting louder and more intense with every sentence that she spoke, and the knife was waving wildly in her hand. Jackson's gaze was shooting between the blade and her lips, not knowing what to focus on and being just as nervous about both.

'You can be angry at the world all you like,' Julia continued, wiping the saliva that had formed at the corner of her lips, 'but that doesn't give you the *right* to take your pain out on it. Yes, you might be devastated over the loss of your wife and I have – well, I *had* – sympathy for you because you're a good boy, but what you did has snowballed into something so much worse. And now, me and many others feel just the same as you did.'

She took a step forward and Jackson tensed backward, almost becoming part of the wall.

'Do you think that's fair, Jackson? Do you think that is *just?*' she asked.

'Julia, I—'

'No! I want an answer. You're going to answer for what you've done. I don't want a half-assed apology from you that I know you don't mean. I want you to tell me if you think that this is fair?'

'Of course it's not fair!' Jackson shouted, with a crack in his voice as if he were about to burst into a flood of tears. He couldn't tear his eyes away from the knife. 'It's cruel, and I regret every moment of it now that I've seen what it does to people. I'm sorry, Julia, I really am. I just—I don't know what to do anymore.'

She lowered the knife and glared at him with a deep and burning judgment, and said, 'Let me make this a bit easier for you, then.'

Jackson untensed and lowered himself from the wall, relaxing his shoulders and suddenly realising that his teeth had been clenched whenever he wasn't speaking.

'I don't under-understand,' he muttered slowly.

'You're a killer – you're heartless, and you don't care about anyone other than yourself and the petty problems that you have. I'm going to give you a choice.'

'A choice?'

'Correct,' her stare was intense, but her face looked relaxed and her arms hung by her side, and the grip she had on the knife seemed to be loosening.

'What kind of choice?'

'Option A – you can get the hell out of my house like I originally wanted you to. Now, with this option, you have to bear in mind that I fully intend on calling the police as soon as you shut the door. You deserve to rot in jail for the rest of your life and I will make damn sure that happens.'

'Or...?' Jackson said with a gulp. He didn't want to move but he could feel his legs becoming achy and numb the longer he stood in the same spot.

'Or... you can take this knife, and kill me right here. You can add another victim to your ever-growing list and you can leave here absolutely no different than when you came in. But, maybe you'd have a cleaner conscience after confessing everything.'

Jackson looked at her without blinking for at least a minute before calmly shaking his head and sighing sharply. Julia raised her eyebrows trying to hurry him for an answer but he just stood in place, trying to make as little noise as possible. Finally, he spoke, in a hoarse and tired voice.

'I can't make that decision, Julia,' he said, speaking to her with his eyes closed.

'Well, you're going to. That's the only way out of this situation.'

'I-I can't, Julia. That's way too hard.'

'It's not hard at all. You can't just suddenly be a coward now after the damage that you've done. You're *not* a victim!' She jabbed the knife at him as she shouted, narrowly avoiding his hip.

'Don't make me!' he shouted back.

'Get out, or kill me. It's simple. It's *really* simple.'

'No!'

'You want to kill me, don't you?' she whispered, with a wry smile forming on her wrinkling face, 'You want to put this knife straight into my stomach because you need to feel that adrenaline rush. I bet you do.'

'Stop it,' he said, almost under his breath. His forehead was beginning to give off a light glow as the sweat appeared.

'You want to kill me, but you also want to get more sympathy, don't you? Is it because you've adopted this—this persona of a 'victim' and you don't want to break character? I bet you're just itching to grab this knife—' she held it up in the air with the end of the handle between her thumb and forefinger '—and just *jam* it into me.'

Julia jabbed a finger from her other hand into her stomach a few times, where her liver would be.

'Right here,' she said threateningly, 'Do it right in there.'

'Julia, stop it,' Jackson said, louder that time but still without force, and still under his breath.

'I bet you're looking at this knife and it's turning you on, you sick freak,' she yelled, 'I know you want to kill me because that's all you're good at. It's getting you horny just looked at the shiny blade. Isn't it?!'

'I can't do this!'

'But you can! You've killed all those people – you killed *my son* – and you did it so viciously when they didn't even deserve it. Why can't you kill someone who wants to die?!'

'Julia, stop this!' he screamed, as a tear began to roll down his blood-stained cheek.

'I want to die!' she shouted again, feeling her own eyes well up.

She tightened her grip on the knife, squeezing as hard as she could, and grabbed Jackson's arm with her free hand. It felt warm and slimy from the sweat, and she could smell the sweetened stench of blood emanating from his face as she leaned in closer. She moved her hand down his arm, feeling the hairs tickle against her palm, gripping it hard enough to leave a light, red bruise. She placed her hand on his and guided it towards the handle of the knife, spinning it so it pointed at her.

'Do it,' she whispered. Her stomach was tense and saliva had begun to build up her mouth.

'I can't!' he shouted again, not able to stop her advances. The adrenaline was now surging through *her* body. He didn't have much energy; he felt weak and unable to summon the strength or the courage to push her away.

'We both want this, Jackson!' she screamed.

Still guiding Jackson's hand, Julia wrapped his fingers around the handle and slowly moved it towards her. After a few struggled seconds, the tip of the blade pierced her skin and he felt a soft pop. Her eyes were fixated on his and could feel her burning gaze – and he could see it in the corner of his eye – but all he could look at was the blood that was slowly dripping out of her stomach.

She didn't loosen her grasp on his hand.

As the knife effortlessly slid into her body like it was a stick of butter, the blood began to slowly come out of her mouth. It dripped from her lip and landed on Jackson's arm, wrapping itself around his thin hairs and sending a warm sensation through his body.

He didn't know where to look. He didn't know what to say. He didn't even know what the hell was going on. He just wished it was another terrible nightmare.

But it wasn't.

Julia began to cry as more blood came out of her mouth and stained her clothes.

'This is what I want,' she managed to whisper through the tears and the blood.

Jackson could only stare, not able to pull his hand away from the knife and not being able to pull his gaze away from the knife that was now fully inserted into Julia's stomach.

With her last remaining ounces of energy, she jiggled the knife slightly. A small stream of blood shot out of her mouth along with her final, sharp breaths. She stumbled and let go of his hand, which caused him to let go of the knife. The momentum sent her tumbling backward and crashing into the glass coffee table. The impact of her body shattered the glass and sent the contents of the table flying in different directions across the room. Beneath her body, hundreds of small shards of glass at implanted themselves in her back.

Jackson looked down at her, wide-eyed and trembling. Her eyes flickered for a few seconds and then went out; he could only watch her die, still not being able to comprehend what had just happened.

And then he began to wonder how he'd managed to do that six other times.

40

Air. He needed a lot of it.

He wanted to feel the wind blowing through his blood-soaked arm hairs and into the creases and crevices of his clothes. He wanted to feel it splash against his face and softly propel his hair into a tidy quiff. He wanted to soothe the wound on the side of his head, even though it stung intensely, and wouldn't stop.

Julia Renshaw's living room was suddenly way too hot and he felt like he was about to pass out. It was stuffy and his clothes were sticking to him. His nose was blocked and he felt like there was a lump in the back of his throat that was preventing him from swallowing.

It was all beginning to get too difficult.

He left Julia's house, still in a deep state of shock, and walked slowly to his car. His vision seemed blurred the whole, and he felt like a robot being told to go to a specific location. His head didn't move; his arms didn't swing; he just walked blindly until the gleaming white of the Jaguar filled his eyes and his attention returned to the world. He stood by the driver-side door for a few minutes – taking in the cool air and reliving what had just happened repeatedly in his head. All he could hear was Julia screaming; her grief-stricken, blood-curdling screams. They got louder every time, and he had to close his eyes and cover his ears just to make it go away.

After finally returning to the real world, he got into his car and drove back to the motel. The journey was just as blank as his walk from Julia's house to the car. He had too many thoughts racing around in his head to be able to properly concentrate on the road in front of him – both literally and metaphorically.

He couldn't remember what adrenaline felt like – he couldn't even remember what smiling felt like. All of the surging emotions that he'd felt before had quickly vanished and had been replaced by guilt and frustration. He wished he could scream everything but he couldn't.

And it was killing him.

He thought about Lily and what she was going through. He remembered the colour in her face draining with every minute as she tried to wrap her head around her brother's death. He remembered the majestic stream of tears that fell down her face when she found out she could've been an aunt.

Then, he remembered the last name on the list.

41

Jackson got back to his motel room and threw his belongings onto the bed as he passed. His car keys caromed off the pillow and tumbled to the wooden floor with a loud clatter.
He went into the kitchen and splashed his face with water a few times, wincing through the pain. The wound on his head was still open, but all he could do was clean it. He took a small cloth from one of the dining chairs and wiped around the opening, tidying it as best he could, making sure there weren't any small shards of glass still lodged in his head.

After cleaning it, he went over to his desk and sat down, placing his phone in front of him and went through every drawer that was there, taking out every piece of paper that he'd written on, and sprawling them out across the length of the surface.

As he looked over every note he'd made since beginning his quest for revenge on Arthur, he noticed how deep he'd gotten into that life and how intensely he was overcome by it – that, and how he couldn't seem to stick to just one style of handwriting.

He had to finish his plan – one way or the other – but there had to be a change.

After giving all of his notes a quick scan, and being satisfied with what he knew – as satisfied as he could be in that situation – he moved all of the pages to one side and placed a fresh piece of paper in front of him. Just as he'd picked up a pen ready to put ink to page, his phone starting buzzing in front of his face. The screen lit up and his stomach let out a nerved rumble.

It was Lily.

A selfie of her holding a hot-dog bigger than her head popped up and illuminated the room. He just stared at his phone, too nervous to answer. A million questions and thoughts began floating through his head and a sharp sense of paranoia was beginning to creep in.

What if she knows? What if she found Julia's body? Are you stupid? You've just left her house. What if I got caught on CCTV somewhere? Oh my god, she knows, doesn't she? She's gonna put me away. Everyone I know is going to hate me.

The deep, grating noise of the phone rumbling against the wood of the desk went straight through him. Jackson couldn't bring himself to answer it, and he couldn't bring himself to decline it, so he just watched as it vibrated for a minute and then went off.

If she didn't know before, maybe she's a bit suspicious now. Damn, I should have just answered it, now she suspects me.

He quickly shook those thoughts out of his head and began writing on the piece of paper in front of him. He knew everything that he needed to say. For the first time in a long time, he thought he could see everything clearly. After he finished writing a couple of pages, he folded the paper and slotted it into an envelope he found in the desk drawer.

He needed to pay Andre Nelcourt a visit.

Luckily, he didn't need to do any research, since he already knew where he lived. When he was in Chase's kitchen writing the note, he'd noticed an unsealed letter that had Andre's address written on it. It made the rest of the plan a whole lot quicker and a whole lot smoother.

Wasting no time, he stuck the envelope into his pocket and stood up to leave, collecting his car keys on his way out of the door. He rushed through the hallways and through the lobby area – not seeing a single person on his way out. When he got out of the double doors and into the parking lot, the cold air hit him straight away and the darkness that had taken over was refreshing. The rain was lightly falling, almost like a fine powder, brushing against the parts of his skin that were showing. The moisture felt good and soothing.

He rushed to his car, as the rain was slowly starting to get heavier, and exited the parking lot as quickly as possible. The roads were clear, so he still didn't bother to look both ways before exiting the junction and leaving the motel in his rear-view mirror, turning the corner out of sight on the way to Andre's house.

As the brightness of his white Jaguar disappeared off into the horizon, he saw nothing but dim, flickering streetlights behind. What he didn't see, was a familiar black Lexus pulling into the motel parking lot.

42

The rain was getting heavier as he drove. The sky was a deep purple and there was a light mist cloaking the city. The dim streetlights penetrated the haze and cast an eerie shadow on the streets as he passed through – it gave a slight resemblance to a horror movie.

The rain splashed against his windscreen and, as it got heavier, thick droplets splashed on the roof of his car with a bang. It seemed more like hailstone than it did rain. Jackson took his time on the way over to Andre's. He could barely see six-foot in front of him and, that late at night, there were no sounds other than the rain hitting off his car at all angles and the dull calling of birds trying to fight for space in the trees that lined the roads.

His mind was still racing back and forth, and his thoughts kept returning to the phone call from Lily that he'd ignored.

It could have been really important – but she would have left a voicemail if it was that *important, wouldn't she?*

During the 20-minute drive to Andre's house, Jackson barely made a sound. For the most part, he felt like he didn't actually breath – nor did he feel himself even blink. It was like his body had just taken over and put itself on autopilot while the rest of him was left to doze off. His right arm stayed outstretched, gripping the top of the steering wheel while his left hand rested nervously on his thigh – he felt himself scratching at his jeans as his fingers trembled softly. For a minute, he felt himself drift over to the opposite side of the road and was driving into oncoming traffic. But luckily, there was traffic to drive into; just an open, lonely road.

Halfway through the journey, he decided he had to pull up on the side of an empty road and return his mind to the present. It seemed as though he was a car crash waiting to happen.

Deep breath in. Hold it. Deep breath out.

Close your eyes, and listen to the noise of the rain. Remember where you are and what you're doing.

Deep breath in. Hold it. Open your eyes. Deep breath out.

When his eyes opened and he saw what lay in front of him – he didn't seem to notice it before – the mist that was submerging the roads had gotten thicker and had begun to surround the still-dim streetlights that lined them. A faint glow tried to force its way through to illuminate the path but it struggled. The way the rain was falling had Jackson mesmerised. He turned the wiper blades off temporarily and watched as the rain droplets formed perfect lines as they streamed from the top of the windscreen to the bottom. It was like they were racing, and he couldn't take his eyes off them.

But then he remembered why he was there. He'd wasted too much time waiting.

He flicked the wiper blades onto their quickest setting and checked all of his mirrors – as far as he could see. Putting his full-beam headlights on, he drove slowly off. He took his time, trying not to go over 20mph, just in case something jumped out at him or pulled out of a junction without warning and it took him a week to stop the car in the heavy rain.

After another 20 minutes – a 20-minute journey ended up taking him 45 – he arrived at Andre's house. He pulled up across the road with the driver side door facing into the road; he had to be ready to make a quick getaway. He rolled down his window and stared at the house. Lacking a driveway, a ten-foot concrete walkway led from the side of the road up to the front door, which was an old-looking wooden door – a dull shade of white with a black handle – and sat in a deep alcove. There was large bay windows on either side of the door, one of which was illuminated a bright yellow.

He was home.

Jackson sat still for a minute or two, letting the cold air hit him and feeling the rain splash against the window opening and into the car. It sent a refreshing tingling sensation over his face and he soaked it in before collecting what he needed and getting out of the car.

Finally looking over his surroundings – as far as he could see, which wasn't very far – he crossed the road. His hair was immediately soaked and flopped over his forehead, and he could feel his clothes clinging to him again as they took in litres of water from the sky. The walkway to the house was cracked and dipped, and puddles had formed along the edge of the stone, growing bigger as the minutes passed and the rain got heavier. He got halfway up and reached into his inside pocket, feeling the envelope between his damp fingertips.

Suddenly, a voice echoed behind him, 'You didn't answer my call.'

Jackson stopped in place and raised his eyebrows, directing his pupils to the bottom of his eyes like he was trying to look behind him. He knew who it was, but he didn't want to see her. He wasn't prepared for that.

'I couldn't. It was too hard,' he said to the ground in front of him, closing his eyes.

After half a minute of silence, he wiped the rain from his face and turned around.

And there she was.

Lily was standing on the side of the road with her arms hung loosely by her side. Every so often, she wiped her face which was soaked with a combination of rain and tears. Her lightened butterscotch hair was tied up in a short ponytail and her dark blue shirt was turning a shade of black as it got soaked.

The streetlight directly above her was casting a dull yellow hue across the top of her face, making her eyes look pale.

'I found your notes,' she exclaimed through the noise of the rain that was starting to crash to the ground.

Jackson didn't reply; he couldn't find the words.

'You know,' she continued, 'I really didn't want to believe that it was you. I didn't want to believe that the guy that's been ruining my life – this—this *vicious psychopath* that's been keeping me awake most nights – was actually my *boyfriend.*'

She picked up a small rock that was laying by her feet and inspected it.

'Are you fucking—' she hurled the rock towards him, hitting his shoulder with a painful thud '—*serious?*'

'Oh, and by the way,' she said as she stepped forward, 'I found the piece of paper with all the names on, too.'

'Lily—'

'Arthur Renshaw,' she shouted, interrupting him, 'Jacob Davies. Grey Sullivan. Chase Morgen. Jordy—' she exhaled sharply and stopped herself from tearing up '—Jordy Renalto. Andre Nelcourt. And last but not least…'

'Lily, please—'

'No!' she shouted, holding up her palm to shush him, 'And *last but not least*… Lily Harrod.'

43

Lily was able to quell her own tears, but she couldn't do anything for Jackson's, which began slowly rolling down his cheek as she read the names off his note. He took a step forward and she almost flinched, like she was both disgusted and scared.

He rubbed his shoulder, trying to soothe the bruise that was forming, then turned his attention back to his girlfriend – probably his ex-girlfriend now. She had come slightly out of the streetlight's rays and her eyes now looked shrouded in darkness. From the whites of her eyes, he could see she'd been crying before she even arrived there, and she was in desperate need of some sleep – but maybe she'd be able to get some since she had finally caught the "Irvine Impaler".

He didn't like that name. Hopefully, the news only refer to him as Jackson and not the moniker the police had given him.

'You don't understand, Lily,' Jackson said solemnly.

'Oh, I understand perfectly, Jackson. It's not complicated anymore,' she turned her attention back to the note and continued speaking. 'Arthur, Jacob, Grey, Chase, *and* Jordy's names are all crossed out. That's because they're all dead. It's not that hard to decipher. Or do you just think I'm dumb? Huh?'

'Of course I don't think that.'

'This is your hit-list, isn't it? You're a *monster*. I should have connected the dots a long time ago. You kept leading me astray with the case, you kept feeding me so much shit to make sure I wouldn't suspect you. But, you once told me that you think the murders were just part of a hit-list. You said it could be random, or it could be planned, but I never thought it would be *yours*!'

'It wasn't like that at all! I really wanted to help.'

'You're lying! You never wanted to help, you just wanted to get away with it. How did I *ever* love you?'

'Because what we had – what we have – is real. I love you, Lily,'

'No, Jackson, you don't. You love the *idea* of me. If it wasn't for the fact that I was the lead detective on *your* case, you would have left a long time ago.'

'That's not true,' he wiped his face again and took another step forward. She noticed and took a step back, into the full glow of the streetlight.

'Yes, it is. You can't deny that. You haven't loved anyone since Hannah died, and you're the only one that doesn't see that,' her tone seemed sympathetic, but she lacked proper emotion or feeling towards him.

'You need to believe me, Lily.'

'I can't believe anything you say anymore, Jackson. You've manipulated me, and *lied,* for so long, just to throw me off your scent. You acted like you were trying to help me catch the guy when really, you were just putting different scenarios in my head to make me think it wasn't you. And I had no reason to suspect you, either, because you were always so normal, so *boring*.'

Jackson quickly lifted his brows, and whispered, 'Ouch.'

She pointed at the door behind him. He turned around and followed the invisible line her finger was drawing, then turned back to look at her.

'I know where we are. This is Andre Nelcourt's house, isn't it?' she asked.

'Would you believe me if I told you I'm not here to kill him – or hurt him in any way?' Jackson replied.

'What have I *just* said?'

'But I'm telling the truth this time, I promise. I'm not a killer anymore. Please—'

'Where are the other names?' she interrupted, speaking matter-of-factly.

'What?' he replied with a confused furrow of his brow.

'The other names. Where are they? You've killed more people than this. What about Jordy's wife?'

'She walked in while I was with him. I couldn't let her go. If you go to Julia Renshaw's house, you'll find her dead as well.'

'W-what?'

'I went over to apologise, and I don't know what happened but—'

'Just… shut your mouth. Please,' her hand moved so it was loosely on her hip. She wiped her face again and shook her head backward to get the loose bits of hair away from her eyes.

The rain was still heavy and had completely drenched both of them. The distance between them seemed longer than it was due to the mist that had completely surrounded them. It was like they were talking inside a cloud. The only thing that was stopping the walkway from being shrouded in darkness was the makeshift spotlight hanging a few feet above Lily's now-dark red hair. A faint smell of smoke drifted in from down the street and they heard groups of people cheerily shouting, and then cars revving.

'Lily, what are you doing?' Jackson asked, ignoring the noises.

'Why is my name last? Were you—were you planning on killing me from the very beginning?' Lily replied, passing over his question without a thought.

'I-I didn't want to get caught. That was before I really—'

'And you had the nerve to say you *loved* me?' she muttered, tears beginning to drip gently from her eyes. She thought she'd cried enough since she was put as the lead on the case, but her body had other ideas.

'That was *before* I really loved you, Lily. Please believe me. I'm changed now. I can't live that life anymore. It's too much for me now.'

'Oh, bullshit,' Lily retorted.

'It's not bullshit, Lily. I mean it. Ask me anything you want.'

'Okay,' she replied sternly, folding her arms, 'Was I just a loose end? Or did you actually have feelings for me?

'You—'

'And don't you dare lie to me—' she placed her hand back on her hip, hovering a few millimetres above her gun holster '—or I swear to God I will put a bullet straight through your god damn head.'

Jackson stared at Lily's hand, following every little twitch and every slight movement in her arms. Her eyes were fixated on him; following him just in case he made a rash decision and she wanted to be prepared. The mist had begun to thin as their standoff got to the peak of its intensity, but the rain was still fiercely ripping through the thick, humid air.

Jackson could finally see Lily's face in all of its glory. He saw the freckles that ran in a thick strip along her nose and on both cheeks. He saw the growing dullness of her hair as the rain got deep into the fibres, and her once-full, peach lips looked thin and tired.

Lily could finally see the bags under Jackson's eyes, seeing now how much the stress was affecting him; thinking he was actually telling the truth about *some* of it. She could see his light-brown-turned-jet-black hair that was flatter than the concrete he stood on and his fringe flopped unflatteringly on his forehead, stopping just above his eyebrows. It was a face she loved, but now she could only see the monster that he'd turned out to be.

'When we first met... had you already killed someone?' Lily asked, already worried about the response she'd get.

Jackson sighed and slowly nodded his head. Lily took a long blink and looked around the sky above her, trying to hold back the tears by not looking at him.

'I went to that bar as soon as I'd left the garage in Little Joaquin Valley,' he said disappointedly.

Lily stared at him with shock in her eyes; it was a fierce shine that she couldn't hold in.

'You… you'd already killed th-*three* people?'

'Yeah.'

'Wait,' Lily stopped and tilted her head in confusion like she'd just figured something out. 'How long after killing them did we meet?'

'I don't know, I wasn't really paying attention to the time.'

'Well… just guess,' Lily said forcefully.

'Half an hour?'

'Seriously?!' she shouted.

'I'm sorry, Lily, okay?!' Jackson shouted back, 'but that was *not* my fault. You walked in and we got to talking, you can't possibly blame me for that. But you have to believe that I've changed now. When it started, I really liked you; we got along well and you were *so* beautiful. You still are.'

'Don't,' she whispered, dabbing the corner of her eye with her knuckle.

'When you got assigned to my case,' Jackson went on, 'I didn't know what to do. I was so torn. I'm not sure I really loved you as much as I do now – as much as I've really grown to. So, yes, I wrote your name at the bottom of the list because originally, I didn't want there to be any loose ends; I didn't want to get caught. But then…'

'Then what?' Lily asked impatiently.

'Then I found out who Jordy was, and I—'

'What?' she whispered again.

'—and after that, I felt so guilty after seeing what it was doing to you, and I couldn't take it anymore. I couldn't bring myself to do any of it.'

'And you think that makes it *better* do you?' she screamed, 'You killed my big brother; you killed my sister-in-law; you killed their unborn child! Do you think feeling "guilty" makes it more acceptable? Huh?!'

'Of course I don't!' Jackson shouted back.

'Do you think I'm going to feel better about the entire situation because you're *sorry* and you *regret* what you've done?'

'You don't know the whole story, Lily. He would have died regardless of whether I killed him or not. There was a target on his back and *you* should have known about it.'

'No, no, no, don't turn this back around on me, Jackson. You're a manipulative liar, and I'm not gonna let you rope me into this.'

Jackson sighed and told Lily everything he knew about Jordy – raping the little girl, confessing to Jackson in floods of tears, the $25,000 hit on him, the three men plotting to kill him – and Lily stood in shock. Her face was blank and colourless, and Jackson couldn't tell if she was believing him or not – or whether she was just astounded at how well he'd crafted the "make-believe" story.

'No,' Lily said monotonously when he'd finished.

'What?'

'No. You're lying.'

'I'm not lying, Lily. Hannah died because of what *your* brother did to a little girl. How do you think that made *me* feel, huh?! Did you ever stop to think about that?'

'You *are* lying, Jackson,' Lily said, wiping a tear that had begun to slip down her cheek, 'Jordy would *never* do something like that. He was a kind man; he loved his family, and they loved him back. He was caring, gentle, and he was too nice for his own good.'

She wiped more tears away and sighed dejectedly to herself, looking down at the ground and watched the raindrops dance around her feet. The rain and the mist were beginning to lighten up, but the water still felt heavy as it dropped onto her body with a tiny thud.

'*You*,' she said angrily, suddenly void of any sadness, '*you* took him away from me. You... you... monster. You deserve to rot in hell for what you've done.'

'Lily, I promise I'm—'

'Enough!' she bellowed, loud enough for the entire neighbourhood to hear. She couldn't hold back the raw emotion any longer.

Jackson stood frozen in place, a look of fear covering his face. He was taking sharp, calming breaths, and he couldn't comprehend the anger that had just released itself from Lily's body.

Then, without warning, she pulled her gun from its holster and pointed it straight at him, aiming the barrel precisely between his terrified, mahogany eyes.

44

'Jackson Yardley, you are under arrest for the multiple kidnappings and murders of—'

'Lily, don't do this,' Jackson said, tearing up.

'—Arthur Renshaw, Jacob Davies, and Grey Sullivan; and also for the multiple murders of Chase Morgen—'

'Please, Lily…'

'—Jordan Renalto, Dana Renalto, and Julia Renshaw.'

'Okay, I get it,' Jackson said again, sniffling wildly.

Lily sighed disappointedly and continued, 'You have the right to remain silent. Anything you do say can and will be used against you in a court of law. You have the right to have an attorney present during questioning. If you cannot afford an attorney, one will be provided for you. Do you understand these rights as they have explained to you?'

Jackson wiped his eyes with the tip of his fingers and nodded slowly.

'I'm sorry, Lily, I really am,' he mumbled. 'Please, this doesn't have to be it.'

'I'll take that as you understanding,' she replied plainly.

'I know how much I've hurt you,' he pleaded, 'and I know the suffering that I've caused you and your family, but please don't let this be it. I'm begging you. I don't want to go to jail.'

'You should have thought of that before you started.'

Lily took a small step forward, for no other reason than to stretch her legs. She'd been standing in the same spot under the streetlight for far too long and she could feel her calves aching like she'd just completed a long, vigorous workout at the gym. Jackson stayed in place, unable to move from nervousness and his new-found fear of her.

She wiped the hair from her face and tightened her grip on the handle of her pistol.

'The law doesn't work the way you think it does, you know? You should have thought of the consequences before you kidnapped Arthur. Do you not understand that?' Lily asked.

She had begun to slightly tremble, noticing the pistol wobbling gently in her hands; themselves beginning to sweat. The reality of the situation had dawned on her; that she was pointing a gun at the man she thought she'd loved. Maybe she still loved him – she felt like she did. Every time she looked in his eyes, she tried to push away the memories that they'd created, the time they'd spent together. She didn't know whether it was real, but it felt real to her.

As if he could sense her hesitation, Jackson stepped forward a few inches.

'I love you, Lily,' he said regretfully.

'Don't do that,' she muttered as she started crying, doing her best to hide it but the tears gave her eyes a faint glimmer. She wiped her eyes roughly with the back of her hand and refocused the gun, holding it tightly so it didn't wobble in her grasp.

'Don't do what?' Jackson replied, taking another small step.

'That's far enough,' she warned him, but he didn't seem to listen.

'Am I not allowed to tell you I love you?'

'I mean it,' she warned again, more stern this time.

Jackson took another step forward so that they were only separated by slightly longer than five feet. He felt like he could hear her cold breaths and the odd aroma of mint that came out with them. He was close enough to see that she was just as scared as he was.

'Alright, stop!' she shouted, and cocked the gun. The click echoed through the air – now thin and humid, even though was rain was still steadily pouring - and created a deafening silence immediately afterwards.

He was staring blank-faced down the barrel and every thought that was in his head suddenly alluded him, making way for the terror to return. The small, circular abyss that was looking straight at him looked vast, like it was ready to swallow him whole. He couldn't take his eyes off it, even as they both spoke.

'I don't feel sorry for doing this anymore, now that I know who you really are,' Lily said. 'So, put your hands behind your back, and just give up.'

Jackson sighed intensely and wiped the last remaining tear from his face. He held his hands above him and bowed his head, signalling his reluctant surrender. Lily sighed too, glad that the standoff they were having was finally coming to an eventual climax.

'Slowly,' she instructed.

He took a slow step forward and moved his arms from above his head to behind his back, clasping his hands together.

'You win,' he whispered as he walked towards her.

Lily quickly holstered her gun before reaching out to grab his left shoulder, keeping him from going anywhere or making any rushed movements. With her other hand, she reached behind her to pull out a pair of handcuffs from one of her pockets.

'This is just as hard for me as it is for you, you know?' she said quietly.

'You have no idea,' Jackson replied.

Picking the perfect moment of vulnerability – as her head was turned trying to rummage for the cuffs – he pulled the knife that he had stashed in the back of his trouser waistband and quickly lunged forward. In one swift motion, his right arm extended outwards and his left arm swung around her neck to hug her tightly, and keep her firmly upright.

The blade penetrated her skin with ease, slicing straight through her intestines with a loud *squelch*. Her head stiffened for a few seconds and her eyes went wide before it slumped onto the welcome support of Jackson's shoulder. The blade burned inside her and she went numb, and a painful tingling sensation travelled the length of her body.

'I still love you,' Jackson whispered softly in her ear as her eyes fluttered and the colour drained from them.

He felt the warmth of her blood slowly covering his hand and seeping through the webs between his fingers. He held on to her as tight as he could. Then, he started weeping, as yet another woman he loved died in front of him.

45

Jackson held Lily, tightly, in his arms for as long as he had the strength to. Holding on as if he never wanted to let her go. He knew she'd crumble to the floor the same way Grey did when he killed him, yet this time was so much worse and he didn't know if that was something he could watch.

As he felt his shoulders begin to struggle under all of her weight, and the blood began to grow thicker, he decided to lean forward and gently let her down to the floor. He released his hold on the knife and shook the excess blood from his hand before putting it on the small of her back to cushion her landing to the cold, wet ground. As he was letting go of her head, he kissed her soft, rosy cheek and whispered sadly into her ear that he was sorry, and that he never meant for it to end the way it did.

Throughout his meticulous planning, he never imagined that he'd kill Lily like that – a small part of him thought he would never actually go through with it. A small part hoped he would never have to. Once again, something had taken over him and he couldn't seem to control it. Maybe the fear had brought the adrenaline back for one last "hurrah".

Jackson stared intently at Lily's dead body, trying to find a way to grieve, wondering if he even had the emotions to feel anymore. He reached into his pocket and pulled out the letter that he'd originally come to deliver. He wondered the whole time how Andre hadn't heard the shouting and come out to see what it was. Maybe he wasn't even home, and he'd left the light on as a security measure to make would-be intruders think that he was home. Trying his luck, he posted the letter through the letterbox and sighed.

He turned around to look at Lily for the last time. He didn't want that to be the last image his brain remembered of her, but he still wanted to look at how graceful she was, even in death.

He took in her image, and then banged loudly on the door before sprinting away towards his car. He tumbled in and sat slouched, hiding from outside view, but still being high enough to start the car and make a quick getaway when necessary. He used the cover of the dim, flickering streetlight above his car to blend into the environment if Andre happened to look his way.

Seeing that there was continuously no activity, he was beginning to get doubtful that Andre was even in. Just then, a light appeared in the glass above the front door and Jackson slid down his seat, just far enough that he could still peak over the window.

The front door opened slowly and Andre appeared with Jackson's letter in his hand, wiping his eyes vigorously like he'd just been rudely awoken from a nap. He looked around to see who had knocked at the door, before spotting Lily lying on the ground. He gasped and ran over to her, shouting for help and frantically looking around the street to see if there was anyone – but it was deathly quiet. He didn't look Jackson's way; all he saw was a parked car in the corner of his eye and didn't concern himself with its presence.

With no-one around to help or close enough to hear his shouting, Andre ran back inside and emerged a minute later with a phone to his ear. He wasn't wearing his glasses and the shine from the streetlight at the end of the walkway flickered brightly in his face, making him squint.

He looked slimmer than he did in the picture on his website, but his clothes were ragged and over-sized. He held his hand over his nose as he spoke into the phone, either trying to contain his crying or maybe his vomit – Jackson couldn't tell which one.

Clearly stricken with grief, he put the phone down and crouched next to Lily's body, inspecting the wound and the puddle of blood beneath her that had begun to mix with the rainwater, and was making a thin paste along the concrete. Andre kept looking around to see if anyone was coming but the world was empty, and it was getting cold. The rain was barely existent now, but the clouds were still a worrying grey – ready to split open again any point and drown the world.

Andre looked up from Lily's body with a confused look on his face and glanced towards Jackson's car - a still-shimmering shade of white that seemed out of place in the dullness of the neighbourhood. He tried to slump down further to avoid being seen, but he might have been too late.

Andre stood up and began to walk towards the edge of the pavement; the confusion on his face changed swiftly to that of investigation. Jackson didn't want to stick around to see how far he'd come, so he quickly pressed the ENGINE START button and wasted no time driving off. He heard Andre shout at the car a few times, almost tempted to run down the street to chase after him, but he decided against and went back to tend to Lily's corpse. He felt like he needed to keep her company until the police arrived.

As Jackson got a few blocks away on his drive back to his motel room, he heard the distant sound of sirens that pierced the eerily silent night, echoing through the city like they were playing on an industrial speaker. Fifteen minutes later – getting back a lot quicker than he got there – he parked as quick as he could in the parking lot of the motel and sprinted back up to his room. His clothes were still dripping as he ran through the lobby and up the few flights of stairs, leaving a thin trail of water behind him. The receptionist that he'd passed on the way in shouted a complaint to him about the mess, but he ignored it and ran straight through to the stairway, hidden around the corner of the elevator wall that was opposite the front desk.

He burst through the door into his room and stopped abruptly, noticing how it was a lot different from when he'd left. The spread of papers he'd left on his desk was scattered aimlessly over the floor in front of it, and some of his drawers had been left open.

How could you be so careless?

Jackson walked over to the mess and glanced down at all the pages, circling on the spot as he suddenly got extremely flustered, and every thought he'd been piling onto his conscience came crashing down. He felt hopeless, angry and scared all at the same time.

He walked around the desk and sat down, leaning back in his chair for a second before springing himself back. With an intense and angry *ugh*, he flung the entire contents of the desk to the floor with one swift sweep of his arms, and then slammed his fist down as hard as his body would allow him to with an angry grunt that was loud enough to wake the neighbours. Breathing heavily, he sat in the chair and stared gormlessly at the door for what seemed like an eternity.

After finally calming down, he reached into his inside pocket and pulled out the list of names that he'd retrieved from Lily's body after she died, and placed it on the table. Reading through it, the regret and the guilt had boiled over and he felt only anger towards himself.

Then, he did the only thing he could think to do at that moment, as painful as it was.

He crossed Lily's name off the list, and crumpled it up, throwing it to the floor to join the rest of the mess.

III

46

The blaring of horns and the incessant shouting of crowds of people awoke Jackson from the deepest slumber he'd had in months. A dull shade of yellow light was trickling in through the curtains and cast a glare into his eyes. He sat up in his bed, appreciating his new surroundings, and the fact that he hadn't seen his blood-soaked wife in weeks. He seemed to have left her memory in the motel room, along with everything else. It was as though this was where he'd always lived, and he'd been having a recurring nightmare of living in a rundown motel room – and being a deranged serial killer.

Thinking back on it, it all seemed so surreal. But he knew what he'd done.

It had been a couple of weeks since Lily had died, and part of him had accepted it, but the other part was still hung up on her death – like he was trying not to blame himself for it.

It was an accident, after all. Wasn't it? You need to believe that it was an accident or self-defence.

No-one had contacted him since, and it was worrying. Doing as much as he did, that doesn't just *go away* – he murdered the lead detective on his own case, people were bound to find out. Or maybe they had, he hadn't turned a TV on in a while.

He wasn't even certain that Lily was the only who knew it was him. He figured she would have been told by someone, and she refused to believe it, so she went to the motel room when he wasn't there and found everything. She wouldn't have accepted it otherwise.

Jackson stood up from his new, more comfortable bed and stretched his body out. His t-shirt was a size too big and hung low over his underwear, brushing lightly against his bare thigh. After he killed Arthur, he'd gone out a bought a SLAYER t-shirt as a way to remember his "first", and they didn't have his size, so he was forced to make do. He knew wearing it was strange and he didn't want to remember it anymore, but the t-shirt was soft and comfortable, and the size of it let air circulate around his body while he slept.

He walked over to the curtains and flung them open with force, being immediately blinded by the sun that was creeping over the top of the buildings on the opposite side of the street. They opened to a set of clean French windows that led the balcony of his apartment, overlooking one of the busiest streets in the city. Downtown was a different beast to the suburban surroundings he'd grown accustomed to. He was used to looking out of the window and seeing a parking lot with damaged perimeter walls that lead to the outskirts of the city. This much activity right in front his new home made him nervous – any one of those people down there could know who he was and what he'd done.

Still paranoid, then? Get over yourself, Jackson. You might actually get away with it.

As the light that was beaming in unobstructed was hurting his head, he walked over to the small flat-screen TV that sat atop a long chest of drawers in the corner of the room. When he flicked it on, it was showing the morning news. And he couldn't have picked a worse time to watch it.

"Good morning, this is ABC7 News,' the news anchor began, 'I'm Allison Bazemore. Our top story this morning remains the ongoing manhunt for the so-called Irvine Impaler, now identified as 35-year-old Jackson Yardley. Mr. Yardley is responsible for the murders of at least seven people in and around Irvine, but police believe that figure to be higher.'

Allison had blonde hair that looked like it had been recently dyed, as the brightness of each strand of hair radiated through the lens of the camera in front of her. Some of her roots were a dirty blonde and were doing their best to creep through to the surface. The makeup that had been done for her looked natural – the foundation blended well with her slightly tanned skin tone and her eyeshadow was a neutral blue.

Jackson watched as her vibrant blue eyes followed the teleprompter in front of her, He could almost see the reflection of the camera crew in her pupils. She looked down to the pages of notes on the desk in front of her, then looked back towards the camera.

'One of the confirmed deaths is 31-year-old Lily Harrod,' Allison continued, 'who was the lead detective for the case. Chief of the Irvine PD, Mark Hayley has said that the entire force is "beyond devastated" over the passing of Ms. Harrod and that "even in her short time with the IPD, she made an indelible mark on all of her fellow officers and she will be sorely missed".'

Allison delicately swallowed some saliva that had brought its way up to the back of her throat, then she took a sip from a small glass of water on the desk to her left. She looked back towards the camera with a subtle glare, as if she were about to address Jackson directly. She spoke again, slightly softer this time.

'Police have been going through Ms. Harrod's case files and diving as deep as they can into Mr. Yardley's history in order to figure out a motive for his surprising reign of terror. For more on this, we go to our expert on this case, Simon Morris. I must warn you; this report contains some flashing and distressing images,'

The screen changed from Allison's youthful, gleaming face to a montage of various clips of the city where Jackson's victims had been found, edited together to make it look as upsetting as possible for those watching it. The camera movements were slow, making sure to keep the dried blood in the centre of the frame for as long as possible. The picture then changed to the walkway outside Andre's house and a recording of police investigating the scene and dabbing the knife for fingerprints. Halfway through the segment, Simon's voiceover began.

'A case everyone in Irvine has struggled to wrap its head around for weeks, even months, might finally be coming to a welcome conclusion,' he said, 'Residents of Irvine have been left in a terrifying limbo since Jackson Yardley's killing spree began a couple of months ago, and only now are they seeing the prospect of safe, bloodless streets. Police believe that Mr. Yardley's deep-rooted anger began in 2000 when his younger sister committed suicide aged 14 as a result of bullying. One of the deceased, Chase Morgen, was believed to be one of those bullies. Chase's best friend at the time – and still – Andre Nelcourt is still alive and under police protection until Mr. Yardley is apprehended.'

The picture on-screen changed to Jackson's old house, and as soon as he saw it – the door he burst into; the window that he'd knew Hannah had been peeking out from – his stomach knotted and he felt sick. He thought he was fine, and that it didn't affect him anymore, but something felt different. The camera scanned through the interior of the house and then a picture of him and Hannah together flashed up in the corner of the display. His stomach tightened again, seeing her radiant face and the smile that she gave to everyone.

'Police found that the spree started following the rape and murder of Jackson's wife of ten years, Hannah. The three men who were responsible for her death – Arthur Renshaw, Grey Sullivan, and Jacob Davies – were his first three victims. Police are still trying to figure out the proper timeline of events, and the motives behind each one, but they've told us they recovered at least six pages of handwritten notes from Jackson's motel room and are using them deeply in their investigation. Using some of the notes, police have also arrested one other man on suspicion of contract murder, and he remains in custody.'

The picture switched to a pre-recording of the exterior of Irvine Police Station, the camera panning around its perimeter before coming to a stop on the top half of Simon – who was wearing a long, thick, grey trench coat that hung over a spotted light blue shirt, open at the collar. His black hair looked tidier than the last time he appeared on camera, although it looked crispy to the touch. His cheeks were dry and it looked like the makeup team had tried to hide the bags under his eyes, but they were still visible.

'Although they want us to believe that the streets of this city are safe,' Simon spoke again, using plenty of hand gestures, 'and that the killings were planned, residents are still wary of going out at night by themselves – and they have a right to do that. It's clear from the pictures, that Jackson Yardley could snap at any moment, at anyone, and continue his reign over the city. It's undoubtedly clear that no-one will have a proper nights sleep until one of the worst serial killers in California history is arrested and brought to justice – and even then, that might not be enough. For ABC7 News, I'm Simon Morris.'

The report ended and Allison appeared on the screen again with her head bowed. As soon as the camera's gaze was thrust upon her, she looked up as if she'd been waiting like that since Simon's report started. Jackson turned the TV off again and stood up. After throwing on the first pair of trousers he came across, he walked back to the open windows and stepped out onto the balcony.

The outside world hit him like a brick. The brisk wind slapped him in the face as it blew by, and the noise of car horns, engines and drivers filled the surrounding area. Directly opposite his apartment was a huge new office building that seemed to pierce the clouds as it towered over the rest of the area. Across the front of the building just above the highest window were huge gold and black letters that read MARITECH. Far below that, just above the plaza entrance was a banner that had been strung across the face. NEW MARTITECH IRVINE HQ – OPENING AUGUST 2019, it read.

Jackson leaned over the balcony, feeling the cold steel against his bare forearms, and smiled to himself. He was looking at the brainchild of Chase Morgen and his team, and he had admitted to himself that the building was a magnificent creation. But what really caught his eye was the metal plaque that had been attached to the entranceway, just below where the banner hung.

He took a few tense breaths, but before he could relax again, he heard his front door crash open behind him and almost fly off the hinges. He heard at least four different voices shouting towards him. He turned his head to look over his shoulder and saw a SWAT team advancing carefully through his apartment dressed in heavy combat gear, and holding assault rifles to their shoulders. A few unarmed police officers trailed behind them, quickly checking in each room for the presence of weapons or – hopefully, they probably thought – more bodies.

'Down on the ground!' the two lead officers shouted in unison.

Jackson turned back to face the street below and sighed disappointedly. He felt like they played him. They let him relax and think that the case had come to a standstill when in reality they were plotting to get him.

Careless, yet again. This is your own fault, Jackson. You deserve to go to jail.

He felt the soft rumbling of the floor beneath as the thick boots of the two lead officers trudged towards him, still locked into their combat walk, just in case he had a weapon hidden on him – they'd learned from the mistake that Lily had made.

'Hands on your head, now!' they shouted again, but he remained calm and unmoved – at least on the outside.

He kept staring at the metal plaque that bore the name of the new building as one of the officers bundled into him, feeling as if he was going to fall over the balcony and land on a passing car. His head was pressed forward over the edge, and his hands were pulled behind him and he felt the cold steel of the handcuffs as they were wrapped uncomfortably tight around both of his wrists.

'Got you, you sick bastard,' the soldier whispered in his ear before he pulled Jackson's head back up straight, sending a rush of blood towards his brain and dizzying him temporarily.

A man then appeared on the balcony next to him and looked out onto the city, acting like he was alone. The cologne he was wearing immediately attacked Jackson's nose, just like it had in his motel room, and he knew immediately who it was.

'Bell,' Jackson muttered with a humoured shake of his head.

'Long time no see, Mr. Yardley,' Officer Bell said with a smug look on his face.

Bell's hair was just as spiky as it was the last couple of times the two men had crossed paths, but he'd gain a light stubble over his chin and his breath smelled fresher when he spoke. He stood up straight with his shoulders back, looking every bit the proud, powerful cop that he knew he was.

'I figured you might show up at some point,' Jackson said, turning to face him.

Bell kept his attention on the road beneath him, and the plaque in front of the building across the street.

'Oh, I wouldn't have missed this for anything,' he said.

'Couldn't have just left it alone, could you?'

Bell turned to face him, and said, 'I told you in the motel; I knew it was you, and that I'd be the first face you saw when you got caught. You acted like you were innocent, and that I was wasting my time. Now, look where we are.'

Jackson smirked at him and nodded, 'Yep, look where we are. I guess you were right. Actually, I'm surprised it took you so long.'

Bell turned around and looked at the SWAT team that had come to apprehend Jackson and chuckled, then turned back to look over the balcony.

'It's funny…' he muttered.

'What is?' Jackson replied.

'You outdid yourself.'

'What d'you mean?'

'Well, I thought you were just sleeping with Lily to get information; to make sure you'd get away with it. But you went and killed her, too.'

'That was an accident,' Jackson bowed his head.

'Oh, I'm sure it was. I'm sure the other six were accidents, too. Strange how murders work out like that, isn't it?'

Jackson looked up again and stared Bell dead in the face.

'I bet you wish I would have an accident as well, right?' Bell asked, laughing.

'Are you done?' Jackson replied, accepting his defeat.

Officer Bell looked back at the officers inside the apartment then back at Jackson, then smiled with a quiet *hm*, then said, 'Yeah, I'm done. And you know what? So are you.'

He grinned and patted him lightly on the back.

Jackson took one last look at the Sienna Yardley Memorial Building and smiled sadly before the SWAT team hauled him away.

47

A strong aroma of charred wood combined with a mixture of various perfumes swam around the interior of the courtroom and gave Jackson's nose hair an uncomfortable itch – which he couldn't scratch because of the handcuffs. His orange jumpsuit was stained and smelled dirty – most likely because he didn't think it had been washed in the two weeks he'd been living in it. Being in solitary confinement wasn't doing his hygiene any favours.

The rows stacked full of people behind him were talking amongst themselves, creating an inaudible noise for his ears. He knew at least of few of the groups were talking about him, since he heard words like "guilty" and "monster." He even heard Hannah's name a few times and it sent a chill through his body. *Still.*

Along with various residents of the city that came to watch a killer get the justice he deserved, the rows were populated by prominent figures in the case. Lily's boss, Benji, sat at the back row in a crisp black suit, looking like he'd aged at least 10 years since she'd died. To his left was Officer Bell, slouching as if he was hiding because he didn't belong there, and not being able to hold back his proud smile. To his right was Officer Hamasaki, sitting with perfect posture and a blank but focused expression plastered across his face.

Jackson sat in an old wooden chair in the section designated for defendants that felt like it was going to give his butt multiple uncomfortable splinters – that's if they could penetrate the rock-solid exterior of his jumpsuit. In the two seats to his left were the public defenders that had been assigned to his case – because absolutely no-one would willingly take it on because it would be a guaranteed loss. The two men were discussing their notes between themselves, promising each other they'd done all they can for Jackson. They seemed to be convincing themselves that, during the few days that the case was actually being tried in court and they were giving all their opening and closing arguments, they gave it everything they could to make the jury see it from an innocent, vengeful perspective. That's all he had. It's not like he could plead insanity, because no-one would have bought that for a second.

He'd already accepted his fate. Subconsciously, he'd accepted it as soon as his knife first entered Arthur Renshaw's stomach – he knew where it would end, he just didn't know when.

Well, now he did.

After ten minutes of sitting in silence – eavesdropping on every conversation within earshot – and nearly dozing off, he was startled awake by the booming voice of the bailiff that echoed around the hollow walls of the room.

'All rise,' he shouted with a voice that was deep and resonant, 'This court with the Honourable Judge Mulroy presiding, is now in session.'

Everyone in the room stood up in unison as the door to the chambers swung open and Judge Mulroy emerged with a swagger that suggested he never took any stick from anyone in his court. He was a relatively tall man, but his face and body had sagged with old age. He moved around like he was still youthful. His thick silver hair was combed back with marvellous precision, with not a single strand out place. His thick moustache-goatee combo was equally as impressive. This was a man with a calm, but confident swagger. He knew the power that he had, but he was in no way arrogant about it.

The Judge sat down in his chair and instructed everyone to be seated and to remain quiet as the session went on. Jackson shuffled uncomfortably in his chair as Mulroy glared disgustedly down at him. There was a strange intent emanating from his old, brown eyes and Jackson felt like he knew the verdict even before he started speaking.

'This court is now in session,' Mulroy repeated as he lightly rapped his gavel against the block beneath it. 'This is the final session of this case. Both parties have made their arguments, along with their opening and closing statements, Prosecution, are you happy to proceed with the verdict?'

The prosecuting lawyers looked at one another, accompanied by the Chief of Irvine PD, and then nodded at the Judge.

'Defence, are you happy to proceed with the verdict?'

'We are, Your Honour,' one of Jackson's lawyers replied.

'Mr. Yardley, do you have any final words before you find out your fate?'

Jackson looked the Judge in the eyes and pursed his lips. 'No, Your Honour,' he replied, 'I've made my peace.'

'I'm sure you have,' Mulroy remarked before turning to the jury and asking, 'Jury, have you come to a unanimous decision?'

The lead juror stood up – an overweight woman with shoulder-length hair that looked too curly to be real, wearing an unflattering sweater and shirt combo – and confirmed that they'd reached a decision. The bailiff approached her cautiously and she handed him a small brown envelope that she'd been keeping next to her on her seat. He took the few steps back over to the Judge's bench and handed Mulroy the letter. He inspected it for a few seconds then placed it in front of him, just next to his gavel.

'Before I read the verdict for the many, many charges you are facing,' Mulroy said to Jackson, 'I have something of my own to say,'

Jackson leaned forward and rested his forearms on the table in front of him, interlocking his fingers.

'After reading through your case files myself,' Mulroy began, 'and hearing everything that both parties have argued, I have no doubts in my head that you are a monster, and a vile human being. I do not say that lightly. I have tried a lot of murderers in this courtroom – some of them I know have made a mistake, and some of them I know had intent – but you are something that I can't quite work out. I'm still not fully certain what goes on in your head, and how your brain was triggered and poisoned so easily and so viciously after the death of your wife.

'Throughout the duration of the case – from the kidnapping of Arthur Renshaw on May 9th, 2019, to the murder of Lilian Harrod on the night of July 22nd, 2019 – you showed little remorse for your actions. Each of your murders was more gruesome than the last, and even after you feigned guilt and regret, you still had no problem killing. If you felt had *actually* felt this "guilt" and "regret", then you would have turned yourself in and ended up saving multiple lives – one of which was a valued and respected police officer in this community.'

Mulroy looked down at the envelope and picked it up, sliding his finger underneath the flap and then pulling out several sheets of paper. He scanned quickly through them before setting them back down on the bench next to him, ready to be announced to the waiting spectators.

'It is for those reasons that I will not be setting a bail, and – at risk of letting my personal feelings interject – feel like you should be punished to the fullest extent of the law,' Mulroy finished.

Jackson sat back and looked up to the heavens, just wishing for the day to be over.

'I will now read the verdicts,' the Judge said.

Everyone behind Jackson sat forward in their seat, making sure they heard every single word.

They might as well have brought pom-poms and fireworks to celebrate, Jackson thought to himself.

Judge Mulroy cleared his throat then picked up each piece of paper page-by-page next to him; one for each charge that was presented.

'As to the multiple kidnappings of Arthur Renshaw, Grey Sullivan, and Jacob Davies; the jury has found you guilty on all counts,' he said.

The crowd behind Jackson erupted into applause of the first verdict, and Mulroy immediately slammed the gavel down and loudly called for silence until all verdicts had been read.

'As to the multiple murders of Arthur Renshaw, Grey Sullivan, Jacob Davies, Chase Morgen, and Jordan Renalto – all in the first degree – the jury has found you guilty on all counts,' Mulroy continued, flicking quickly through the pages. 'As to the murder of Dana Renalto in the second degree, the jury has found you guilty. As to the manslaughter of Detective Lilian Harrod, the jury has found you guilty. You are also being charged with two counts of Breaking and Entering, relating to the properties owned by Mr. Jordan Renalto, and Mr. Chase Morgen – both of which you entered under false pretences in order to murder both men. Again, the jury has found you guilty on both counts.'

The rows of spectators were trying their best to hold back their rowdy applause, and joy over the guilty verdicts. They'd settled for quiet murmuring, expressing their happiness between one another instead. Judge Mulroy insisted on silence again, rapping the gavel down softly but with enough force to echo around the open air of the courtroom.

'Having read these verdicts,' Mulroy summarised, 'and after hearing the arguments and statements from both sides – one a lot more convincing and reasoned than the other – I hereby sentence you to death by lethal injection.'

The crowd erupted once again; the sound of a hundred people all banging their hands together at once was deafening. But Jackson phased it out, too shocked to notice anything. His head fell to the bench and the cold wood tickled his forehead. He held his hands to the back of his head and fought to stop himself from crying. Somehow, the prospect of death had never occurred to him.

Judge Mulroy banged the gavel multiple times, shouting as loud as he could for quiet and order in the courtroom, but doing little to suppress the raw emotion of everyone in the seats.

'Your execution date will be confirmed to you in the coming days,' Mulroy shouted over the clapping, still banging the gavel down. 'You will be taken to San Quentin State Prison and held in solitary confinement on Death Row for the duration of your sentence, and until your execution date arrives.'

With one last slam of the gavel, Judge Mulroy stood up and shouted, 'This court is now adjourned.'

The applause continued as the bailiff approached Jackson and grabbed him roughly by the arm and pulled him up from his seat. The Judge glared at him as he was dragged across the floor and towards the exit. Jackson turned his head to look at the officers, residents, and family of the deceased in the crowd that were hugging and smiling, trying to stop himself from shedding a few tears. His nightmare was getting worse, and whether he deserved it or not, there were one hundred people in front of him celebrating the fact that he wouldn't get to see his 36th birthday.

48

Jackson's cell was dark, dingy, and a nightmare for those with claustrophobia. The grey brick that made up the 8x5 living space was cracked and covered in scratches. Some bits had begun chipping away and he'd woken up a few times to find his bed covered in dust and small pieces of the walls. He couldn't even call where he slept a bed; it felt more like a slab of concrete. The thin mattress that lay atop the rusted frame felt like it was filled with gravel, and he had a constant ache in his shoulders from it.

The only source of light was via a small window at the back of the room. It had been permanently boarded up, making him unable to see the outside world, but there were tiny holes in the wood and cracks between each panel in which small rays of light filtered. Even through the protection, the light felt warm against his skin – seeing those soft, yellow spots dotted along the ground had become one of the highlights of his day.

Just below the window was a small toilet that wouldn't be out of place in the vast jungles of a third-world country. Jackson thought he'd contract a skin disease every time he sat down. The seat was always warm and uncomfortable – and so was his new life. Across the ceiling were several exposed pipes that gave the room a faint, but horrible smell. It was as if he were living underneath a sewage plant and all of the substances travelled through those pipes to get where they were going.

He might be a killer, but he no longer felt like someone with any element of power. He felt useless, hopeless, and weak. Prison was *not* for him. He'd known about solitary confinement from TV shows, documentaries, and interesting articles he'd come across online, but he never thought it would be as bad as it was. His body always seemed to be itching, and he'd killed at least five spiders a day in the week that he'd been living there – if living was what it could be called.

For the past half an hour or so, Jackson had been standing shakily on the toilet seat, trying to peak through the small cracks in the wood to get a view of the outside. The gap was only a few millimetres wide, but he saw parts of overgrown grass, old and brown. At the edge of the grass was a thick metal fence that spanned the entire perimeter of the prison complex. Its bars were thick, with little space between each one, and decorated with barbed wire along the top.

Beyond the fence was a narrow road that followed around the prison, then the ground sunk down to form a steep hill that led to the San Francisco Bay, stretching far and wide along the horizon. Jackson stared at the murky, greenish water of the bay in the distance and took multiple deep breaths. He looked long enough so that the image was frozen into his head, and he could see it perfectly when he closed his eyes.

He turned around on the seat and his pupils dilated to adjust to the darkness of his cell. Closing his eyes, he revisited the image of the bay, pretending he was on the other side of the fence, looking out on it.

Then, he took another slow breath, and jumped.

The blanket that he'd wrapped around the ceiling pipes and fashioned into a noose tightened from the trauma and his neck snapped almost instantaneously, jarring his body backward, then he swung gently from side to side for a short while. He would hang there, finally at peace, until someone came to discover the body during inspections.

Just like that, Jackson Yardley was dead.

49

'Andre! Andre! Here!'

'Can you say something about Chase?'

'Tell us about the building!'

'Are you aware that the Irvine Impaler was apprehended just across the street?'

'Andre! Andre!'

The reporters shouted in unison as Andre Nelcourt approached a wooden podium that had been set up for him outside the entranceway of the new MariTech building. His dark blue pinstripe suit flatteringly hugged his slim figure and made his shoulders look bulkier than they actually were. He wore his thick, square-rimmed glasses perfectly on the top of his nose, looking straight ahead and making eye contact with everyone that was there.

He smiled as he stood at the podium, and checked the microphone that sat on top of it to make sure it worked. The reporters kept shouting his name to get his attention; some held recorders and phones towards him, while others extended thick microphones to get a clearer sound. He calmed them down by pressing his palms through the air and then coughed to clear his throat.

'Good morning,' he said proudly, 'I'm glad so many of you have turned up to what is one of the happiest, proudest days of my life.'

He turned around and looked up at the building, before looking back to the reporters and flashing a smile – part out of genuine pride and happiness, part out of wanting to give the reporters a good photo to use for their articles.

'As you all know,' Andre continued, 'This building is, ultimately, the creation of Chase Morgen – whose death will forever be mourned by myself, and everyone at IDS. We all loved him, and his architectural mind was unmatched. It was also a huge personal loss for me, because Chase and I grew up together, and we'd been friends since we were ten years old. It was—' he took a long, calming pause and temporarily removed his glasses to wipe the sweat from his head '—boy, it was tough to take when I first found out. But I worked side-by-side with Chase for this project, and after years of planning, arguments, and construction obstacles, it's finally ready to open and become a staple of this great city. I'll now take a few questions.'

Immediately after he finished his sentence, the reporters burst out into shouting again. They kept gently shoving each to try and get some position in their assigned space, trying to sneak into Andre's view so he'd pick them. He fielded questions from a few of them – all business or architecture-related – giving them as much detail as he could before one reporter near the back of the pack shouted something at him.

'Hey, Andre, did you pick the name of the building?' he shouted.

The rest of the crowd turned around to look at whoever asked the question, then turned back at Andre as they realised they were all similarly interested in that question. Andre replied with another smile, like he was trying to contain laughter, then nodded slowly. He'd been expecting that question – hoping for it, even.

'I knew that would come up,' Andre said, 'and I've properly prepared to give you as honest an answer as I can, even if it hurts me.'

The reporters looked confused. Andre smiled again, then reached into the inside pocket of his suit jacket and pulled out a folded up letter, laying it down on the podium.

'When I was younger,' Andre began, trying to make eye contact with every reporter, 'I was a completely different person. I will wholeheartedly admit that I wasn't a very nice person, and I feel like I didn't understand common decency or the values that I hold dear to me today. Chase and I; we were bullies. We bullied one girl for – in hindsight – no reason at all, but we did it relentlessly. Her brother even told us to stop, but we never did. Then, one day, that girl committed suicide because she felt like it was the only way out. She was fourteen years old.'

The reporters were following along to his every word; all seemingly raising their eyebrows in unison. All of the microphones were held steadily out towards Andre, not wanting to miss anything he was saying.

'You may be familiar with the name on the building because it's been in the news a lot lately. The little girl's brother was Jackson Yardley, the so-called "Irvine Impaler". Jackson murdered Chase because of what we did to his sister all those years – and it was horrible to see because that could've so easily been me, and Chase could be the one standing here today.'

Andre held up the letter that he'd taken from his jacket, showing it clearly to all of the watchful faces, who immediately began flashing their cameras.

'This letter,' Andre said, placing it back on the podium, 'was posted through my letterbox by Jackson. He could have killed me, but he didn't. He decided to write a letter instead. As I read it, it opened my eyes. I saw inside the mind of the man that temporarily brought Irvine to a halt, and I feel like I began to know the man that he was *before* this all started.'

He opened up the letter and placed it flat on the wooden surface. He quickly scanned over it, refamiliarizing himself with it then looked back towards the crowd.

'Now, as you all know, Jackson was awaiting execution on Death Row in San Quentin State Prison for his crimes. But, as some of you might *not* know, Jackson hung himself in his cell almost a week ago, on August 30th. And I brought the letter with me, because I know there would be a press conference, and it seemed like a perfect opportunity for me to give you a different side of the story, and why this building is so important to myself, and the city.'

Andre removed his glasses again and wiped the lenses with a small cloth that he had in his pocket, then placed them comfortably back on the bridge of his nose.

'It's quite long, but I'm going to read part of the letter that really stuck with me, because I think you all deserve to hear it.'

He cleared his throat, took another look at the reporters, then began. '"Seeing your 14-year-old sister hang themselves in their own bedroom when you're only sixteen; that stays with you forever, whether you find future happiness or not. The worst part about it was that there was nothing I could do about it. I knew who was to blame, and I knew why she did it, but there was still nothing I could do, and that hurt just as much. I never wanted to feel that way again. When Hannah was killed, I was thrown right back into that hole – that deep, dark abyss. It affected me more than anyone will ever know, because I tried not to *let* it affect me. And for some reason, after the police didn't do anything, I took it upon myself. I didn't want to feel helpless yet again.

'"And so I thought that revenge was the easiest avenue to go down; the right path that I needed to follow. But along the way, I realised that I'd ruined so many lives. I didn't think of anyone or anything else – I just stayed focused on my own heinous, selfish plans. I destroyed five different families, and I did it without a second thought. It was like I was the only one that was allowed to hurt. And all it did was lead me here. I took so much more than just life – I took everything. And now, I don't feel like I deserve my own.

'"The news and all of the different media outlets will spin this whatever way they see fit to get a story, but that doesn't bother me. I just want you to hear me, and understand that I'm truly sorry for what I've done.

As the city heals and moves on, I just want you to remember one thing: I might be a lot of things, but I am not a psychopath."'

Andre folded the letter back up and returned it to his inside pocket.

'No more questions, thank you.'

Printed in Great Britain
by Amazon